Princess of the Savoy

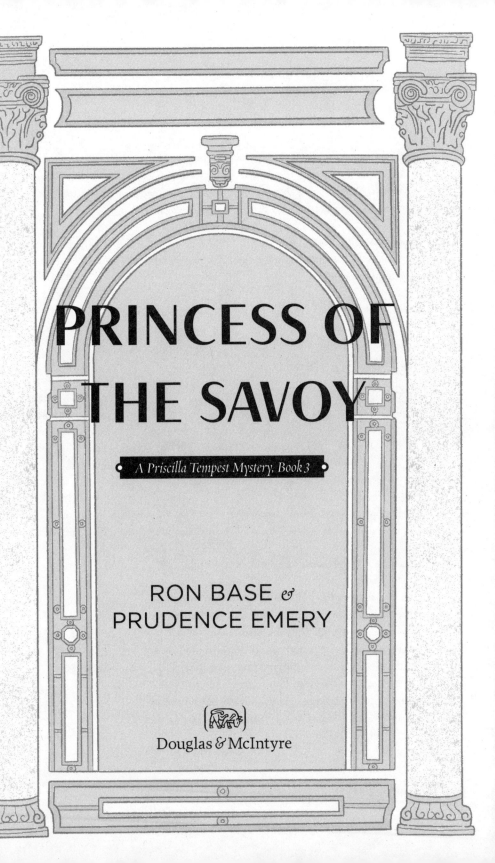

PRINCESS OF THE SAVOY

A Priscilla Tempest Mystery, Book 3

RON BASE &
PRUDENCE EMERY

Douglas & McIntyre

1 2 3 4 5 — 28 27 26 25 24

Douglas & McIntyre (2013) Ltd.
4437 Rondeview Road, P.O. Box 219, Madeira Park, BC, V0N 2H0
www.douglas-mcintyre.com

Edited by Pam Robertson
Text design by Carleton Wilson
Printed and bound in Canada
Printed on 100% recycled paper

Canada Council   Conseil des Arts   Canadä
for the Arts   du Canada

BRITISH COLUMBIA | BRITISH
ARTS COUNCIL | COLUMBIA

Supported by the Province of British Columbia

Douglas & McIntyre acknowledges the support of the Canada Council for the Arts, the
Government of Canada, and the Province of British Columbia through the BC Arts Council.

Library and Archives Canada Cataloguing in Publication

Title: Princess of the Savoy / Ron Base and Prudence Emery.
Names: Base, Ron, author. | Emery, Prudence, 1936- author.
Series: Base, Ron. Priscilla Tempest mystery ; bk. 3.
Description: Series statement: A Priscilla Tempest mystery ; book 3
Identifiers: Canadiana (print) 20230568418 | Canadiana (ebook) 20230568424 | ISBN
    9781771624053 (softcover) | ISBN 9781771624060 (EPUB)
Subjects: LCGFT: Detective and mystery fiction. | LCGFT: Novels.
Classification: LCC PS8553.A784 P75 2024 | DDC C813/.54—dc23

"Everyone likes flattery; and when you come to Royalty you should lay it on with a trowel."

—Benjamin Disraeli

Contents

CHAPTER ONE

The Prince Arrives

Not long before Miss Priscilla Tempest quite possibly saved British democracy, she found herself atop the roof of the Savoy Hotel having her picture taken, listening to Antony Armstrong-Jones observe, "It's London, 1968. A new and exciting time in this city. All bets are off. Everyone is either married, gay or a Russian agent."

"Which of those are you?" inquired Priscilla. She was posed in her Kelly-green Mary Quant minidress so that her lovely long legs were on full display. Her russet blond–tipped locks had been softened and shaped to perfection by Kenneth, Jackie Kennedy's hairdresser, during his current London visit. Behind her, the graceful curve of the Thames, from Tower Bridge to Westminster, was a misty backdrop, perfect for the photo Armstrong-Jones—everyone called him Tony—had in mind.

"I'm not a Russian agent, although, God knows, it's just about the only thing the tabloids haven't accused me of," he stated, peering through the lens of his Leica camera. Armstrong-Jones, who suffered under the weight of being known to all as Lord Snowdon, the short, blond, devilishly handsome husband of Princess Margaret, had been hired by the Savoy to photograph daily life at the world's most famous hotel. As head of the Savoy's press office, Priscilla was tasked with assisting him in any way he saw fit so that his photos reflected the protective fortress of luxury that the Savoy had established over its long and illustrious history.

There was the real world beyond the imposing statue of Count Peter of Savoy. And then there was the world of elegance and calm and reason—and discretion!—that existed within the walls of the hotel. Here there was no bad news; here the impossible was always possible. Here everything was as it should be and always had been. If for some reason it wasn't, that deficiency was soon corrected by the attentive staff—with three staff members in the service of each guest, it was said.

Occasionally, however, despite the staff's best efforts, the miseries of life intruded. Priscilla had been reminded all too often of the truth of this.

For the time being, though, she was preoccupied with the complications of dealing with a particularly feisty and amorous member of the royal family.

"Well, that's good news," Priscilla said carefully. "Your wife will be relieved."

"The point I am trying to make is that there are no labels now," Armstrong-Jones continued, his blue eyes glinting mischievously as he approached her, holding out a light meter as if offering a gift. "You are what you need to be at any given moment in time, depending on your mood and the circumstances."

He bent down, moving around the light meter, so that he was able to easily kiss Priscilla's neck. She flinched away, groaning inwardly. "Don't," she said aloud.

He moved back, smiling. "The circumstances called for it," he explained. "The pale, irresistible exquisiteness of your neck demanded a kiss."

"My mood calls for allowing you—against my better judgment, I might add—to take my picture, nothing more. Besides," she added pointedly, "you may not be a Russian agent, but you *are* a married man."

"A harried man," said Armstrong-Jones, leaning in for another kiss.

That was the moment Susie Gore-Langton, Priscilla's assistant in the press office, chose to make her appearance. Already out of breath, eyes wide with alarm, growing to saucer size when she spied Armstrong-Jones at Priscilla's neck. "Priscilla!" Susie cried.

Priscilla sprang away as though she had just heard a warning gunshot. She gathered herself together enough to say, "What is it, Susie?"

"Mr. Banville is waiting in the Front Hall," she announced breathlessly. Susie announced everything breathlessly. "Prince Teodoro, Duke of Vento, is due to arrive. Mr. Banville demands your presence."

"Duke of Vento?" Armstrong-Jones said dismissively. "An *Italian* duke? There's no such thing."

"I am simply following orders," Susie said. "The duke is to be greeted in the Front Hall by Mr. Banville, accompanied by Priscilla."

"Phony royalty," Armstrong-Jones went on with a sneer. "Accompany me along the Strand, ladies, and I will introduce you to real English princes, all of them grovelling at the royal trough—boring lads, but the real thing." He gave Priscilla a mischievous look. "Tell you what, Priscilla: I'll set you up with a prince, you can marry him, and that way you will become Princess of the Savoy. You can thank me and we will have an affair."

"No thanks," Priscilla said. "I'm not the marrying type, I'm afraid, prince or no prince. Oh, and I should add, I don't have affairs with married men."

"You don't?" Armstrong-Jones feigned surprise. "I'd heard rumours that there is one girl in London who doesn't sleep with married men. Now I know who she is."

"I wouldn't mind marrying a prince," Susie said hopefully.

Tony put his arm around her waist. Susie didn't object, Priscilla noticed. "How about a lord?"

Susie smiled and said, "That's right, you are a lord. Lord Snowdon." Then she frowned and moved away from his arm. "But a married lord."

"Why does everyone always have to remind me?" groused Armstrong-Jones.

"I am leaving you Susie, Lord Snowdon. She will be glad to help you with anything else you require. Right, Susie?"

"Of course," said Susie eagerly.

Armstrong-Jones looked at Susie. "What I require..." he allowed the sentence to drift away. There was a wolfish gleam in his eye that Priscilla didn't like the look of.

Mr. Clive Banville, the Savoy's imposing general manager, a gentleman through and through in his morning suit with waistcoat and striped trousers, appeared to have been sent from central casting to oversee and maintain the perfection of the Savoy. This morning he waited impatiently in the Front Hall, keeping a close eye alternately on the entrance and his self-winding Rolex Tudor Oyster watch.

Around him—and he viewed the hubbub with great satisfaction—whirled the incoming and outgoing guests of the hotel. Well-to-do men accompanied by their fashionably dressed women, the latest arrivals taking in the Front Hall's fine marble pillars and floors set off by gleaming mahogany panelling as they made their way to the reception desk overseen by Mr. Vincent Tomberry, the assistant reception manager. The hotel had been faithfully obsessing over the comfort of its guests ever since theatrical impresario Richard D'Oyly Carte opened the establishment in

1889. In those days, when English hotels were little more than roadhouses, the thought of bringing elegance to one's travel was largely unheard of. Not only did D'Oyly Carte desire that his guests be as comfortable as they would be in their own homes—goodness, bathrooms in every suite!—he also insisted they be well-fed. This was unheard of. Why would the rich leave the comfort of their mansions and estates housing their private chefs to eat in a... *hotel?*

Who could ever imagine it?

Now, after years at the helm, having weathered numerous storms, Banville could relax enough to allow himself to bask in the Savoy's continued success under his guidance. There was deep gratification in knowing that the rich and the famous and the aristocratic, despite the winds of change blowing so harshly just outside the hotel's doors, could still find safe refuge here.

Banville spotted Priscilla crossing the hall. Not all was perfection at the Savoy, he thought, and coming toward him was the evidence of that. Miss Tempest remained one of his continuing sources of irritation. He had had nothing to do with her hiring, except to agree reluctantly with the higher-ups who for some mysterious reason decided she should head the press office. Gossip about her he was determined not to hear—but heard! Certainly her previous experience was thin—a brief stint at a minor public relations agency before arriving on his doorstep. A woman, for heaven's sake, in a job that previously had been held very effectively by a man. Not that he was prejudiced, but there was also the matter of her nationality. She was... *Canadian!* From somewhere around Toronto, it was said. What had Canadians to offer the world? Not much if Miss Tempest was any indication. But he was stuck with her and her questionable lifestyle and unorthodox methods.

For the time being.

Whatever her qualities, Miss Tempest was the worst possible thing in Banville's estimation, she was—

"*Late*, Miss Tempest! You are *late*." Banville arranged to look properly displeased, not hard to do when he was dealing with Priscilla.

"So sorry, sir," said Priscilla. "I was busy dealing with Lord Snowdon."

"Very good, Miss Tempest," Banville gave in. "But it is your responsibility to balance the demands of Lord Snowdon with the requirements of your regular job—which, I would point out, include being at my side when important guests arrive. As is about to happen this morning."

"That would be Prince Teodoro," Priscilla put in helpfully.

"Duke of Vento," Banville stated firmly, as though that confirmed his status. "A regular, therefore very important, guest at the hotel."

"I understand, sir." Priscilla could not help thinking that until now, Mr. Banville had seldom made time for minor European royalty, let alone waited in the Front Hall to personally greet them.

Banville looked at his watch and frowned. "An important guest who is also running late, I might add."

No sooner were the words out of Banville's mouth than a commotion erupted at the entrance. A stylish grandee exploded into view. He was dressed in a fawn-coloured suit, beautifully cut and double-breasted, his handsome head topped by a white Panama hat. A line of porters, pushing and pulling at carts bearing his luggage, quickly followed.

"Prince Teodoro," announced Banville with, to Priscilla's ears, an unusual note of enthusiasm.

"Signor Banville!" cried Prince Teodoro. Immediately he advanced, throwing his arms around the startled Banville, whose sudden unease was compounded by the addition of loud kisses to both cheeks. By the time he was released, Banville had turned a beet red.

"Your Grace, it is a pleasure to have you back with us here at the Savoy," Banville said formally, pulling himself together following the prince's affectionate assault.

It was doubtful Teodoro heard a word of Banville's greeting, his attention already redirected to Priscilla. "*Mio Dio!* Who is this lovely creature?"

Banville couldn't stop himself from looking momentarily chagrined before forcing a smile. "Your Grace, I'd like to introduce you to Miss Priscilla Tempest. Miss Tempest heads our press office."

"Welcome to the Savoy, Your Grace," Priscilla said, flashing her best smile, silently thankful that she had been styled by Kenneth and dressed by Mary Quant to be shot by Snowdon. "Should you require help with press inquiries while you're staying with us, please let me know."

His face lit with expectation, Teodoro took Priscilla's hand and kissed it with the passion one might expect from an Italian prince. "Priscilla!" he announced gleefully. "You are my princess. Princess Priscilla, Princess of the Savoy!"

Priscilla retook possession of her hand. First thing in the morning, and this was the second time she had been deemed royal material. Not a bad start to the day, she thought wryly. However, she could see that not everyone thought of her so highly. A glum Banville was poised close by.

"Uh, let me help you get checked in, Your Grace, and then I'll direct you to your usual river suite," he said.

"Could not Signorina Tempest show me?" Teodoro inquired.

That had the effect of further perturbing the ordinarily imperturbable Banville. "I'm afraid Miss Tempest has other duties that require her immediate attention."

Priscilla silently pondered what duties those might be, other than the duty to stay away from amorous Italian princes.

"But I must insist!" Teodoro had dropped the facade of the merry Italian prince and become the spoiled child Priscilla might have suspected.

"Come with me, sir," said Priscilla, daring to interrupt in an attempt to end further debate. "I would be pleased to escort you to reception so that you can check in."

"*Bellissima!*" cried the prince. Then he turned to Banville—his face immediately lost its expression of delight, and his voice fell to a whisper that Priscilla barely overheard. "It is important that we talk as soon as possible."

"Yes, I understand," Banville replied quickly.

Understand what? Priscilla wondered.

At that point, Mr. Tomberry appeared, the soul of Savoy calm: "Your Grace," he announced in the perfect plummy tone he had addressed so many guests with over the years, "your suite is ready."

"Wonderful!" cried Teodoro, resuming his merry expression. "It is wonderful to be back at the Savoy, the world's greatest hotel!"

He allowed Mr. Tomberry to lead him away. Priscilla was left with Mr. Banville, who was looking unexpectedly distracted.

"Anything wrong, sir?" Priscilla inquired.

He quickly pulled himself together. "Not a thing, Miss Tempest. After all, we do the impossible here at the Savoy, do we not?"

"We do, sir."

"Even when it comes to pleasing Italian princes," Banville added grimly.

He marched away. Already, Teodoro and his luggage had disappeared from reception. The Front Hall had calmed and taken on an air of flower-scented tranquility.

Priscilla had paused for a moment to breathe in that air when she noticed the peculiar rake-thin little man come through the front entrance. He might have been a priest in his black suit, except for the lack of an ecclesiastical collar. He moved lightly, almost floating across the Front Hall toward reception, weighted to the earth by the small brown suitcase he carried. His skin was a deathly white, as though it had been drained of colour so that it was almost translucent. Everyone, of course, had a place at the Savoy, Priscilla reminded herself. But even so, this little fellow seemed out of place, an ethereal figure, his ghostlike face resolutely set, his jaw rigid as though on a mission he was determined to complete, no matter what.

Peculiar indeed, thought Priscilla as she watched the little man approach Mr. Tomberry at reception.

But then again, even the peculiar were welcome at the Savoy.

CHAPTER TWO

The Little Prince

"What did you do with Lord Snowdon?" Priscilla asked Susie when she got back to Room 205. Known as just 205 among the staff, the press office could be found down a corridor off the Front Hall. It featured a reception area where Susie was stationed and an office for Priscilla. The walls were of blond wood panelling. One of those walls was devoted to photographs of the many celebrities who over the years had graced the Savoy with their presence. Thus far, save for a grumpy Prince Philip, the wall was short on princes.

"He sped off in his sports car shortly after you left," Susie answered. She gave Priscilla a speculative look. "I think he likes you."

"Lord Snowdon likes anything in a skirt or a pair of trousers, depending on, as he says, his whim of the moment."

"He is rather dreamy, don't you think?" Susie, Priscilla noticed with mounting annoyance, maintained that speculative look.

Priscilla entered her office and took a seat behind the desk, which she liked to think was her refuge from the vagaries of the tiny universe she occupied at the Savoy. The trouble with that, she had long since learned, was that the desk, with three phones devoted to bringing her nothing but trouble, provided no refuge at all, and was merely a trap from which escape was impossible once the proverbial shit hit the proverbial fan.

She was about to press the waiter telephone, one of three within reach on her desk that would summon a much-needed infusion of coffee, when, as though by the magic that was only possible at the Savoy, Karl Steiner, Austrian class personified, arrived with that needed infusion mounted on a silver tray.

"You are a lifesaver, Karl," Priscilla declared as he deposited the tray on her desk. "You will note I am resisting the temptation to call for champagne."

"Your iron discipline is an example to us all," Karl said.

"It's crumbling fast," said Priscilla.

His services no longer required for the time being, Karl made his escape, slipping past Susie as she took his place in front of Priscilla's desk. Her face was flushed with excitement. Not unusual for Susie. It did not, Priscilla had learned, take a whole lot to excite her.

"Not another crisis," Priscilla groaned. "It's too early. I haven't had my first sip of coffee."

"Not a crisis at all," she reported eagerly. "Gordon Scott."

"Who?"

"Gordon Scott. Don't you know? The movie star?" Susie stood bravely in the face of such ignorance.

"Gordon Scott is a movie star?"

"He played Tarzan." She said this in a way that suggested there was no excuse for not knowing who had played Tarzan in the movies. "He has arrived today."

"I must admit I haven't been keeping track of my Tarzans," Priscilla said.

"I've had the worst crush on him."

"Then I will leave Tarzan in your capable hands," Priscilla said.

"I was hoping you would say that," Susie said with satisfaction.

Priscilla sipped her coffee. She did not want to think of what Susie might get up to with Tarzan, but at least there was one less possible crisis on her plate.

No sooner had that thought crossed her mind than the office door opened and in popped the curious little priestlike fellow in a black suit that Priscilla had noticed in the Front Hall. His translucent skin shone against pale-blue eyes lit by a zealot's fervour.

"Good day," he said crisply in accented English, inspecting her with wide, unblinking eyes. "Do you mind if I step in?"

"Not at all," said Priscilla.

"So sorry to bother you," the little man said, moving further into the office. "I understand you are the press representative here. Is that so?"

"Priscilla Tempest." She held out her hand. Instead of shaking it, he bent forward and gently kissed it.

"It is my honour to meet you," he said. "My name is Constantino. I am the Prince of Parma."

Priscilla could hardly credit what she was hearing. Another Italian prince?

"Your Highness," Priscilla gulped. Was she supposed to stand when royalty entered her office? Was this guy really royalty? He certainly didn't look very royal. Nothing like Prince Teodoro, that was for sure. Well, he was a guest whatever his title, she decided, therefore deference must be paid. She struggled to her feet. Susie lingered behind the prince, her face a muddle of uncertainty.

"Please, please," begged Prince Constantino. "Do not stand on my account. And you must call me Constantino."

Priscilla plunked herself back down. "A pleasure, Your Highness. Can I offer you something to drink? We have coffee or tea. Or something stronger, perhaps?" Her welcoming host mask was firmly in place.

"No, no, I do not touch caffeine or spirits."

"Then please, how may I be of service to you?"

"First of all, I wish to apologize for my cousin," intoned the prince politely.

"Your cousin?" Priscilla didn't understand.

"Teodoro, if I am not mistaken, has also checked into the hotel."

"Prince Teodoro is your cousin?"

"Unfortunately, yes, that is correct. The man is a monster, a criminal." Constantino reported this quietly, as though it were a given that his cousin was a monster and a criminal. "I must say I am surprised he has been allowed into this great hotel."

"Can I ask you what brings you to the Savoy, Your Highness?" Priscilla asked carefully.

"Please! You are such a beautiful woman. I do not stand on ceremony like my cousin. I am the people's prince. You must call me Constantino."

"I'm so sorry, but the rules of the Savoy do not allow me to address guests by their given names." Priscilla, sticking to the Savoy playbook. Such a good, dependable employee, she thought to herself.

"First of all, I should explain something about myself," he said.

"If you would like," Priscilla said encouragingly.

"I am not a religious man, you understand, but ever since I was a boy, I have heard voices, experienced visions. These voices and visions have led me through life. They have taken me along a righteous path, one of abstinence and discipline. They have also made me understand what a terrible man my cousin is. Thanks to the visions I have experienced, I have found a path of light, while Teodoro has chosen the way of darkness."

Constantino paused, his pale-blue eyes burning fiercely. A zealot's flame, Priscilla thought. Light and darkness? Best to keep her mouth shut, she decided.

"Lately, my beloved uncle, the man who practically raised me, has come to me," the prince continued reasonably. "He has told me that my cousin, Teodoro, has disgraced the duchy of Vento and that I must take his place as duke and restore its reputation. He has brought me here to London to continue my quest."

"Your uncle told you this recently?"

The little prince shook his head impatiently. "No, no. My uncle died twenty years ago. He lives on in my visions."

"Apologies," Priscilla said in haste. "Your uncle has advised you in a vision, is that it?"

"That is true," Constantino confirmed.

"And this vision of your uncle has brought you to the Savoy?" asked Priscilla. A visionary uncle who appreciates luxury, she thought cynically.

"In order to expose my cousin," Constantino hurried to explain.

"And how will you go about doing that, Your Highness?"

"That is what has brought me to you, Miss Tempest. I will have a press conference!" declared the prince.

"You will?" Priscilla, caught by surprise.

"It is at this press conference that I will denounce my cousin for the fraud that he is and lay out my rightful claim to the title of—*Duke of Vento.*"

The words were delivered with a feverish certainty. This precise little man in his black suit with his intense white face struck Priscilla as a person who might be a priest, but hardly a prince, let alone a prince now declaring himself a duke.

Priscilla bought some time by clearing her throat as she thought desperately of the best response—the most diplomatic response.

"I see," Priscilla said cautiously. "And when would you like to hold this press conference?"

"Immediately," he said. "Time is of the essence. Every day that my cousin spreads his devious lies is another day when I should rightfully possess this title."

"Yes, I can see that you are terribly dedicated, Your Highness," Priscilla said in a conciliatory voice. "But I am not exactly sure how we here at the Savoy will be able to assist you."

"It begins with a press conference," Constantino asserted. "Alerting the world to Teodoro's criminal behaviour." He leaned forward and dropped his voice, as though the world might overhear him otherwise. "He is a fascist, you know."

"No, I didn't," responded Priscilla, thinking that if the Savoy checked each of its guests' political beliefs, it would be a very empty hotel.

"He should be in prison," asserted Constantino. "Such a man should not be the Duke of Vento."

"I see," Priscilla said noncommittally, not sure she should be encouraging the imprisonment of the hotel's guests.

"Can you please be so kind as to arrange this press conference for me, Miss Tempest?"

"Let me see what I can do," Priscilla said, measuring her words. "This is a very busy time at the hotel. Most of our conference rooms are booked up. However, give me a few days, if that's satisfactory, and I will get back to you."

"I am not to be put off, Miss Tempest!" Constantino's blue eyes burned even brighter.

Priscilla was desperately trying to think of what to say in reply when Susie reappeared. "Excuse me, Miss Tempest," she said in her most professional voice. "I've just received a call from Mr. Banville, our general manager. He wishes to see you immediately."

"I apologize, Your Highness," Priscilla said, rising to her feet. "But as you can see, duty calls. My boss demands my presence."

Constantino looked disappointed. "Very well," he said in a resigned voice. "But you will let me know about my press conference, yes?"

"Of course," Priscilla said.

"As soon as possible."

"I will be in touch."

"Let me show you out, Your Highness," Susie said, taking Prince Constantino gently by the arm.

As he headed for the door, the prince, shoulders back, head held high to give the impression of a height he didn't possess, cast a final, fleeting look back at Priscilla. "*Ci vediamo presto!*" he purred in what Priscilla could only imagine was his idea of a seductive voice.

The little prince exited. Susie reappeared a moment later. "Is he really a prince?"

"Apparently," Priscilla said.

"Do you believe him?"

"Whatever he is, Prince Constantino is a guest at the Savoy, where all our guests are royalty, no matter what."

"Jolly good," agreed Susie. "Prince Constantino it is."

Priscilla moved back to her desk and her unattended coffee. "Incidentally, thank you."

"For what?"

"I had no idea how I was going to get rid of him until you appeared with that excuse about Mr. Banville wanting to see me. Clever thinking on your part."

"No," said Susie, shaking her head vehemently. "That was no excuse. Mr. Banville *does* want to see you. *Immediately!*"

Meglio Stare Attenti, Priscilla!

In order to enter the lair of general manager Clive Banville, one first had to pass Banville's gatekeeper, Sidney Stopford, dubbed El Sid by a fearful hotel staff. Today, Priscilla observed as she entered, there appeared to be a much different Sidney standing guard. The perpetual sneer embedded into that small, moist mouth, beneath the carrot-coloured mustache, was absent. The eyes that usually glinted with malice behind gold-rimmed glasses were subdued, darting nervously in the direction of the gentleman in the grey suit seated on a sofa not far from Sidney's desk.

A narrow face like a knife blade dropped down from slicked-back black hair, framing eyes like black marbles coated in ice. Those icy black marbles glinted as they ran up and down the length of Priscilla.

The hard mouth worked itself into something resembling a smile. "Hey," the gentleman in the grey suit said, "who have we here?"

"You sit there quietly, do you understand?" Sidney's snarl had returned full force.

The gentleman in the grey suit seemed unperturbed. He stood to approach Priscilla, extracting a coin from his trouser pocket. "See this?" he said. He then proceeded to roll the coin across his knuckles. "How do you like that?" He flipped the coin into the air and caught it adroitly.

"Impressive," Priscilla said.

"My pal George Raft taught me how to do that," he said.

"You don't say," said Priscilla.

"I do say." As if to prove the point, he rolled the coin across his knuckles a second time, and then bounced it into the air. Priscilla caught it.

The gentleman in the grey suit's narrow face fell a bit. Priscilla handed him the coin. "*Scarface*. I believe that was the film that made Mr. Raft a star."

"I guess you think you're pretty cute, sweetheart." The idea did not appear to please the gentleman in the grey suit.

"I guess I do," Priscilla said. "And, believe me, I am not your sweetheart."

The gentleman in the grey suit broke out a wide smile. A smile that lacked any warmth, Priscilla thought, that made you want to run for cover. "Don't be so sure about that," he said.

Afraid this character could turn out to be a guest at the Savoy, Priscilla ignored the remark and addressed Sidney. "I believe Mr. Banville wants to see me."

Sidney blinked a couple of times behind his gold-rimmed spectacles. Was Priscilla seeing things, or did El Sid actually look impressed?

"Go right in," he said. "Mr. Banville is waiting for you."

Priscilla moved toward Banville's office door. She could feel the cold eyes of the man in the grey suit boring into her. She knocked and, as she always did before entering the lion's den, took a deep, calming breath.

Banville was seated in one of the armchairs beside the big window spilling pale sunlight into his otherwise gloomy—and, to Priscilla, foreboding—office. With him, to Priscilla's surprise, was Prince Teodoro, sprawled across an adjacent armchair, looking as though he had settled in for the afternoon. Without his Panama hat, his short hair feathered artfully across his fine head, the prince resembled one of those Roman emperors who show up in Hollywood biblical epics to lament the state of affairs in Palestine. The evil Roman emperor at that, Priscilla thought. Caligula reborn?

"There you are, Miss Tempest," Banville announced, rising to his feet. Teodoro stayed where he was, Priscilla noticed, restricting himself to beaming happily in her direction. "You were introduced earlier to our friend, Prince Teodoro."

"Such a pleasure to see you again," said the prince, actually raising himself up a bit to acknowledge her presence. Whatever his possible fascist shortcomings, Priscilla mused, Teodoro possessed a much more princely demeanour than his cousin.

"The reason I've called you here today, Miss Tempest," Banville went on, "is that I believe you can help our friend with a rather delicate matter."

Mystified, Priscilla nonetheless nodded. "Anything I can do, of course."

"It would be most appreciated," Teodoro said. His eyes remained firmly on Banville, who cleared his throat—a bit nervously, Priscilla thought.

"His Highness has heard rumours that a certain tabloid newspaper plans a story about him that is most scurrilous and totally untrue."

"I see," said Priscilla, wondering how a story Teodoro had not seen could be automatically scurrilous and untrue.

"An abomination," announced Teodoro angrily.

Priscilla addressed him. "If you don't mind my asking, does this story have anything to do with your cousin?"

"My cousin! That idiot? What about him?"

"Prince Constantino has just checked into the hotel," Priscilla reported.

The prince reacted with surprise. "I did not know this." He waved a dismissive hand. "But it is of no consequence. Pay no attention to him and his ravings. He is a lunatic. Thinks he hears things."

"Frankly, the prince is not certain what form this story might take," Banville said. "That is where you come in, Miss Tempest. You know the reporter who we understand is doing the story."

"Who is the reporter?" Priscilla did not like the way this was going.

"It's that blighter Percy Hoskins at the *Evening Standard*," Banville said, frowning and shaking his head in evident disgust. "Nothing but trouble, that chap."

Priscilla shuddered inwardly—*Percy, oh God!* She worked to maintain an expression of professional concern. "You're sure we don't know what the story is about? Has Mr. Hoskins attempted to contact His Highness?"

Teodoro frowned. His dislike of Priscilla's questions was obvious. "No one from the press has contacted me as yet," he said sullenly.

Banville hurried to fill the uneasy silence. "What we'd like you to do, Miss Tempest, is find out exactly what this Hoskins has up his sleeve. Glean any details you can pertaining to the story."

And do what? Priscilla asked herself.

"This is a terrible situation," lamented Teodoro, sadly shaking his head. "The man is a liar and a criminal. He should be arrested!"

It was Priscilla's turn to nervously clear her throat. "Yes, well, I will certainly do my best." Thinking at the same time about how the blazes she would ever be able to stop Percy once he was in pursuit of a story. "But I would be remiss not to point out that controlling the London press in any way tends to be... difficult."

Banville and Teodoro exchanged unhappy glances. "You *will* do your best, I'm sure, Miss Tempest." The warning tone in Banville's voice was unmistakable: *Get the information I require. Or else!*

"Yes, sir," Priscilla said, her stomach sinking.

"You will report back to Prince Teodoro as soon as you have the information he requires." Banville issuing the marching orders. "Naturally, you will keep me informed as well."

"Very good, sir." The army sprog responding with hollow enthusiasm just before being sent over the top to certain death in no man's land.

"I must emphasize that the utmost discretion is required in this matter," Teodoro put in, looking very grave. "Is that understood, Miss Tempest?"

"Yes, certainly."

With Priscilla firmly entangled in his web, Prince Teodoro was on his feet, once again full of oily charm. He took Priscilla's hand. "I look forward to working closely with you," he said, bending to kiss that hand.

It was all Priscilla could do to stop herself from yanking it away.

"And please, Miss Tempest," the prince added, "ignore my crazy cousin. He has no idea what he is talking about."

"Thank you, Miss Tempest," Banville stated formally. "That will be all for now." The sprog dismissed. *Get over the top! Die for your country! No further questions!*

In something of a daze, Priscilla found her way back out to where El Sid had resumed the familiar smug expression he now aimed in her direction. There was no sign of the gentleman in the grey suit.

"Do you still have a job?" inquired El Sid snidely.

"I'm afraid so," Priscilla said.

"More's the pity."

Priscilla resisted the urge to strangle El Sid on the spot. Instead, she moved out of his accusatory range and into the corridor, where she was immediately confronted by the grey-suited man. "I thought I'd introduce myself," he said.

"I'm sorry, but you're in my way," Priscilla said in an agitated voice.

"A close friend of Prince Teodoro's. Al Cellini is the name."

"I thought you were a friend of George Raft."

"Al Cellini has many friends here in London and in New York and Rome. Al Cellini is a very popular fellow."

"I'm happy to hear that," Priscilla said. "But Al Cellini is in my way."

"He is." Al Cellini grabbed her arm. Up close, the icy black marbles were even blacker.

"You are hurting my arm!" Priscilla tried to pull away. Cellini only tightened his grip. A vise-like grip, she couldn't help thinking.

"Yeah, I *am* hurting you," Cellini said agreeably, practically whispering in her ear. "No matter what the prince told you in there, you listen to me, you got that? Find out what that reporter is up to. Get the information. Don't play around. You don't get the information Teodoro wants, he's nice to you still. You don't get that information, Al Cellini is not nice. You get it?"

Priscilla looked directly into those scary black eyes. "Let me go," she said angrily. She tried again to pull away from him. He didn't let go.

"Do you get it, girlie?"

"Hey there," a voice said.

Cellini jerked around in surprise, allowing Priscilla to rescue her arm and lurch away from her tormentor. A tall, tanned man in a beige suit said, "Excuse me, miss, but do you work here at the hotel? I'm afraid I'm a little lost."

"Yes, yes, I do," Priscilla said, pulling herself together. She took some pleasure from the sullen expression on Cellini's face.

"I hope I'm not interrupting anything." The tall, tanned man was looking directly at Cellini.

Cellini cast a dark glance at Priscilla. "*Meglio stare attenti,* Priscilla!"

"He says that you had best be careful," the tall, tanned man said, eyes fixed on Cellini. "I'm not sure that's particularly good news."

"Al Cellini's gonna remember you, pal," Cellini said to the tall, tanned man.

"Most people do," he answered.

Cellini cast one last dark look at Priscilla and then slunk off along the hallway.

"Are you okay?" The tall, tanned man turned to Priscilla.

"I'm not sure," Priscilla said, still shaky after her encounter with Al Cellini. "But thank you."

Even in her unsteady state, Priscilla could see that the tall, tanned man had a pleasantly sharp smile. "Was I right?" he asked. "Do you work at the hotel?"

"Definitely," Priscilla said, regaining her professional composure. "Are you really lost?"

"I'm always slightly lost," the tall, tanned man said with a grin. "Perhaps you could direct me to reception."

"I'd be only too glad to escort you there. I'm Priscilla Tempest, incidentally."

"Gordon Scott," the tall, tanned man said, maintaining that wonderful smile as he shook Priscilla's hand. The hand that, to her relief, he did not try to kiss.

Then she realized where she had heard that name before.

Tarzan! thought Priscilla, somewhat deliriously. She had been rescued by... *Tarzan!*

CHAPTER FOUR

"Things Are Seldom as They Seem, Skim Milk Masquerades as Cream..."

Priscilla arrived back at 205 to find Susie even more agog than usual. "He's here!" she exclaimed.

"Who is here?"

"Gordon Scott! I just heard he has checked in."

"I know," Priscilla said.

"You *know?*"

"I met him outside Mr. Banville's office." No need to go into details, Priscilla thought, entering her office. She eyed the trio of telephones on her desk as though they were enemies not to be trusted. For the moment, their evil was at rest and they remained silent. That would soon end, she speculated.

"You *met* Gordon Scott?" Susie was in the doorway, practically palpitating with excitement.

"Susie, really, you must stop repeating everything I say."

"But you met him! You *met* Gordon Scott. What did he say? What was he like?"

"He said, 'Me Tarzan. You Jane.'"

"You're making fun of me," Susie said petulantly.

"Not at all." Priscilla made herself pick up the receiver. "Actually, he turned out to be a very nice chap." In more ways than one, Priscilla thought. "But a reminder, Susie—no matter what your hormones are telling you, you must stay away from him." As

34

she spoke, Priscilla forced herself to dial the number she knew only too well. "After all," she added, "he is a guest at the Savoy, and therefore off limits."

"You're so mean to be even thinking what you're thinking," Susie sulked.

"Only because I know what *you're* thinking." The phone was ringing. And ringing.

"I hate you." Susie flounced away. "For the next few minutes, anyway," she added.

Ah, thought Priscilla as she put the receiver to her ear, the many, many loves and passions of Susie Gore-Langton. Gordon Scott today—tomorrow? That was the ongoing fascination of Susie, wasn't it?

"Be still my beating old heart," Percy Hoskins said when he came on the other end of the line. "Priscilla Tempest has actually called."

Priscilla took a deep breath and said, "We must talk."

Despite the heavy grey skies over London and the attendant threat of rain, Priscilla insisted on meeting Percy Hoskins in the Victoria Embankment Gardens, behind the Savoy but far enough away so that she was not likely to be spotted conspiring with a member of the tabloid press.

For his part, Percy insisted they meet not at the Henry Fawcett Memorial, their usual rendezvous point, but rather on a bench at the Sir Arthur Sullivan Memorial in the same park. She found Percy already seated when she arrived. Only it was a Percy she hardly recognized. The shaggy Fleet Street reporter was shaved, his hair neatly cut, and he was wearing a raincoat that looked as if it had just left the cleaners. What's more, as he greeted her, his usually bloodshot eyes were clear and sparkling. He actually looked as though he'd had a good night's sleep.

Priscilla could hardly believe what she was seeing as she joined him on the bench.

"What have you done with Percy Hoskins?" she demanded.

Percy looked bemused. "Whatever are you talking about?"

"An alien from outer space has inhabited Percy's body," Priscilla said with feigned seriousness. "Please tell me that you come in peace."

"Very funny," Percy said. "Actually, I've been drying out this last while."

"Which I suppose you're going to use as an excuse to explain why I haven't heard from you."

"I wanted to make sure that the next time we met, you saw the new me."

"Or you've decided to put your best foot forward so you can more effectively pry information out of me." A cynical assertion, considering that Priscilla was there to extract information from him.

Percy responded with a look of innocence. "You will notice that, with my new personality in hand, I've decided to meet with you at what is known as the 'most erotic statue in London.'"

He nodded in the direction of Sir Arthur, his proud head cast in bronze—conservative British upper-class hauteur topping a granite column. A woman, naked except for a length of drapery around her buttocks, had thrown her breasts forever against the column. Lusting after the composer of operatic comedies in collaboration with W.S. Gilbert? Hard to imagine the plump, moustached face looming over her, seemingly oblivious, inspiring lust in anyone.

"Not exactly the last word on eroticism," Priscilla observed, keeping her eyes on the woman's impressive back.

"Pretty damned good for a London memorial, I would say," Percy ventured. "Actually, I believe she's supposed to be Euterpe, the muse of music, mourning Sir Arthur's passing. But I like to think she's a beauty who simply finds him irresistible—much the same as you find me irresistible."

"I find you entirely resistible," Priscilla said.

"Then what, pray tell, are we doing here?"

"The Duke of Vento," she asserted. There, she thought. Might as well get right to it.

Immediately, Percy's innocence was replaced with an expression of darkening suspicion. "Why would you want to know about Teodoro?"

"Because he is staying at the hotel." As good a reason as any for why she wanted to meet with Percy. Also, the only one she could come up with on short notice.

Her feint did little to assuage the suspicion clouding Percy's face. "Why would you want to know about him?"

"His cousin, Constantino, is also at the hotel," Priscilla offered. "He's the little prince. So different from Teodoro. Constantino says he is rightfully the Duke of Vento, not his cousin."

"Why does he think that?" asked Percy.

"He says he received a vision from his dead uncle."

"A vision?" Percy rolled his eyes. "A prince who has visions."

"He hears voices, too," Priscilla added.

"Don't we all."

"He claims Teodoro is a fraud and a criminal and wants to hold a press conference to expose his cousin. Before I allow something like that, I want to know as much as I can about what is going on between the two of them—and whether Constantino's allegations against his cousin have any validity."

That actually sounded pretty convincing, Priscilla thought. Carrying the ring of truth certainly helped.

"Well, any visions or voices aside, he's right about Teodoro," Percy said. "But what makes you think I might know anything about a couple of squabbling Italian princes?"

"You're always telling me you know just about everything," Priscilla shot back.

"And to think, up to now, I was certain you didn't believe me."

"Do you know anything or not?" Priscilla asked impatiently.

"As it so happens, you're in luck. I happen to know quite a lot."

"Do tell," prodded Priscilla.

"For starters, they're both a couple of idiots, if that's any help," Percy offered. "Both of them laying claim to something that doesn't really exist."

"The dukedom of Vento," Priscilla said.

"Teodoro's probably got more claim to what's left of the Italian monarchy," Percy went on. "He did inherit the title from his father."

"Okay, but that doesn't stop his cousin, Constantino, insisting that he is the rightful heir. I'm nervous about him having a press conference at the hotel and making all sorts of wild accusations."

Percy rolled his eyes. "Your little prince is banging his head against the castle wall if you ask me. The best you can say for Constantino is that he is the innocent in comparison to his older cousin. He's spent years trying to claim his place in Italian royalty without anyone paying much attention. He was married to an actress, but she dumped him last year. The word is he's wandering around, desperate to put his hands on some sort of validation—and cash, in order to maintain his lifestyle, which apparently includes staying at the Savoy."

"What about Teodoro?" Priscilla pressed. "What's so terrible about him?"

"Teodoro is why I know anything at all about these two. He is the bad guy, through and through," Percy explained. "He was charged with murder five years ago, and he's said to be involved with a secret pro-Nazi group in Rome—evil lads dedicated to doing what they can to end democracy through corruption and political influence peddling."

"Are you working on a story about him?" Nothing ventured at this point, Priscilla thought, nothing gained.

"What makes you think I'm doing a story?" Suspicion already set into Percy's face, now crawled into his voice as well.

"What with your status as the best reporter in London..." Priscilla stroking the part of Percy that was most vulnerable—his ego.

"There is that," Percy agreed. Some of the suspicion was gone from his eyes.

"I simply imagined, based on what you've told me, that you are chasing a story about Prince Teodoro."

"All I'm prepared to say right now is that I'm on to Teodoro. He's up to something in London. My job is to find out what it is."

"Knowing your unerring eye for a story, you must have some idea," said Priscilla, maintaining her Percy the Great theme.

Percy shot her a wary sideways glance. "What is it you're not telling me?"

Damn his intuition, anyway, Priscilla thought. "I can't imagine what you're talking about," she said aloud, shooting him the innocent-little-girl look that had worked so effectively over the years with men.

"Don't give me that innocent look you love to produce when you're lying through your teeth," Percy demanded.

Double-damn him, Priscilla thought. "I am not giving you any look—and I am not lying through my teeth." Priscilla did her level best to sound hurt that Percy would even suggest such a thing.

"I know you too well, Priscilla. What's this all about?"

"And I know you even better," Priscilla retorted angrily. "You wouldn't have agreed to meet me unless you wanted something. What is it?"

Percy stretched his arm across the back of the bench so that he could draw closer to her ear. "Like I said, I'm interested to know what Teodoro is doing in London. This meeting tells me you are open to helping me accomplish that."

"No, I am not!" Priscilla responded in an incredulous voice. She pushed away from him.

"Yes, you are," Percy countered, straightening.

Priscilla paused long enough to make sure Percy could see clearly that she was fuming. "Besides, there's nothing I can do to help you, anyway."

"There most certainly is."

"What?"

"It wouldn't be much, really," Percy answered casually. "All you would have to do is take a look around his suite and see what you can find."

"What? Are you totally mad?" Priscilla reared back in shock— feigned shock, but she wanted to make certain her dismay was evident.

Percy's imperturbability when it came to the most outland-ish suggestions was on full display. "You work at the Savoy, after all. How hard can it be to get into a guest's suite when he's not there? I'm sure it happens all the time."

"It does not!" Priscilla protested emphatically. "In fact, it *never* happens. If I ever did such a thing and got caught, I would lose my job and probably end up in jail."

"You won't get caught," Percy said confidently. "You know your way around the hotel. You can get away with just about anything if you put your mind to it."

"I'm not going to do it," Priscilla asserted. "Don't even begin to think I will."

Percy gave her one of the self-assured smiles that she found so irksome. "Say anything you like, it doesn't matter. You're a snoop. What's more, you can't resist a challenge."

"You don't know me at all," she replied petulantly. She was determined not to fold her arms defensively as she spoke—and then folded her arms.

"Here's the other thing about you."

"And what is that?" she asked, against her better judgment.

"I'm not sure why, but I'm betting that you want to know what our good-for-nothing prince is up to as much as I do."

"You couldn't be more mistaken." Priscilla rose to her feet. "I can't listen to any more nonsense. I've got to get back to work."

"Teodoro is a Nazi sympathizer who has murdered people," Percy said soberly. "I'm trying to expose him. That's what my story is about."

Aha, thought Priscilla, so that's it—and why Teodoro, having somehow got wind of Percy's intent, might be worried.

"You can help me," Percy continued, "and at the same time protect the reputation of the Savoy."

"The reputation of the Savoy doesn't need me protecting it," Priscilla said, thinking at the same time that there were those who would dare to suggest she was a detriment to that reputation. Nonsense, of course—as long as she wasn't caught breaking into a guest's suite.

"Let me know what you find out." Percy gave her one of his insouciant grins. She found those grins even more annoying than his self-assured smiles. Everything about him was irritating, in fact. Why she ever had anything to do with him was beyond her. Even if he had cleaned himself up a bit.

"Call me as soon as you're out of his suite," Percy said.

41

"Go to hell," she said as she strutted away, leaving behind the most erotic statue in London—not very erotic at all, in her estimation—and moving far, far away from Percy Hoskins, the least erotic male in all England, in her estimation!

CHAPTER FIVE

Flower Girl

"Lord Snowdon has been looking for you!" Priscilla was certain she detected an accusatory tone in Susie's voice as soon she entered 205. As though to suggest she and Antony Armstrong-Jones had been up to something.

Or was she imagining things? Possibly.

"What did he want?" Priscilla asked.

"What Lord Snowdon wants, I suppose, depends, doesn't it?" said Susie enigmatically.

"On what?" demanded Priscilla.

"On what he wants," said Susie.

There was much too much of an impish gleam in Susie's eye for Priscilla's liking.

"Lord Snowdon is on assignment for the hotel and that is the end of the story," Priscilla said definitively.

"I doubt that is ever the end of the story as far as Tony is concerned," Susie replied.

"At this hotel we refer to him as Lord Snowdon."

"Right-o. Lord Snowdon it is." Susie's grin had transformed from devilish to cattish. Priscilla didn't like that grin in any form.

Whatever her many shortcomings, Priscilla thought as she entered her office, Susie did serve to take her mind off any consideration about breaking into the room of a prominent Italian prince—who might also be a fascist sympathizer involved in who-knew-what nefarious activities here in London.

CHAPTER FIVE

Unthinkable!

Teodoro was not only a prince, royalty no matter what one thought, but, much more importantly, a *guest* at the Savoy! Not only a guest, but a guest with a personal connection to the general manager. One simply did not break into the rooms of Savoy guests. One did not even *think* of such an idea.

In fairness, she thought further, taking her seat behind her desk, she had been asked—no, *ordered*—by the general manager himself to discover what Percy planned to write about Prince Teodoro. If she did decide to do as Percy suggested—*if!*—would that not fall under the category of discovering what Percy planned to write? Even if it turned out that she inadvertently—*somewhat* inadvertently—helped him with his story?

She called Susie. Almost immediately her head popped into the doorway.

"I'll tell you what I'd like you to do," Priscilla said. "Order an arrangement of flowers from our Front Hall florist. The card will read, 'Compliments of the Savoy Hotel.' You will then arrange to have the flowers delivered to the suite of Prince Teodoro, the Duke of Vento. Have you got it so far?"

"Roger that," confirmed Susie. "But why—"

"No questions," Priscilla interjected. "Have them call you the moment the flowers are ready. Tell them it's a rush order, but further instruct them not to deliver the flowers until I say so. Understand?"

"Sort of," Susie said dubiously.

"Get on with it, please." Susie disappeared from view. Moments later she heard Susie on the phone. She picked up the receiver and asked the switchboard, "Put me through to Prince Teodoro's suite, please."

"Various people have been trying to call him today, but he's not answering," reported the operator. "I would imagine he's out. Would you care to leave a message?"

"No, it's fine," said Priscilla, hanging up.

Three-quarters of an hour later, Susie waved from the outer office. "Your flowers are ready," she called.

Priscilla made her way to the hotel's floral department next to the Embankment entrance. Here a staff of twenty worked away creating the lavish flower displays that had been initiated by the hotel's first manager, César Ritz, and were now a Savoy tradition. They had outdone themselves for Priscilla with a carnival of colour, from yellow and red dahlias to purple lilacs, blue hydrangeas and yellow roses. "We're about to send them," said the young woman on duty.

"Not to bother," Priscilla said. "I'm on my way up there, anyway. He's gone for the day, but I want to make sure the flowers are properly arranged. Can you let me have a master key?"

"We can take them," said the young woman insistently.

"I appreciate that, but the prince is a very finicky guest. I would prefer to do it myself."

The young woman hesitated, and Priscilla worried she was about to offer further objections. But then she shrugged and reached under the counter to produce a house key that she handed to Priscilla. "I hope he likes the flowers," she mumbled.

"He will be thrilled," answered Priscilla, taking the arrangement.

She hurried back through the corridor to the lift, praying that she would not have to share it with anyone who might later serve as a witness to her deception. Luckily, she was alone as it rose to the sixth floor.

Priscilla was barely able to breathe, heart pounding madly as she lugged the arrangement along the hallway to Suite 610, repeating to herself that she was doing nothing more than delivering complimentary flowers to a valued guest. At the suite, she knocked on the door. If someone answered, it would be simple enough to present the flowers with the Savoy's compliments. Teodoro might actually be charmed. His Princess of the Savoy, personally delivering a beautiful flower arrangement. On the other hand, if no one answered, well, what could she do but leave the flowers in the suite? No one could fault her for that. Could they?

She knocked again and still there was no answer. Her heart pounding even more furiously, she inserted the key into the lock. The door clicked open and, holding the arrangement in front of her like a shield, she stepped inside.

"Hullo," she called as she crossed the threshold. "Priscilla Tempest from the press office. Is anyone here?"

Priscilla received an answering silence. She backed against the door, feeling it close behind her. The drapes had been drawn so that the sitting room in which she found herself was cast in shadow. Placing the flowers on a nearby coffee table, she took a deep breath, hoping to settle her racing heart, promising herself that she would take no more than a quick look around and then get out of there.

Official-looking papers were stacked atop the desk, but they were all in Italian, Priscilla discovered as she quickly leafed through them. Anything that might provide insight into the prince's illegal activities would be in a language she did not understand. Great, she thought.

Moving the papers carefully, she discovered a battered loose-leaf daybook. She stared down at it for a time, hesitant to move it in case the prince returned and noticed that his papers had been disturbed. Very carefully, she lifted up the book and opened it to the day's date, hoping it might provide some clue as to Teodoro's activities.

Scrawled across the page in pencil was a single notation: "Wanderworth Group riunione 20 hr. Wanderworth House."

Riunione? Italian for what? Priscilla wondered. Meeting? A meeting of a group at 8 p.m. at a place called the Wanderworth House.

She spent time replacing the daybook so that it was positioned exactly how she found it. She crossed the sitting room and poked her head into the bedroom. Suitcases were piled on luggage racks in a corner, but otherwise there was no sign that a prince was a guest here. Either the vast canopied bed had not been slept in or the housekeeping staff had already cleaned the suite. It was hard to tell, given the fastidiousness of the hotel's maids, but the suite gave off the sense that nobody actually lived in it.

Priscilla made her way to the door, heaving a quiet sigh of relief that she was getting out of there. She opened the door, and stepped into the hall, feeling her heartbeat settling. She had taken a tremendous risk for which there wasn't much reward, she thought, but at least she had gotten away undetected.

"Hey there," a voice called.

Priscilla jumped in alarm. She swung around quickly as Gordon Scott sauntered toward her.

CHAPTER SIX

La Dolce Death

"We meet again," Gordon Scott said, coming to a stop as she finished shutting the door, petrified at having been caught red-handed exiting a guest's suite.

"No threatening Italians this time, I'm glad to see," Gordon added with a grin. He wore a tan suit that went nicely with his tanned face, Priscilla thought, and also with the blond highlights shot through thick, curly hair.

"No, just dropping off flowers at a guest's suite," Priscilla said, making it sound as though she did this all the time.

"Must be a very special guest," Gordon said.

"What makes you say that?" Was that a nervous edge she was hearing in her voice?

"Well, an attractive young woman has yet to drop flowers off at my suite," Gordon said.

Aha, Priscilla thought, feeling suddenly on firmer ground. Tarzan flirting. She could handle that. "Yes, but you've just arrived," Priscilla said. "You must be patient, Mr. Scott. The Savoy prides itself in taking care of its valued guests."

"That's reassuring," Gordon said. "I'm not feeling quite so hurt now."

"At the Savoy, we work very hard to make sure no guest's feelings are hurt."

"If that's the case, then would you be willing to walk with me down to what you call the Front Hall?"

"Of course," said Priscilla. Was that her heart picking up speed again? It had better not be, she reminded herself.

As Gordon escorted her along the corridor, Priscilla assured herself that this was a good thing, Tarzan functioning as an alibi. As they waited for the lift to arrive, Priscilla asked, "What brings you to London, Mr. Scott? If you don't mind my asking."

"I'm meeting with some English and American producers," Gordon said. "They want to make a movie called *La Dolce Death*.

"Well, it's an interesting title," Priscilla offered diplomatically.

"I'm trying to change my image," Gordon explained.

"You're Tarzan, aren't you?"

"Not for a while. Now I make sword-and-sandal pictures in Rome. This would be a more contemporary type of character. I wouldn't have to wear a loincloth."

"I see."

"I'm kind of stuck in a rut," Gordon continued. "The money's good, and I don't have to spend a lot on clothes, but still, maybe it's time for a change."

The lift arrived. Gordon held the door while she stepped in.

"Are you going to do *La Dolce Death*?" Priscilla asked as the lift descended.

Gordon shrugged noncommittally. "It depends on whether they can raise the money. The script is pretty bad." He grinned at her. "However, that's never stopped me before. After all, I'm the guy who got talked into playing Hercules—twice."

"I didn't know that," Priscilla said.

"Understandable," Gordon said with a grin. "You don't strike me as someone who has seen a lot of Hercules movies."

Or Tarzan, Priscilla thought to herself.

"I'm supposed to meet some prospective investors this week out at a place called Wanderworth House. Do you know it?"

Priscilla couldn't quite believe what she had just heard. "Wanderworth?"

Gordon nodded. "Apparently, it's a pretty spectacular estate about an hour outside London."

"I'm afraid I don't know it," Priscilla said. "Of course, Britain is full of spectacular houses."

"In America, we would call them palaces."

"The British like to understate things," Priscilla offered, her mind still reeling.

"You don't sound very British, if you don't mind my saying."

"I'm Canadian, actually."

"Ah, Canada. No wonder you're so polite."

"I'm part of the Savoy staff," Priscilla said. "We are all polite. Day and night."

They laughed together as the lift came to a stop at the ground floor. Gordon followed her into the Front Hall. "Well, here we are," he said, facing her.

"Yes," Priscilla said.

"I'll be waiting for those flowers—politely," he said.

"Yes, how could I forget? Good luck with *La Dolce Death*."

Gordon made a face. "I'll let you know how it goes—when you deliver the flowers."

Right, Priscilla thought as she headed back to 205. Flowers for Tarzan. Mustn't forget.

Relieved to be back in the comparative safety of her office, Priscilla spent some time comforting herself with the notion that as mad as what she had done was, she appeared to have gotten away with it. Not that she had learned much about Prince Teodoro's activities—except for a meeting at a place called Wanderworth House. The same Wanderworth where, coincidentally, Gordon Scott said he was going to be meeting potential investors.

A prince having a meeting was nothing unusual—was it? Unless it was. And would Tarzan himself, by any stretch of wild imagination, have anything to do with what Teodoro was up to? To be a good snoop, she decided, one also had to be suspicious— of just about everyone. Even Tarzan.

Susie was back and poking her head into Priscilla's office. Her round, peaches-and-cream face was aglow. "I just *talked* to Gordon Scott," she gasped.

"As long as that's all you did with him," Priscilla said.

"He is just so dreamy," swooned Susie. "I wouldn't mind at all if Mr. Scott were to swing down on a vine in nothing but that animal-skin loincloth he wears in the movies, his body oiled and glistening, and sweep me off to his jungle lair. I would bear his children and we would live happily ever after."

"In the time you have left before you leave for the jungle, step in here so I can ask you a question."

"Certainly," Susie said, abruptly sobering. She closed the door as she came in. "What is it, Priscilla?"

"Do you know anything about Wanderworth House?"

Susie's face brightened. "Wow, yes. That house is amazing. My cousin and I used to spend weekends there with my parents."

Susie was one of the Gore-Langtons, a very rich, very establishment family. Or they had been a rich establishment family. There was talk that the elder Gore-Langton had lost most of his fortune in a series of ill-advised business ventures. Nonetheless, the Gore-Langtons managed to cling to a certain pedigree in London society, which raised the question of what exactly their only daughter was doing basically slumming in the Savoy press office.

"We were all very frightened of Lady Wanderworth, of course," Susie continued, as if it was a well-known fact that children in general were afraid of this woman.

"Lady Wanderworth?"

"You are from Canada." Susie's tone suggested that might not be such a good thing. "Otherwise, you would almost certainly know of Lady Daphne Wanderworth. There were all sorts of nasty stories about her before the war."

"What sort of stories?" Priscilla asked.

"Well, they were more than simply stories. There were claims back then that she was a German sympathizer. You know, that she supported the Nazis and didn't think Britain should go to war with them."

"But you didn't know that when you visited, did you?"

"I was a child, and it was obviously after the war." She lowered her voice to a conspiratorial level. "I knew nothing about Nazis. I just thought she was a witch."

"What made you think that?"

"For one thing, she *looked* like a witch. You know, very small and hunched over with these deeply set, haunted eyes. Long, lank hair that we were certain she had dyed black. We were always afraid she would cast a spell on us. Turn us into toads or something."

"But she never did," Priscilla observed.

"As you can see." Susie did a quick pivot to display the evidence that she was anything but a toad. She stopped and asked, "What makes you ask about Wanderworth House?"

"It happened to come up in conversation," Priscilla said vaguely. "I'd never heard anything about it. But then as you like to point out, I'm a stranger in a strange land."

"As far as I know, she's still out there at Wanderworth, casting spells and wishing Adolf Hitler were the prime minister of Britain."

As well as entertaining an Italian prince later this evening, Priscilla mused—and perhaps an unexpected guest.

The Witch of Wanderworth

Wanderworth House shone out of the darkness amid masses of encroaching oak, beech and ash forests. Seemingly set in the middle of the nowhere that was Buckinghamshire, it perched on the ridge of one of the Chiltern Hills, a balustraded, Italianate structure as far away from a house as Priscilla could imagine. The wonders of English understatement, calling this mass of brick and stone that had been around since the 1700s a house, she thought. She drove past a marble nymph mounted upon a cockleshell at the head of a wide gravel drive that cut through an emerald-green lawn to the residence.

Priscilla peered out the windscreen of her Morris Minor at the brightly lit finials and balusters that adorned Wanderworth's facade. Expensive vehicles gleamed in a line outside the main entrance, driven, Priscilla assumed, by guests present for the eight o'clock meeting. She glanced at the dashboard clock. It was eight fifteen. She was running a bit late.

But late for what, exactly? A rendezvous with Gordon Scott? How would she handle that if he were present? She was about to find out, wasn't she? Improvising all the way. She found a spot in a parking area adjacent to the house. She turned off the engine and adjusted the rear-view mirror to check her makeup. With any luck she would pass muster inside Wanderworth House.

A couple of hulks guarded the porticoed entranceway. Someone had made the mistake of stuffing them into evening clothes.

One of the guards was in charge of smiling; the other, glum-faced, wasn't. The smiling guard held a clipboard.

"Good evening, ma'am," he said to Priscilla. "Could I have your name please?"

"Priscilla Tempest. I'm with Prince Teodoro."

The smiling guard checked his clipboard. "Yes, the prince has arrived."

"I'm running a bit late," Priscilla said. "The prince will be wondering where I am."

"The guests have all gathered in the great room," said the smiling guard. "Do you know the way?"

"Of course," Priscilla said, not having a clue, but not about to admit it to these ominous guardians of the gate.

A long gallery was flanked by a series of austere, hollow-eyed aristocrats of noble lineage, cast in marble, set upon pedestals. Ahead, Priscilla could hear the murmur of voices. She came into a great room, subtly lit by lamps with fringed shades set on end tables around plush crimson and canary-yellow sofas. Elderly men in bespoke three-piece suits, fitted to perfection by their Savile Row tailors, occupied the sofas while other elderly men in similar suits stood together on the opulent Axminster carpet, cocktails in hand. Conversation came to a halt as the group spotted Priscilla. She swallowed hard and then declared, in a tone suggesting the comfort she wished she felt: "Good evening, gentlemen."

Murmurs approximating greetings from the gathered gentlemen followed. A red-coated waiter approached. "Would you care for something to drink, ma'am?"

"A glass of champagne would be lovely, please," Priscilla said. She glanced around, hoping Gordon Scott might appear. He didn't.

A plump, red-faced man, an impressive white moustache on display, a blue polka-dot bow tie at his throat, wandered over. "Hullo there," he said. "Ashbury's my name. Colin Ashbury."

Priscilla took his offered hand. "Priscilla Tempest."

"I must say, it's unusual, but a pleasure nonetheless, to have a woman join the group," Ashbury said. "The others are in a bit of shock, I'm afraid."

"Are they?"

"Indeed. You are new, are you not?"

"Prince Teodoro is a friend," Priscilla replied noncommittally.

"Ah, yes, the prince." Ashbury didn't look particularly happy as he said this.

The waiter was back, presenting her with a flute of champagne on a silver tray. Relief, Priscilla thought, taking a sip. Then she quickly took another sip, nerves settling. That felt much better.

Ashbury leaned in and said, "Have you seen her tonight?"

"I'm sorry?"

"Her. Lady Daphne." He leaned closer and dropped his voice. "On a bit of a tear, I hear."

"Oh? Why is that?" asked Priscilla.

"They're not coming." Ashbury's voice was down to a whisper. "Cancelled at the last minute."

"I'm sorry," Priscilla said, mystified. "Who is not coming?"

"The duke and duchess."

"Of Windsor?"

Ashbury moved his head up and down. "They are great and good friends of Lady Daphne, since before the war."

"I had no idea," Priscilla said.

"I knew him a bit before they plunked a crown on his thick head," Ashbury went on *sotto voce*. "A lot of fun back then. But now he's a bit bonkers, if you ask me. Too much sun in the Bahamas, I suspect. She's a handful. Never forgiven us for failing to embrace her. What did she expect? A divorcee and all that. A couple of bores, if you ask me. But they do support the cause, I suppose."

"The cause?"

Ashbury gave her a sly look. "The cause, my dear. We must all support the cause, you know."

Distracted, looking over Priscilla's shoulder, Ashbury announced, "Ah, here they are. The dark prince and the lady of the house."

She turned to see Prince Teodoro, resplendent in a black cape slung across his broad shoulders, entering, pushing a wheelchair containing a tiny, wizened woman with a mat of black hair, wearing dark glasses and a black gown. A shadowy spectre.

The other guests turned to greet her with light applause. The woman made an impatient face and announced, "Enough! Enough!"

"Lady Daphne remains in high dudgeon, I see," Ashbury whispered with a certain amount of satisfaction. Priscilla couldn't help but recall how Susie had described her: the Witch of Wanderworth. All she needed, thought Priscilla unkindly, was a broomstick.

Teodoro wheeled Lady Daphne to the centre of the room as the applause subsided. He looked around at the assembled guests and spotted Priscilla. His eyes narrowed as though trying to place her and then they widened suddenly with recognition. Lady Daphne had begun to speak in a loud, nasal drawl. "Thank you all for being here this evening. I'm so sorry the Duke and Duchess of Windsor could not be with us. I am told His Highness has a cold. We wish him a speedy recovery. But the duke assures me that we of the Wanderworth Group continue to have his full support. He promises to visit us soon with the duchess."

She craned around so that she could see Teodoro standing behind her. "We are thrilled to have Prince Teodoro with us once again this evening, one of our most dedicated supporters. *Benvenuto*, Prince Teodoro!"

"*Grazie mille*, Lady Daphne," responded the prince happily. "It is such a great pleasure to be back in Britain with all of you and to be part of your ongoing quest to bring about the changes necessary to return this nation to its former glory. We are working toward the same goals in Italy and throughout Europe. Working together to end the terrible blight of democracy and the parliamentary system and embrace stricter government, more rigid centralization that brings the order and prosperity to our nations that is so lacking. Undaunted by the forces arrayed against us, we can succeed—we *will* succeed! We come again!"

The prince's words were met with a chorus of "We come again!" from the collected guests. Colin Ashbury did not join in.

"At this rate, I am not so sure there is any chance in the world we will *actually* come again—if you ask me," he said quietly to Priscilla. "I mean, how is a thug like Teodoro going to help us change anything?"

"I don't know," Priscilla said. "Is that what he is?"

"We achieve the change we advocate by convincing people ours is the better way," Ashbury said, his voice low. "We don't achieve it with the jackboot tactics favoured by Teodoro and his lot." Ashbury was shaking his head. "For the life of me, I can't understand why she has anything to do with him. Makes me think twice."

"Does it?" Priscilla asked. "What does it make you think?"

"Things I should not be thinking—not here at Wanderworth House, that's for certain..."

"Ah, here she is to surprise us, my lovely Princess of the Savoy!" Teodoro was suddenly at Priscilla's side with a smile that looked as though it had been screwed into his face and was about as sincere. He glanced at Ashbury. "Has Colin been telling you horrible stories about me?"

Ashbury looked slightly alarmed and then quickly recovered. "Merely filling in this young lady as to what sets you apart from the others here, Teodoro."

"Colin and I go back so many years," the prince stated with forced conviviality. "We met in Rome after the war. We know each other only too well. Each other's secrets." He regarded Ashbury icily. "Do we not, Colin?"

"I am afraid we do," Ashbury acknowledged grudgingly.

"So tell me, Colin, what sets me apart from the others?"

"Perhaps it is the little things, you know, such as your ruthless desire to upend the institutions that are the foundations of Western democracy."

"Is that not the desire of everyone here tonight?" Teodoro asked.

"Perhaps not everyone," Ashbury replied sullenly. "Remember, Teodoro, I know all your tricks, everything you're capable of."

"I am capable of bringing about change." He shot Priscilla a quick glance as he spoke. "As are you, Colin—if I can convince you to stay the course."

"I do believe I need another drink," Ashbury said in a choked voice.

"Yes, Signor Ashbury, I believe you do," Teodoro answered coldly. Threateningly?

"It has been a pleasure meeting you, Miss Tempest." Ashbury had turned to Priscilla. "Please take care of yourself." Was that a warning? wondered Priscilla.

Ashbury cast a furtive glance in Priscilla's direction before turning abruptly away.

As soon as Ashbury was gone, Teodoro's face darkened. "What are you doing here?"

"For starters, suggesting that it's probably not a good idea to make a scene," Priscilla shot back.

"Yes, you are right." Teodoro kept the obligatory smile rigidly in place as he spoke. "No scene is necessary. We are all friends, are we not?"

"How could we not be?" answered Priscilla tightly.

"But still, you have not answered my question."

"Perhaps I'm a supporter of your cause—of the Wanderworth Group—and I wanted to see for myself what it is all about."

Teodoro's dark eyes were full of doubt. "No one was supposed to know about this meeting."

"Well, I knew, didn't I?"

"And who do we have here?" Lady Daphne had wheeled herself over to confront Priscilla and Teodoro.

"A friend to our cause," Teodoro answered quickly. "Miss Priscilla Tempest. Priscilla, I present our hostess this evening, Lady Daphne Wanderworth."

"It's so nice to meet you," Priscilla said, smiling.

"Nice?" Lady Daphne flared. "Nice? Well, that doesn't say much, does it?"

"I'm sorry—" Priscilla began, before being cut off.

"Young woman, your skirt is too short and you are wearing too much makeup," admonished Lady Daphne.

"I—I'm sorry you feel that way," Priscilla gulped.

"I do like the English rose aspect of young women like yourself. I do not like tramps."

"I will try to remember that for the next time we meet," Priscilla said.

"Please do," the old lady snapped. "*If* there is a next time," she added.

Teodoro, Priscilla noticed, did not rush to her defence. Burning with embarrassment in the wake of the nasty old dowager's attack, Priscilla tried to change the subject. "You know a friend of mine, I believe, Lady Daphne. Susan Gore-Langton? Her parents used to visit here. She has fond memories of Wanderworth House."

Or more precisely, remembered horrors of an evil spell-casting witch, Priscilla thought. Out of the corner of her eye, Priscilla could see Colin Ashbury sliding out of the room.

"Susan, you say?" Lady Daphne's eyes were like flints.

"Yes, she's a friend in London," Priscilla said.

"Don't like her. A hussy, I am led to understand by her parents." Lady Daphne had become upset about Susie's descent into hussiness.

"I don't think that's the case at all," Priscilla countered in defence.

"That is most certainly not what I hear from her parents. Fine Anglo-Saxon stock, I must say. But their daughter? Little Miss Round Heels!" Lady Daphne appeared to be working herself into an even higher dudgeon than Colin Ashbury might have imagined. "What is more, I have it on the best authority that she has embraced *communism!*"

"Oh dear," said Priscilla, adopting a suitably shocked expression, at the same time doubting that, politically, Susie was much of anything, let alone a communist. "I had no idea."

"This country is headed for *ruination* thanks to the likes of our young Miss Susan. Promiscuity. Popular music. Today's theatre—the far left at its devilish work. They have infected our politics and culture with their poison, allowed this country to become invaded by aliens. Perdition is in store for us all, unless people like ourselves act and act quickly to turn things around and make Britain great again." Lady Daphne's eyes were like lasers drilling into Priscilla.

"I am sure Priscilla could not agree more," Teodoro said gently.

"I'm not sure I do, if you'd care to know the truth," Priscilla said brightly.

"Yes, well, that is enough," interjected Teodoro. The smile he had worked so hard to maintain was gone.

Lady Daphne shot daggers at Priscilla before turning to Teodoro. "I wish to speak to you privately." Without another word, she swung her wheelchair around and wheeled away.

Teodoro clutched Priscilla's arm with such force it caused her to gasp with a combination of pain and fright. The temperature in the room had dropped perceptibly. Priscilla suspected she was no longer Teodoro's princess. "I think it is time you left," he said to her angrily. "I want you gone by the time I come back. Do you understand, Priscilla?"

He let go of her arm and turned to follow Lady Daphne. Priscilla was left standing there alone, awkwardly holding her champagne. Others in the room, the bespoke gentlemen, had become silent. Everyone ignored her. Okay, she thought to herself, time to make an escape. But first she needed a stop at the loo before starting the long trip back to London.

Priscilla left the great room with all eyes, she was certain, following her out. She entered a wide, marble-floored hallway. This time, rather than nobles on pedestals, the walls on either side were lined with gilt-framed oil paintings displaying history's great Wanderworth worthies. Supremely well-fed and self-satisfied gents if their smug countenances were any indication. She reached an oak staircase with carpeted runners. She could hear voices coming from above. One of those voices sounded as if it belonged to Lady Daphne.

Priscilla glanced around. No one was in sight. Swiftly she climbed the stairs and found herself at the end of a carpeted hallway. The voices were coming from a slightly open door further along. She went toward it.

"...all well and good, Prince Teodoro, but that is not why I invited you to spend time with us." Lady Daphne's high, brittle voice carried into the hallway. "We come again, yes, all well and good—but we must come *now*."

"I am at your service," Priscilla heard Teodoro say. "I dislike mere talk as much as you, my lady."

"My thinking is of a series of targeted attacks much as you have orchestrated in Italy," Lady Daphne replied.

"We were very successful in disrupting the government in Rome, making the people think twice about so-called democracy and question its value." Teodoro spoke with great pride. "We have targeted certain politicians, employing methods of coercion to bring them to our movement. My agents, disruptors we call them in English, they are very good at this sort of thing."

"This is what we must do here," agreed Lady Daphne with enthusiasm. "I've already put together a list of susceptible politicians. You are bringing in your people?"

"They will arrive soon." Teodoro's voice again. "But what about the others in your group? Are they prepared to take more... forceful action?"

"They are overfed fools, swilling drinks in their evening finery," Lady Daphne snapped. "Well-meaning, but useless, preferring to stand around as they are tonight, talking but afraid to take the actions necessary. You are different, Prince Teodoro—you have demonstrated your ruthless courage many times. So admirable. That is what is needed—"

"Hey!"

Priscilla jerked around to see Al Cellini, dressed in regulation gangster black, his thin face twisted with anger, hurrying toward her from the other end of the hall.

She turned and clattered back down the stairs. At the bottom, she paused to remove her Charles Jourdan heels just as

Cellini reached the top of the stairs. He shouted to her again, and as she ran away she caught a glimpse of him bounding down behind her.

A pair of French doors opening onto a terrace became visible as she shot around a corner at the back of the house. She burst through the doors and onto the terrace and ran to a staircase that led down to the gardens. Shoes in one hand, gripping her shoulder bag with the other, she leapt down the stairs to a series of parterres intersecting multicoloured rose gardens. Behind her, Cellini yelled down from the terrace. As she started through the gardens, Priscilla heard the distant rumble of thunder.

A wall of forest rose at the end of the gardens against a blue night lit by sudden streaks of lightning. Rain began to pour down as she reached the forest. Oak trees towered around her, and the darkness and the uneven ground of the forest slowed her as she ran in her stockinged feet. She found herself groping blindly forward. A lightning flash showed an opening in the trees and she started for it. There the forest gave way to the ridge along one of the Chiltern Hills. She started down the slope but tripped over something in the grass. Stumbling, she cried out, desperately trying to maintain her footing and failing. Down on all fours, she still managed to cling to her shoes. Mustn't lose the shoes, she thought.

The lightning flashed again, casting brief light on the body she had just fallen over. The man lay on his back, eyes wide, staring up into the falling rain. Priscilla cleared the water from her eyes to get a closer look. Thunder followed by lightning lit the face of Colin Ashbury in vivid blue. She had an instant to notice the slit in his throat, from which poured the blood that had stained his white moustache and bow tie.

Then everything around her went dark.

CHAPTER EIGHT

Telephone from Heaven

Priscilla wasted no time in regaining her feet and restarting her run.

If they could murder Colin Ashbury, which they appeared to have done, then the guests at Wanderworth House could most certainly kill her.

She raced blindly through the rain, underbrush tearing at her nylons, until she reached an unpaved country road just as the downpour began to let up. She didn't have to follow the roadway very far before it dipped down into a shallow valley, allowing her a view of rooftops surrounding a church steeple. A sign further along welcomed her to the village of Stokes End.

The tiny houses on either side of what soon became a main road were dark and shuttered, occupied by decent people who went to bed at a proper hour and didn't want to overthrow British society or murder a hapless young woman who had ruined a very good pair of shoes.

She was about to knock on a nearby door and throw herself at the mercy of the good people of Stokes End when she spotted a petrol station at the end of the street. A red phone box, its interior drenched in pale light, stood like a beacon in the rainy darkness. A telephone sent from heaven, Priscilla thought with relief. She opened the door and fell into its warm, rain-free interior. She lifted the phone off its cradle. Now the conundrum. Who was the saviour she could call at this time of night? Not a lot of candidates out there.

However, there was one prospect, although she hated—*hated!*— to admit it.

"Was it?" Percy Hoskins asked in a slurred voice when he came on the line at the very moment, after countless rings, she was certain he wouldn't.

"It's me," Priscilla said, the words coming out in a garbled rush.

"Who me?" Percy sounded irritated as well as inarticulate. His beauty sleep had been disturbed.

"It's Priscilla," she said impatiently. "I need you to come and get me."

"Priscilla?" Percy suddenly sounded more awake.

"Yes, that's what I said." It was Priscilla's turn to be annoyed. What was wrong with him, anyway? "I need you to come for me."

"Where are you?"

"In Buckinghamshire. A village called Stokes End."

"What the blazes are you doing out there?"

"I'll tell you when you get here. I'm at a phone box by a petrol station. Bring a blanket and some towels."

"Towels?" Percy sounded confused. "What do you need towels for?"

"Just do it, Percy. And hurry. My life is very likely in danger." Not only melodramatic, but also quite possibly true.

"Come on," said Percy doubtfully. "Your life in danger? Give me a break."

"Percy—now!"

He issued a ragged exasperated sigh. "Take it easy, luv," he said. "I'm on my way."

Lady Daphne had sent word to the great room that due to the absence of the Duke and Duchess of Windsor and the inclement weather everyone should go home. They would meet again at a later date. She sat apprehensively with Teodoro in the library, its walls lined with shelves full of books. Al Cellini, drenched to the bone, entered looking pale and exhausted.

"She got away?" Teodoro asked in a disappointed voice.

"Al Cellini is too goddamn old to be chasing broads through the rain," Cellini replied.

Teodoro rose from the armchair where he had been sitting. He had removed his jacket and had been nursing a snifter of what he considered to be very good brandy. "I believe you could use a drink, my friend," he said to Cellini.

"Yeah, that's for sure," Cellini said.

Teodoro went to the trestle table at one side of the room that had been turned into a makeshift bar with an assortment of spirits. Teodoro poured brandy into a snifter and then brought it back to Cellini.

"How much do you think this woman heard?" demanded Lady Daphne, irritation masking her concern.

"What do you think, Al?" Teodoro asked by way of deflecting the question.

Cellini took a gulp of brandy before he said, "No idea, but she was listening at the door when I spotted her. What the hell was she doing here, anyway?"

"A very good question." Lady Daphne looked accusingly at Teodoro. "What about it, Prince Teodoro? Did you invite her?"

"I certainly did not," Teodoro said with a trace of nervousness.

"One of the skirts you chase, is that it?" she pressed.

"The noble prince who can't keep his hands off the broads," offered Cellini with a smirk Teodoro didn't like. For that matter, Teodoro did not like Cellini. He had no passion for what they were trying to accomplish. An American gangster, interested only in Lady Daphne's money to fund his business. A rough and loud bull in the china shop. Arrogant. The prince preferred more subtle methods—until it became apparent that subtlety would not work.

"She said she was interested in our cause and wanted to learn more," Teodoro replied defensively.

"Could she be working for Special Branch, trying to infiltrate our group?"

"I hardly think so," Teodoro said. "Priscilla is no more than a miniskirt-wearing nobody who pours champagne for celebrities at the Savoy. If she heard anything at all, it's meaningless. Who would ever listen to her?"

"We were talking about the overthrow of the government," said Lady Daphne darkly. "It is not meaningless. We cannot take any chances."

"Let Al Cellini handle it," announced Cellini.

"Al," Teodoro said in a warning voice.

"This is personal," Cellini said, his voice tight with anger. "Al Cellini knows how to take care of things like this. Not to worry."

"No," Teodoro said decisively. "For now, let me handle it."

CHAPTER NINE

The Rescue

Priscilla huddled and shivered next to the petrol station's garage, out of sight in case her pursuers showed up looking for her. There was little traffic, only the deep silence of the night, the moon out after the rain, dark puddles of water glistening against the slick pavement of the petrol station.

She thought about what she had overheard. A serious plot to overthrow the government? Or nutters talking nonsense, led by a crazy old woman and a comical Italian prince? Except this evening Teodoro had not seemed so comical. Was there someone she could report all this to? But then what would she say? That she had followed a guest of the Savoy into the country and then listened in on his private conversation, not really certain what she was hearing? Wouldn't that go over well with Mr. Banville.

And what about the dead body?

Oh God, she thought despairingly. The dead body.

What was she to do? She was totally lost on a rainy night in the country—and scared.

Very scared.

Percy finally showed up an hour later, behind the wheel of his battered shamrock-green Bentley, the incessant rattle of its faulty exhaust and sputtering motor announcing itself before the headlights appeared.

As the Bentley drew to a stop, Priscilla stepped from her hiding place against the wall and, carrying her ruined shoes and drenched shoulder bag, hurried over and got into the car.

Percy, unshaven, his untamed hair leaping around his head, swathed in a faded brown trench coat that looked as though it had been retrieved from the mud of a First World War battle-field, reacted with shock when he saw her sodden state. "Dammit, Priscilla, this is a Bentley. These are real leather seats," he pointed out anxiously as soon as she was beside him in the car. "You're soaking wet. You're going to ruin them."

"You bastard," Priscilla flared angrily. "I almost got myself killed tonight trying to help you, and you're worried about your *car seats?*"

"Out here? Helping me? How's that?"

"Yes," she retorted. "Helping *you.*" Choking back tears. "Although I'll be damned if I know why."

Seeing Priscilla's distress, Percy spoke more gently. "You were trying to help me. I appreciate that. Tell me what happened."

"I've ruined a pair of perfectly good Charles Jourdan shoes, for starters," Priscilla said.

"I'm sorry about your shoes."

"Did you remember to bring a towel?"

Percy reached into the back and pulled a thin towel off the seat and handed it to her. She glared at it. "This is the best you could do?"

"Hey, it was short notice," he said. "You said you were in trouble. Being the heroic guy I am, I wanted to get out here as fast as I could."

"I *am* in trouble, and heroic guys don't grumble the way you do," Priscilla said, using the towel to dry her hair as best she could.

"This heroic guy came to the rescue," Percy pointed out.

"Okay, heroic guy, right now you'd better get us out of here."

Percy looked as though he very much wanted to say something else, but then thought better of it and put the Bentley into gear. The engine, reacting to being forced to move forward, screamed defiance.

"What's wrong with this car?" Priscilla demanded as Percy turned onto the roadway.

"It's my temperamental baby," Percy said.

"The baby sounds like an old man dying," Priscilla suggested.

"This car is my pride and joy, but I don't drive it that often. Only when I have to rescue someone."

Priscilla let out a deep breath. "Thank you for coming, Percy. I do appreciate it," she said earnestly. She had to give the heroic guy something, didn't she? After all, how many other men in her life would have come for her in the middle of the night? She settled back in her seat, beginning to finally unbend as she used the towel to dry her face and arms.

"What happened? How did you end up here?" Percy kept his eyes on the road as he spoke. The Bentley's headlights cut through an otherwise black night on a roadway with Brothers Grimm forests threatening on either side.

"I'll tell you," Priscilla said, thinking she had to tell him *something*. "But just let me catch my breath. I'm just so exhausted..."

"Take your time," Percy said. When Priscilla didn't answer, he glanced over and saw that she had fallen fast asleep. Even with her hair a mess, her makeup smeared, Percy couldn't help but think there was something utterly beguiling about Priscilla. What was it, anyway? Certainly, there was plenty about her that he disliked, including her predilection for calling him only when she needed something—like tonight for instance. Of course, he admitted to himself, she could say the same about him. She only heard from him when *he* needed something. Maybe that was their fate in life: using each other so they could be together without ever having to concede that's what they both wanted.

He stole another look at her. Ah, the innocence, he thought, Priscilla in repose, that scheming mind of hers stilled for the time being. You could fall in love with a woman who looked like that. Could you not? Falling in love. Good God, he thought. Even the words produced an involuntary shudder. If he ever allowed himself to really, truly love her, then he would have to hope that she loved him. And he had his doubts about that possibility.

Ahead, becoming visible above the trees, below the moon, were the glowing lights of a big house perched on a ridge. Percy vaguely recollected this was the legendary Wanderworth House, home of the highly controversial Lady Daphne Wanderworth.

He picked up speed. The sooner they got back to London and he got the story out of her, the better.

CHAPTER TEN

The Plot Thickens

Priscilla had no choice but to allow Percy to follow her into her flat at No. 37–39 Knightsbridge, embarrassed all over again viewing the mess she had left behind. She was going to clean up the place, she really was, but since she wasn't expecting company there was no hurry. Except now there was company. And the place was a mess.

Where did all these clothes come from, anyway? She couldn't possibly own so many clothes. There must be someone else secretly occupying the flat when she wasn't there. That other person had also left unwashed dishes in the sink. Certainly, she couldn't have left them. It was well known how much she despised anyone who left dirty dishes in a sink.

Trying not to think about how Percy might regard a woman who lived in so much clutter, she escaped to the bedroom, ignoring the unmade bed, the clothes tossed everywhere, the various makeup paraphernalia spilled across her dressing table. Quickly, she discarded her ruined Charles Jourdans, tore off her rain-drenched dress, stripped off her torn nylons and dived under a reviving shower.

Wrapped in a terry-cloth robe and now feeling as though there was at least the possibility of life, Priscilla re-entered the living room to find Percy holding up a glass of white wine. "I thought you might need this." He handed her the glass. From

72

what she could ascertain, he appeared oblivious to the clothes strewn everywhere.

"You're an angel," she said, taking the glass and immediately regretting calling Percy an angel. The relief at being safely home, showered and alive had lowered her defences. Percy was not generally known for his angelic qualities.

Too late. "Aha, I knew it," he pounced. "All I had to do to be recognized was drive out into the country in the middle of the night in the pissing rain, pick you up, bring you home and pour you a glass of wine."

"The wine," she said. "It blurred my thinking. I may have gone too far with the angel bit."

"Doesn't tonight add to my angelic qualities?"

"It certainly helps," Priscilla had to concede. She sipped at her wine, feeling its warmth flowing through her before slumping onto the sofa.

Percy moved to sit beside her. "Maybe it's time to tell me what happened," he suggested. He wasn't drinking anything, Priscilla noticed. Percy Hoskins, ace reporter, sober and on the job.

"You wanted me to search Teodoro's suite," Priscilla started. "And so that's what I did."

"You got into his suite?" The dismay was evident in his voice.

"Don't sound so surprised," admonished Priscilla.

"No, no," he hastened. "It's just that the Savoy is a considerable distance from a phone box in Stokes End."

True enough, she thought. She described how she had come across the daybook entry in Teodoro's suite about a meeting at a place she hadn't heard of before, Wanderworth House. On a whim, she had decided to drive out there. Prince Teodoro had been present, as had the witchy lady of the house, Lady Daphne Wanderworth, and her well-dressed male guests, all members of the Wanderworth Group. The guests of honour were supposed to be the Duke and Duchess of Windsor.

"You're not serious," interrupted Percy with a shake of his head.

"However, they didn't show up."

"Okay, then what?"

"I met Lady Daphne, who went on about the group dedicating itself to making a better, stronger Britain and how great it was to have Teodoro there to help them accomplish this. Then when Teodoro introduced me to her, she immediately suggested that I'm a tramp."

"I wonder where she would get that idea." Thankfully, Percy was grinning when he said it. Still...

She punched him in the arm. "Bastard."

"Go on," Percy urged. "Lady Daphne Wanderworth, notorious fascist sympathizer, wants a better, stronger Britain. Then what?"

"Then I overheard what they really want."

"What's that?"

"As crazy as it seems, they talked about overthrowing the government and blackmailing politicians in order to do it. That's why Prince Teodoro is in London—to help Lady Daphne achieve those goals."

"It may not be so crazy at all," Percy said. "There are a lot of people in this country who would like to do away with democracy—and are willing to go to any lengths in order to make that happen."

"That isn't all," Priscilla said.

"There's more?" asked Percy, disbelievingly.

She went on to describe her escape from the house, chased through the gardens and into a nearby forest by Teodoro's associate, Al Cellini.

"Hold up a minute," Percy interrupted. "Al Cellini?"

"You know him?" Priscilla's turn to be surprised.

"He's a partner in the Colony Sports Club, a hot London gambling establishment. One of his partners is the American actor George Raft. I had no idea Cellini was hooked up with Teodoro."

"Well, he is," said Priscilla. "That's how I got involved in the first place."

"How do you mean?"

"This is what I didn't tell you before," Priscilla confessed. "Mr. Banville called me to his office. Prince Teodoro was there. Cellini was waiting in the outer office. Mr. Banville asked me to find out about a story the prince believes you're writing about him. When I got out of the office, Cellini waylaid me and said I'd better find out what you were up to—or else."

"That's what he said, 'or else'?"

"He certainly implied that, yes."

"That's why you called me?" Percy's astonishment was mixed with emerging anger. "You were trying to use me."

"Who was using who?" replied Priscilla peevishly. "You were the one who urged me to break into his hotel suite."

"You should have told me about Teodoro," Percy replied sullenly.

"I'm telling you now. And there's something else you should know."

"What?"

"The body."

"What body?" Percy demanded.

"The body I tripped over as I was running away from Al Cellini."

Percy grappled with what Priscilla was telling him. "You sure it was a body—a *dead* body?"

"Yes, dead, for heaven's sake. I believe it was a man named Colin Ashbury. I'd been talking to him in the house. His throat had been cut. It was pretty awful."

Percy was on his feet, pacing. "Okay, this is developing into one hell of a story."

"But what *is* the story, Percy?" Priscilla asked in an exasperated voice. "What are *you* not telling *me*?"

"The Wanderworth Group and what they are conspiring to do. Maybe the biggest scoop of my career—"

"It must be my Canadian ignorance of British history," Priscilla said, "but beyond the bits I picked up tonight, I have no idea what the Wanderworth Group is."

"Before the war, a number of British aristocrats, organized by Lady Daphne, came out in support of Hitler. They thought der Führer had the right ideas about how to run a country and Britain should emulate him. Lady Daphne met with Hitler a number of times and was said to consider him a friend. The Prince of Wales may have been part of the group—certainly he was considered a Nazi sympathizer."

"But that was before Britain declared war with Germany. Didn't that change everyone's attitude?"

"You would have thought so," Percy said. "But now with Lady Daphne organizing meetings at Wanderworth, just like in the old days, and Teodoro part of it, and maybe the Duke of Windsor as well, it looks like the Wanderworth Group is back in action. The former king of England, a fascist Italian prince, members of the British aristocracy, a plot to overthrow the government—and a dead body." Percy's face erupted with delight. "I can see the headlines now."

"Colin Ashbury told me he didn't like what he was hearing from Lady Daphne," Priscilla said, "and it was evident that he and Teodoro disliked one another. Maybe that's why they killed him."

"If they have murdered this guy Ashbury, then we must get the police involved," Percy said. "Once they find the dead man, ascertain that it's murder, then that becomes the basis for my story about Teodoro and the revival of the Wanderworth Group."

"The thing is, we can't be in this together," Priscilla admonished.

"Yes, we can," Percy insisted.

"Percy, you must keep my name out of it." Priscilla was suddenly feeling another sort of fear, the all-too-familiar one that came with the prospect of losing her job.

"How am I supposed to do that?" Percy had stopped pacing. "You are the witness to what happened at Wanderworth House. *You* overheard them plotting. *You* discovered the body."

"I didn't *discover* the body," Priscilla protested. "I tripped over it."

"It amounts to the same thing."

"And I'm not really certain what I heard," Priscilla said. "And I shouldn't have been hearing anything. As things stand right now, I get fired, not to mention potentially arrested for breaking into Teodoro's suite."

Percy resumed his seat beside Priscilla, deep in thought. Priscilla watched him, holding her breath. "Okay, here's what I can do," Percy said finally. "First thing in the morning, I'll give a friendly contact at Scotland Yard a call. Give him this bloke Ashbury's name and ask him to check on his whereabouts. If there is anything suspicious—"

"There *is* something very suspicious," Priscilla interjected. "He's dead."

"Fine, but we allow Scotland Yard to discover that for themselves. That way we keep your name out of it."

"What about the rest of them, Prince Teodoro, Cellini, Lady Daphne…?"

"For now, let's deal with Colin Ashbury. I suggest you report back to Banville, as you're supposed to. Tell him that you spoke to me and discovered that I've soured on the Teodoro story. Tell him I haven't been able to find anything and have dropped it."

"Okay. But Teodoro saw me at Wanderworth House. He knows that I overheard at least part of his conversation with Lady Daphne."

"Teodoro really doesn't know anything. And besides, what's he going to say?"

"Yes, but that's the thing, isn't it?" Priscilla said. "Teodoro knows about *me*. Maybe not everything, but enough to be concerned. The others know, too. What's to stop them from coming after me?"

"I'll stay with you tonight," Percy offered. "How's that?"

Her kneejerk reaction to such an offer from Percy Hoskins was to say no. Except she really didn't want to be alone in the flat. "Just don't get any ideas," she cautioned.

"What kind of ideas would I get?" Percy was the picture of rumpled innocence.

"The wrong ideas."

"There are no wrong ideas," Percy countered.

"Yes, there are, and what you're thinking is one of them."

"I'm thinking only of your safety—"

"Reassuring to know." Priscilla was on her feet.

"—although I have to be honest ... you do look quite fetching in that robe," Percy finished.

"Well, I'm off to bed—alone," Priscilla announced firmly. "There's a blanket in the closet if you get cold."

"I'll be fine." He had taken off his coat and was already stretching out on the sofa. He gave her a look out of the corner of his eye. "Doesn't your angel at least get a kiss goodnight?"

"No."

"A mere kiss for the hero who drove through the rain to rescue you. That doesn't seem too much to ask."

She ventured back to the sofa. He looked up at her, his craggy face alive with expectation. Not a bad-looking man, she couldn't help thinking, cleaned up enough to be presentable in public.

She bent over to kiss his forehead. "Good night," she murmured, "and thank you."

"That's it? That's all I get? A kiss on the forehead?"

"More than enough," Priscilla said, heading for her bedroom. "Much more than enough."

Percy called out something, possibly nasty, but by that time Priscilla had shut the bedroom door and didn't hear it.

A ringing telephone.

No, it wasn't possible. Not a ringing telephone. Not at this time of night. Priscilla pried open her eyes, staring at the phone on the nearby nightstand. It refused to stop making that infuriatingly shrill noise. She struggled up and reached for the receiver, trying to shake herself awake.

"In case you thought you got away tonight... think again." The harsh voice on the line was cold and precise. "We know who you are, Priscilla. We know where you live. No one can protect you. We come again."

The Horse's Mouth

Susie was nowhere to be seen when Priscilla arrived at 205 the next morning, her mind still spinning with thoughts of the late-night phone threat she had received. A death threat? How could it be anything else? Although Percy did not seem particularly perturbed when she woke him from a sound sleep to tell him.

"They won't dare do anything, particularly after the police get involved and they find a body on the grounds of Wander-worth House," Percy had reported confidently.

Priscilla wasn't so certain. After all, it wasn't Percy they would be coming after.

It was her.

Settling at her desk had the effect of calming her nerves as much as they could be calmed without hitting the waiter button that would summon Karl with badly needed coffee. Her fore-finger was hovering over it when the door opened and Prince Constantino peeked in. He was wearing his black suit. This morning his blue eyes—a zealot's eyes—burned against the translucent white of his face. Priscilla thought him ready to lead the next crusade as he stood before her, shoulders back and chin up. No match for the overwhelming presence of his cousin, but then Constantino wasn't threatening to kill her.

At least not yet.

"My press conference, Miss Tempest?" Constantino demanded. "Have you made progress?"

Yes, right, she thought, the press conference. Constantino's feud with his fascist cousin. Was the younger prince a fascist, too? Priscilla wondered.

"Miss Gore-Langton is supposed to be making those arrangements," Priscilla explained. Had she not?

"I have heard nothing," Constantino said.

"Miss Gore-Langton isn't in yet, but as soon as she is, I will speak to her," Priscilla said. "The necessary arrangements will be made. When would you like to schedule the press conference?"

"As soon as possible. As I have stated, time is of the essence. My cousin must be held accountable."

"How is your cousin?" Priscilla ventured, thinking that Constantino might know something.

"Why would you ask me that?" demanded Constantino. "I do not speak to him. He is a terrible, terrible man. I am surprised you have not asked him to leave the hotel."

"At the Savoy, we do not pass judgment on our guests," Priscilla stated in the formal voice she employed when making such announcements.

"Well, you should," Constantino muttered.

"Is there not a chance you might speak with your cousin, considering the fact that the two of you are guests here? Perhaps there is an opportunity for compromise before you go public with your accusations."

"I beg your pardon? What compromise? There is no compromise. My cousin is a murdering fascist *pig*," exploded Constantino. "He should be in jail, not staying at the Savoy and parading around London informing everyone that he is the Duke of Vento, when he knows full well that title rightfully belongs to *me*."

"Are you sure he knows that?" questioned Priscilla, finding it hard to believe, based on her limited experience with him, that Teodoro would ever acknowledge anything of the sort.

"I have told him of my vision. He knows my uncle came to me and that he desires for me to have the title."

"How did your cousin react to this news?" Priscilla couldn't resist asking.

Constantino looked pained. "He laughed in my face." Then his expression became resolute, once again prepared to lead the crusade. "But I will tell you this, Miss Tempest: I will have the last laugh. I can promise you that."

"But you are making serious allegations against your cousin," Priscilla pointed out, "allegations you are bound to be questioned about at your press conference."

"These *allegations* as you call them, they are true. Everyone knows them to be true."

"Can I ask you one more question?"

"Ask me anything, Miss Tempest."

"Do you know a woman named Lady Daphne Wanderworth?"

Prince Constantino looked puzzled. "What a curious question. I know this woman, of course, because she conspires with my cousin. They are *fascistas,* the two of them."

"What about a man named Colin Ashbury? Is that gentleman familiar to you?"

Constantino looked even more puzzled as he shook his head. "What has this to do with my press conference?"

"It's nothing." Priscilla waved a dismissive hand. "Please forgive our tardiness. As soon as Miss Gore-Langton arrives, she will be in touch to complete the necessary arrangements."

"Naturally, I forgive you. But please, do not forget."

"Nothing could possibly be more important."

"Then until we meet again." Constantino lowered his head in what amounted to a bow as he backed out of her office.

She looked at her watch. It was almost eleven o'clock. Susie wouldn't be Susie if she wasn't late. But she wasn't usually *this* late. Once again, Priscilla reached for the waiter button, only to be interrupted by the intrusive jangle of the telephone.

That could be either a death threat or a harried Susie desperately trying to explain why she was so late, she thought.

It was neither.

"He commands your presence," hissed the voice of El Sid.

"When?"

"Now!"

As usual when Priscilla entered the Place of Execution, Clive Banville was seated ramrod straight behind his vast desk. The gleaming surface, as far as Priscilla could see in the course of her many disciplinary visits, had never been cluttered with an actual piece of paper.

Banville did not ask Priscilla to be seated. This was hardly unusual. He rarely asked her to sit. She was never quite sure where exactly she was supposed to position herself, or how she was to stand. At attention? Head slightly bowed? How about ladylike guiltlessness signalled by the holding of her small hands daintily in front of her? Adopting this position made it clear that such a perfectly lovely picture of humbled femininity could not possibly be faulted. Thus far that carefully arranged posture had not worked well with Banville. But with no other option, Priscilla decided to try it again today, including the slightly bowed head, thrown in for good measure.

"Miss Tempest," Banville began imperiously, "I have been waiting patiently for you to call with a report on the situation involving Prince Teodoro and the press. There has been no call. Therefore, I've had to take it upon myself to summon you into my presence."

"I understand, sir," replied Priscilla dutifully. "I was about to call you but was tied up with Prince Teodoro's cousin, Prince Constantino."

"Does that mean you have something to report?"

"I do indeed, sir," Priscilla answered brightly.

"Then do tell. What have you found out?"

"I've spoken to Mr. Percy Hoskins, the reporter Prince Teodoro believes is doing a story about him."

"And is Hoskins doing such a story?" Banville demanded.

"No, he is not, as it turns out," Priscilla said, parroting what Percy advised her to say. A bald-faced lie if there ever was one, but needed for the moment, she told herself. "Mr. Hoskins informs me he has not been able to confirm the details he feels are necessary for his story."

"I am, needless to say, pleased to hear that," Banville said, actually looking quite pleased. "But it does sound as though this ink-stained bugger, Hoskins, was planning something pretty nasty."

"If you don't mind my saying..." Priscilla, daring to venture into the unknown waters where the job-destroying dragons lay in eager wait.

"What is it, Miss Tempest?" Banville, having received the answer he was looking for, was already showing impatience.

"I do wonder, given Prince Teodoro's rather shady reputa-tion—at least, shady as far as Mr. Hoskins has been able to ascer-tain—why we at the Savoy would place ourselves in the position of helping him with the press."

Banville arched an eyebrow, a sure sign that he was not happy with a question posed by one of his underlings.

"Miss Tempest, Prince Teodoro is a guest at this hotel. This hotel has prided itself over the course of its long and illustrious history in coming to the aid of its guests in any way it can, with-out question."

"I understand that, sir, and I am happy to maintain that tradition."

Banville hesitated, seeming to consider what he wanted to say next. "Still," he went on, "I must be honest and tell you that the Duke of Windsor might have played a part in my decision to come to the aid of Prince Teodoro."

"The Duke of Windsor, sir?" Priscilla's eyes widened with surprise. "The former Edward VIII?"

"Bertie, for heaven's sake, yes." Banville had returned to the usual tone he employed when dealing with Priscilla, one of dismissive annoyance. "He's a friend, you must understand. I once served briefly as his equerry. Happiest days of my life. Tremendous fellow. A tragedy he gave up the throne for that... woman."

Banville paused again, as though to reflect on those happy days. "Anyhow, Bertie called from Paris asking me to assist Prince Teodoro with this tabloid business. How could I say no to an old friend?"

"I understand, sir," Priscilla said.

"In any event, it's good that we can put this behind us," Banville went on. "I spoke to Prince Teodoro on the telephone just before you arrived. He would like you to go to his suite and personally report to him."

Priscilla froze. Words were abruptly clogged in her throat. "Would it not be better if you informed him, sir?"

"No, no," replied Banville dismissively. "You must speak to him. Horse's mouth sort of thing. He's waiting in his suite now. Go."

Horse's mouth? thought Priscilla. Or lamb to the slaughter?

CHAPTER TWELVE

The Monster in Suite 610

Better to get this over with rather than put it off, thought Priscilla gloomily as she stepped off the lift on the sixth floor and went along the hallway to Suite 610, Prince Teodoro's room—back to the scene of her crime, as it were. She steeled herself before rapping twice.

Teodoro opened the door wearing a snow-white shirt open almost to the waist, showing off an impressively massive chest. The playboy prince, Priscilla thought dimly. Teodoro greeted her with a welcoming smile, as though nothing in the world could be amiss—even though she knew all too well that plenty was.

"You are looking lovely, as always, even under the most trying circumstances," he said, closing the door behind her, the epitome of princely Italian charm today. He added, "You are, forever, my Princess of the Savoy."

"I highly doubt that is the case," Priscilla said coldly. She felt surprisingly confident as she confronted him. After all, inside the safe cocoon of the Savoy, she was at home.

"You are entirely mistaken, Priscilla," Teodoro was saying. "Nothing that has occurred between us changes my appreciation of you."

"Mr. Banville said you wanted me to report to you personally," Priscilla said brusquely. "That is what I am here to do."

"Yes." Teodoro, smiling confidently, drew closer, towering above her.

Too close.

"Would you please back away from me?"

"No." Teodoro held his smile.

Almost casually, he reached down and then suddenly yanked her against him. His thick arms were like iron, coiling themselves around her. His mouth mashed against hers, kissing her so deeply she had trouble breathing. She thought he would pull away after a moment, but he didn't. He just kept pressing his mouth hard into hers, not a kiss so much as an assault.

She struggled to free herself from his embrace, finally managing to push him off. She stumbled back, breathing hard. "What are... you... doing?"

"I'm not going to hit you," he said calmly. "That would leave a mark. There are other ways..."

He grasped her shoulders, wrestling her forward as he propelled her into the bedroom. He tossed her onto the bed and then, before she could move, straddled her, pinning her to the duvet, gripping her wrists so hard she was sure he would stop the blood flow. He was a dark, massive presence closing down the world around her. "You see, my princess?" he breathed. "You see what I can do to you?"

"Get off me, you bastard," Priscilla cried angrily.

She made a whimpering sound of disgust, tried to turn away, couldn't. She felt imprisoned in cement.

"You want to scream, I'm sure, but you can't," Teodoro said, lowering his head so that she had to inhale his stale breath as he spoke into her ear. "You know if you call for help, it will be your word against mine. I am the Duke of Vento, a most valued guest at this hotel; you are merely an employee. They will never believe you, Priscilla. They cannot afford to. You are expendable, while I am accommodated."

Teodoro abruptly released her wrists and heaved himself off her. She sat up in a daze while Teodoro retreated. She pulled at her skirt, which was up around her hips.

Dimly, she could hear Teodoro speaking. She shook her head, trying to clear her mind. "...what you think you heard the other night. But it does not matter. You will not say anything. If you do, what has taken place here this afternoon is merely a foretaste of the terrible things that will befall you."

Priscilla was straightening her clothes, fighting to hold back tears. "Right now, you are very upset, understandably," Teodoro continued in a reasonable, understated voice. "I haven't hurt you. This time, I merely scared you. I am very good at that, as you can see. Please do not make me do something worse."

He rose to his feet. "Do not go back to Wanderworth. Do you understand?"

When she didn't immediately respond, his face darkened. "Priscilla. Do you understand?"

"Yes," she mumbled.

The answer appeared to satisfy him. "Now, you may leave, my princess. You must report back to Signor Banville that you and I had a very good conversation. You find me totally charming—which I am. The Prince Charming, if you will. You will, of course, say nothing about what actually took place between us. You don't want that, I am sure." Teodoro moved aside so that she could rise on wobbly legs. "I will let you see yourself out."

She found herself in the hallway, feeling so weak she thought she might faint. She forced herself to start walking, anxious to get as far away from the monster in Suite 610 as she could.

Back in the richly appointed safety of the lift, she slumped against the wall, exhausted, frightened—*angry*. Teodoro was right, of course. There was nothing she could do. Report that a valued guest had assaulted her? Ha! No, Teodoro's message had been delivered like a hard punch to the gut: Keep quiet or else.

White-hot anger bubbled up, catching in Priscilla's throat. The reasonable voice inside her argued that her best course of action would be to do as Teodoro ordered. But then another voice, the maverick voice, screamed that she had never followed the best course of action.

That maverick voice renewed its furious cry as she came off the lift into the Front Hall and started for her office: *Don't give in! Don't take it!*

Her more rational voice pointed out that she had been badly shaken up. From here on in, she had to be more careful.

She preferred her maverick voice. That was the voice she would listen to.

Get even!

CHAPTER THIRTEEN

The Return of Commander Blood

There was still no sign of Susie when Priscilla got back to 205. That meant there was no one standing guard in the outer office so anyone could get in unannounced, including Commander Peter Trueblood, formerly of the Queen's Guard, and known, with a measure of dread always added, as Commander Blood.

Priscilla was all too familiar with the commander, a tall skeleton with ice-cold eyes and a precise little moustache above a twitchy line that stood in for a mouth. Under other circumstances, he could be mistaken for a sallow-faced undertaker out of a Dickens novel, best suited for the night. But Commander Blood did not operate under other circumstances. His were circumstances that put him in charge of a secret group seconded to Buckingham Palace known as the Walsinghams. The Walsinghams were tasked with protecting the royal family, and their tactics in doing so were known to be extreme. Trueblood had earned the ominous sobriquet of Commander Blood because of his ruthless determination to use whatever means necessary to keep the monarchy safe and to head off any hint of scandal.

"Good day to you, Miss Tempest," he said in the mournful, aloof voice that made his every utterance sound like a death sentence.

"Commander Trueblood," Priscilla said, automatically pulling herself together, determined to put on a resilient front. "What an unpleasant surprise."

"Yes, I assumed I might receive that sort of welcome from

you," Trueblood said mildly. "That's why I thought it best to pop in unannounced."

"Which is exactly what you've done, it appears. What can I do for you, Commander?"

"Do you mind if I sit down?"

Priscilla indicated the chair in front of her desk. Trueblood seated himself, folding his legs carefully and adjusting the crease on his pin-striped trousers. As he did so, he said, "How have you been, Miss Tempest?"

"I've been fine, Commander, but I doubt you could care less."

"I do realize that the last time we encountered each other, the experience was not entirely pleasant for either of us."

"I'm sure that will be the greatest understatement I hear today," Priscilla replied.

Trueblood appeared untroubled. "My job, as you know, is to protect members of the royal family—often, as it turns out, from themselves. I pursue this task with a ferocious dedication, I don't mind saying. I have devoted my life to HRH the Queen and the monarchy in general."

"Which is why they call you Commander Blood." Knowing how much he disliked the nickname.

Trueblood adopted an expression that suggested he had eaten something unpleasant. "Yes, you do try to provoke me, don't you, Miss Tempest?"

"Perish the thought," said Priscilla dryly.

"But if you will, I come in peace this morning."

"I have trouble believing that," Priscilla said.

A thin smile was drawn from Trueblood before he continued. "While I understand that bygones will probably never be bygones, I do believe we can reach some sort of accommodation that will save you embarrassment as well as spare this hotel possible scandal."

"I'm not sure what you're getting at, Commander," Priscilla said, at once genuinely puzzled and fretting that a hammer was about to drop. "What sort of embarrassment are we talking about?"

"Embarrassment that involves Lord Snowdon," he said definitively.

"Yes, Lord Snowdon," Priscilla nodded. Was that what this visit is about? Not surprising, she supposed. Armstrong-Jones would be a handful for anyone, and undoubtedly so for the staid, conservative Walsinghams. "We're pleased to have him here at the Savoy while he completes an assignment to photograph daily life at the hotel," Priscilla intoned diplomatically.

"If that's all he was doing, then this visit would not be necessary," Trueblood said.

Priscilla carefully arranged an expression of bewilderment. "What else would he be doing?"

"As I suggested earlier, it is my job to head off royal scandal before it gets started. Lord Snowdon keeps me extremely busy, I must tell you."

"I'm afraid I still don't understand." Although, with growing trepidation, she was beginning to.

"Come now, Miss Tempest, please do not play naive with me. You know full well what is going on."

"On the off chance, Commander, that in fact I don't know, why don't you enlighten me?"

"Lord Snowdon's involvement with a certain hotel employee." He was gazing pointedly at Priscilla.

She felt a numbness begin to work its way down her body. She was suddenly having trouble moving her lips. What was it about being in the presence of this man that made Priscilla afraid that a firing squad waited with rifles pointed at her?

"Commander, if you're implying that I am involved with Lord Snowdon in anything but a totally professional capacity then you are seriously misinformed." Priscilla thought she had done a fine job working herself into a state.

Trueblood stared at her in disbelief before he did something she had never seen him do before—did not think him capable of. He burst out laughing. Commander Blood actually laughing? She could hardly believe it.

"No, no, Miss Tempest," Trueblood managed once he pulled himself together. "This time, I'm happy to say, I am not talking about you."

"Then who are you talking about?"

"Your assistant—Miss Susan Gore-Langton."

"*Susie?*" The word flew out in a disbelieving explosion of breath.

"She is your assistant, is she not?" The undertaker's mien had returned.

"Yes, but Miss Gore-Langton is not involved with Lord Snowdon any more than I am. We are both trying to facilitate his assignment at the hotel, under sometimes trying circum-stances, no question, but that is the end of it."

"Tell me, is this how Miss Gore-Langton is, as you put it, *facilitating* Lord Snowdon?"

From his inside jacket pocket, Trueblood withdrew a black-and-white photograph and laid it on the desk in front of Pris-cilla. Susie posed seductively—without any clothes covering what Priscilla had to concede was a spectacular body.

"Where did you get this?" Priscilla was sure the question came out as a squeak.

"That's neither here nor there," Trueblood answered. "The fact is it has come into my possession, a photo obviously taken by Lord Snowdon."

Priscilla made a point of pushing the photo toward True-blood. "First of all, I don't know how you can say that this photo was taken by Lord Snowdon. Secondly, even if it was, Lord Snowdon's stock in trade is photographing beautiful people. Miss Gore-Langton definitely falls into that category. It doesn't necessarily mean anything is going on between them."

"We have no reason to believe the photo was taken by anyone else," Trueblood said with the certainty of a man used to speaking authoritatively and being listened to when he did. "As for what else is going on, I would ask you this: Where is Miss Gore-Langton?"

"She is late this morning," Priscilla conceded.

"She is late because she is in residence at Lord Snowdon's Pimlico Road studio."

"You've been following Lord Snowdon?"

"Following is too strong a word," Trueblood said with a slight frown. "More accurate to say that we keep an eye on him for his own safety."

"If he is with Miss Gore-Langton, I have no doubt he is safe." What Susie was under these circumstances was another matter entirely, Priscilla thought.

Trueblood made a face that suggested he'd eaten something even more unpleasant than before. "Miss Tempest, the royal family embodies the British way of life; it is the guardian of the national morality. It is my mission to ensure those two responsibilities are not blemished by scandal. The Earl of Snowdon has demonstrated a breathtaking lack of interest when it comes to morality. I have my hands full persuading him to, shall we say, take more interest than he tends to do."

"I can certainly understand that," said Priscilla. "Although, as guardians of national morality I would suggest the royals are not always the best candidates for the job."

"But that *is* the job," Trueblood stated flatly. He heaved a deep sigh. "What Miss Gore-Langton does in her private life is up to her, but when it involves a member of the royal family, specifically Lord Snowdon, that is another matter entirely—a matter that comes under my purview."

"What do you plan to do?" asked Priscilla, dreading the worst.

"It is not what *I* plan to do," amended Trueblood. "It is rather what I want *you* to do, Miss Tempest."

"Me? What can I do?"

"If I involve myself then everything blows up," Trueblood stated. "Lord Snowdon, as you may know, is a volatile character. He listens to no one—not to his wife, alas, and certainly not to me. But if you talk to Miss Gore-Langton, make it clear to her the potential trouble she is in if she continues to be associated with Lord Snowdon, then hopefully she will come to her senses and break off their relationship. That way potential scandal is avoided. If you do the job I believe you can do, then everyone wins. Best of all, with no one the wiser, Miss Gore-Langton retains her job here at the Savoy."

"Susie can be headstrong as well," Priscilla conceded. "I'm not sure she will listen to me any more than Lord Snowdon listens to you."

"I would hope that is not the case, for the sake of Miss Gore-Langton," Trueblood said. He rose to his feet, pointing a bony finger at the photo. "Hang onto that. You might inform Miss Gore-Langton that if I have the photograph, then it is only a matter of time before it falls into the hands of the tabloid press. And when that happens, well..." he allowed the sentence to drift away menacingly.

"Well what, Commander?"

"Well, I will have to take measures that are—draconian is probably the accurate word. I will do what I have to do, Miss Tempest, and I can do just about anything I choose."

"So I have learned," Priscilla said, acidly.

"I hope to hear from you soon that this situation has been brought to a satisfactory resolution," Trueblood said. "In the meantime, I wish you a good day, Miss Tempest."

He was making his exit when he had another thought and turned to Priscilla. "You know they were Nazis."

"I'm sorry?"

"Miss Gore-Langton's parents. Derek and Sylvia. Before the war, they were well-known National Socialist sympathizers, friends with the Duke and Duchess of Windsor, and with Lady Daphne Wanderworth, all of them thick as thieves in support of Hitler."

"Susie isn't a Nazi, if that's what you're getting at."

"Still, her questionable family background provides another very good reason why Buckingham Palace is not anxious for her name to be linked to that of Lord Snowdon." He shrugged. "Thought you should know."

"Nazis. Are they still a threat?"

"Yes, I would say so," affirmed Trueblood. "To my immense surprise, the National Socialist movement is growing in this country. People who are convinced democracy doesn't work and are willing to take action to end it. Those of us who love this country and its hard-won democratic institutions must be constantly on our guard."

"Thank you, Commander," Priscilla said.

"Are you asking for any particular reason, Miss Tempest?"

"No, no," Priscilla answered quickly. "Curious, that's all."

Trueblood glided away, a skeletal, reaper-like figure, Priscilla thought with a shiver, crouched beneath a black cloud on his way to the cemetery.

CHAPTER FOURTEEN

Oh, My Lord Snowdon!

In the taxi en route to Antony Armstrong-Jones's Pimlico Road studio, Priscilla steeled herself, praying that somehow Commander Blood was wrong. Miss Susan Gore-Langton, as damned foolish as she tended to be, wasn't *that* damned foolish.

Yet where silly young women were concerned—and Priscilla was a perfect example of the sort of silliness that you could so easily fall victim to—it was always best to anticipate the worst.

A laundry stood to one side of the shabby Victorian building that was No. 20, an antique shop on the other. Not a very fashionable area, she thought as she grabbed her shoulder bag and walked along to the studio's arched white doorway. The oh-so-hip lord slumming with his lovely young mistress.

She willed herself to believe that Susie was not inside.

And she wasn't.

There she was in jeans and a T-shirt, hurrying along the street, an informal Susie that Priscilla hadn't seen before. She carried a dark green Harrods bag jammed with wine bottles. She didn't see Priscilla as she fumbled for a key, shifting the bag to her other arm, at the same time managing to insert the key into the door lock.

"Here, let me help you with that," said Priscilla, lifting the bag off Susie's arm just as she got the door open. Susie, her lovely mouth agape, stared in dismay at Priscilla.

Before she could say a word, Priscilla pushed her through the entrance into the studio. "Is he here?" Priscilla demanded, closing the door behind her.

Susie shook her head. "How did you—?"

"How did I know?" Priscilla placed the Harrods bag on a nearby table. "Never mind how I know—I *know*. What do you think you're doing, Susie? Why didn't you come in to work today?"

"To be honest, I was working up the nerve to phone you." Susie spoke nervously, with downcast eyes. "I've decided to quit."

"You've *what*?" Priscilla asked in astonishment.

"Quit—I'm quitting... *have* quit." Susie sounded more nervous than ever.

"You have not quit and you are *not* quitting," stated Priscilla categorically.

"I am and you can't stop me," Susie declared. "Tony and I are in love. He wants me to be with him."

Priscilla had in mere seconds progressed from simple amazement to jaw-dropping astonishment. "Susie, he's a married man... he's married to Princess Margaret, in case you haven't heard."

"Tony says that doesn't make any difference. And frankly, I don't think it does, either."

"I'm supposed to be the one who pulls this sort of irrational, dangerous stunt, not you," Priscilla protested. "You're supposed to be the sane member of this partnership. You have your feet on the ground. You don't do... *this*!"

"Well, I'm sorry to disappoint you," Susie countered fiercely. "But I am doing... *this*."

She flounced over to the table and began removing the wine bottles from the bag. "It's Saint-Émilion, Tony's favourite. I'm going to surprise him tonight with a nice homecooked meal."

"I thought you couldn't cook."

"I'm having it catered by Harrods," Susie retorted. She added meekly, "It's the same as homecooked."

"Susie, listen to me," Priscilla said, coming around the side of the table so she could face her assistant. "No matter what you're fantasizing, this isn't going to work."

"That's what you think," Susie said defiantly.

"You know what he's like."

"I *do* know what he's like and he's not at all what you think. The press paints him as this superficial playboy. There's so much more to him that you don't know about."

"But you do?" asked Priscilla pointedly.

"I know a warm, caring individual who is loving and highly intelligent and who is determined to be with me."

"He won't stay with you. He can't."

"Yes, he can—and will."

"No, you don't understand," Priscilla said, leaning close to make her point. "The reason I'm here is because I've had a visit from Commander Peter Trueblood. You know who he is. I've had a run-in with him before. He is in charge of the Walsinghams. They don't want this to become public—which it will if you continue with him. I don't have to tell you what they're like. They will stop this if you don't."

"I know who they are," Susie admitted sullenly. "I know what they're like and I don't care. Neither does Tony."

"If he tells you that, he's lying."

"No, he's not," Susie insisted vehemently.

"Listen to me, please," said Priscilla. "Trueblood sent me here to speak to you. He knows all about you and Lord Snowdon. He has a photograph of you nude..."

Susie's eyes grew to the saucer size she usually achieved only when Priscilla did something outrageous. "How is that possible?"

"Where Commander Blood is concerned, anything is possible. As certain as the sun rises over the British Empire, that photo will end up on the front page of the *News of the World* if this doesn't end. Trueblood has agreed to give me a chance to persuade you to change your mind before he acts."

"He doesn't scare me," Susie said, maintaining a brave front, but once again looking nervous. "And he doesn't scare Tony, either."

"Yes, right," said Priscilla dryly. "Tony the Lionheart. Off to slay the dragons and save his true love, even if it does mean giving up all the perquisites a lionhearted hero like himself enjoys as a member of the royal family."

"Tony says he loves me, and I believe him. He *is* brave—no matter what you think."

"Declaring his love is not the same as saying he is willing to walk away from his marriage." Priscilla threw up her hands in despair. "He's obviously not making any promises. You can't trust him."

"We're in love I tell you!" Susie practically shouted the words at Priscilla. "Showing up with all your negativity won't change that." She swallowed and threw her shoulders back as though preparing to defend herself against invaders. "I'm afraid you're going to have to leave. Tony will be back soon, and I don't think it's a good idea for him to see you."

"Why not?"

"He doesn't like you."

"He doesn't *like* me? The other day he was nuzzling my neck on the roof of the Savoy."

"He warned me that you would say something like that. That you would lie in order to lure me away. It's not going to work, Priscilla. I've quit. I'm moving on with my life. Now please leave."

OH, MY LORD SNOWDON!

"This won't stand. You're going to call me—I *want* you to call me. I want you back, Susie."

"Tony says you wish to control me. Well, that's in the past. You're not going to control me any longer."

"I'm not trying to control you," Priscilla countered angrily. "I'm trying to make you see common sense."

"Please, I'm not going to say it again." Susie's face had become a cold mask. "Please leave!"

Priscilla issued a deep sigh, shook her head in a show of sadness, and then, with no other choice, left.

Return to Wanderworth

Without Susie manning the reception desk, as Priscilla came back into 205 it was ominously quiet. Priscilla realized that she already missed her assistant's frantic pronouncements of doom, usually centred around her conviction that they were both about to lose their jobs—a conviction not without a good deal of merit.

Susie would be back. Of that Priscilla had no doubt. She had to come back. No way was Lord Snowdon about to leave his wife for an assistant press officer at the Savoy. Was he? It made no sense whatsoever. He was leading her on. That had to be it. Susie was great in bed, Priscilla imagined. Well, she didn't have to imagine—she only had to ask the rumpled figure spread out on the sofa in her office with the beer he must have ordered from Karl.

"There you are—finally," Percy Hoskins announced. If one didn't know better, one might conclude she had barged into Percy's office, instead of the other way around.

"What are you doing here?" Priscilla demanded, immediately on guard. The last thing she needed was Percy finding out about Susie and Lord Snowdon. If that revelation didn't start pumping the printer's ink that had replaced the blood flowing through his veins, nothing would.

"Where's Susie?" Percy asked. "She usually does such a good job of keeping me entertained."

From what she knew had happened between Susie and Percy at the end of a wine-fuelled night, Priscilla had no doubt that she had kept him well entertained. "I thought you weren't drinking." Priscilla pointed to his beer.

Percy looked at the beer as though discovering for the first time that he was holding it. "I never said that," he protested.

"Yes, you did. In front of Arthur Sullivan, no less."

"I can't believe I said that." To her surprise, he actually put the beer to one side. "Why don't you close your office door, and then sit beside me?" He patted the sofa cushion next to him for emphasis.

"What's up?" She closed the door and then sat on the sofa as far away from him as she could to alleviate any possible suspicion of impropriety should anyone walk in.

"Okay," Percy said, leaning into her and dropping his voice, "I checked into this guy Colin Ashbury."

"What did you find out? Is he dead?"

"Missing, at least. No one seems to know where he is."

"He's dead," Priscilla said firmly.

"If he is, the police haven't received a report about it either in London or from the Buckinghamshire authorities. And his name doesn't show up at any of the local hospitals I've checked out. Friends I managed to contact thought he might be at his place in Cap Ferrat. But I can't find any evidence that he even has a place at Cap Ferrat."

"In other words, he's dead," Priscilla offered, feeling the hairs beginning to rise on the back of her neck.

"On the surface, Ashbury is a retired investment banker, worked in the City for many years following the war, moved with all the best people, or at least the people who think they are the best—including, I should point out, Lady Daphne Wanderworth and the so-called Wanderworth Group."

"On the surface?" questioned Priscilla. "What does that mean?"

"It took some digging but I discovered that before he returned to banking, Ashbury spent time in Rome working for MI6. That's where he met Prince Teodoro. I understand it was Ashbury who introduced Teodoro to Lady Daphne."

"From what I saw at Wanderworth House, the two of them had had a falling out," Priscilla said.

"Okay, but I can't find anyone who suspects Ashbury might be dead."

"Well, he is dead," Priscilla asserted.

"Then why hasn't his body turned up?"

"I keep telling you—I tripped over his body."

"You tripped over *a* body," Percy amended.

"It was him," insisted Priscilla. "I had been talking to him not long before I found him."

Percy merely looked more uncertain than before. "I don't know. This all seems pretty far-fetched to me. Why would they want to kill someone just because he may have decided he didn't want to be part of the group?"

"I just had a taste of what Teodoro is capable of," Priscilla stated flatly.

"What do you mean?"

"Mr. Banville made me go to his suite. As soon as I got in there, Teodoro assaulted me. He did it because he knew he could get away with it. He told me he had the power. I had none. And you know what? He was right."

"Priscilla—" Percy started to say.

"He said it would be a whole lot worse if I didn't keep my mouth shut and stay away from him and the Wanderworth Group."

"He assaulted you..." Percy sounded as though he couldn't quite get his head around the fact.

"He's a bad guy. That's what bad guys do."

"Listen, this is serious."

"Yes, it is."

"I don't want you getting hurt." Percy actually sounded concerned. "If he attacked you, if Ashbury was murdered, then we should involve the police."

"No, we shouldn't," said Priscilla adamantly.

"Why not?"

"I keep telling you, I will lose my job." She paused, thinking. "Here's a better idea for now."

"I get nervous when you have 'better' ideas," Percy said.

"We drive back to Wanderworth House and see if we can locate Colin Ashbury's body. If we do, then you have every reason in the world to call in the police."

Percy thought about it, nodding slowly. "When would you like to go?"

"Now," announced Priscilla. When Percy didn't respond, she gave him a poke. "Hey, come on, what's the worst thing that could happen?"

"If Teodoro's about, we could get ourselves killed."

"Teodoro thinks he has scared me off. He's wrong. I want him to pay for what he did to me—and what he could do to the country if he isn't stopped."

"What am I getting myself into?" Percy groaned with a roll of his eyes.

She wasn't about to admit it to Percy, but Priscilla couldn't help wondering the same thing herself.

CHAPTER SIXTEEN

Into the Woods

Priscilla's hopes of finding the body that she had briefly tripped over in a dark wood in the midst of a rainstorm evaporated as soon as she was faced with the mass of Buckinghamshire forest running behind Wanderworth House. By the time she and Percy drove out from London, it was the end of the day, and a grey dusk had turned the surrounding woods into something out of a bad horror movie.

"I probably should have mentioned this earlier," Percy said, huffing and puffing as he tried to keep up with Priscilla moving quickly through the underbrush.

"What?" she called back to him.

"I don't like nature," Percy said.

Priscilla cast an impatient glance back at him. "For heaven's sake, Percy, what don't you like about it?"

"It's full of plants and animals and there are no pubs." Percy came to a halt, breathing hard. "What's more, I might be a bit out of shape for this sort of nonsense. Stop for a minute, will you?"

Priscilla came to a halt and turned to him, seeing his sweaty, flushed face. "What's wrong with you?"

"Did I mention that there is only one thing I detest more than nature?"

"I hesitate to ask," Priscilla said, making a face.

"Exercise. I'm against it."

"Yes, I can see that, Percy. You're very much out of shape."

"I'd prefer it if you'd lie."

"Yes, I'm sure you would. Unfortunately, the evidence is in front of me."

Percy considered firing something back at her, thought better of it, and instead glanced around uneasily at the darkening forest. "Do you have any idea where we are? Or where you saw the body? I'm beginning to think this is a wild goose chase."

"We are not chasing wild geese. We are looking for a body. Come along." Priscilla started moving again.

"I'll follow you anywhere—except through dark woods that I suspect are full of wolves."

Priscilla had moved off into the trees. "Did you hear me?" Percy called. There was no answer. Not wanting to be left alone, he hurried after her.

Priscilla emerged onto a rise. Below, the failing twilight offered a fine view of Wanderworth House with its vast series of parterres, gravel pathways meandering around lush flower beds and low hedges. "He chased me through those gardens." Priscilla was pointing downward as a huffing and puffing Percy joined her. "I entered the woods beyond the gardens and that's when I tripped over the body."

"After all this, you mean to tell me we're in the wrong place?" asked Percy in a tired voice.

"Follow me," ordered Priscilla brusquely once again as she started down the hill.

"I'm beginning to think I don't like following you," Percy called. Too late. Priscilla had once more been swallowed up by the woods. Percy issued another groan before starting after her.

He found Priscilla at the bottom of the hill, staring down at what was left of a rotting trunk. Through the trees, he could make out the lights of Wanderworth.

"This is where I found him," Priscilla declared.

"Well, if this was the place, our friend is not here now," stated Percy.

"Closer to the house than I remembered," Priscilla added, more or less to herself as she looked around. "I don't suppose they would leave a dead man lying about, would they?"

"You sure you didn't trip over that?" Percy pointed to the tree trunk.

"It *was* a body," stated Priscilla definitively. "The body of Colin Ashbury."

"When you were at Wanderworth, did you have a drink?"

"I had a sip of champagne, if that's what you mean," answered Priscilla defensively.

"You had a couple of drinks, you were running away in the dark from a guy who was probably going to do you harm. It was raining. You were scared, maybe seeing one thing, when you might otherwise have seen..."

"What?" Priscilla spoke angrily. "You think I mistook an old tree trunk for a body?"

"I'm just saying it's not impossible," allowed Percy.

Priscilla aimed a nasty look in Percy's direction and then turned and flounced away.

"Where do you think you're going?" Percy sounded alarmed. Music to Priscilla's ears.

"I'm going to Wanderworth."

"Are you insane?" Percy couldn't believe what he was hearing. "What do you think you're going to do there?"

"I'm going to find out what they did with Colin Ashbury's dead body," she called over her shoulder.

Percy shook his head in frustration, wishing he were anywhere else—a good pub, preferably—rather than in this dark, encroaching woodland. Nonetheless, he hastened after her yet again.

A row of plane trees ran along the borders on either side of the parterres. Priscilla kept to the cover provided by the trees as she crept toward the house. As she got closer, a battleship-grey ambulance topped by a revolving blue light came howling along the drive, screeching to a stop beneath the porticoed entrance.

She watched as Wanderworth's front doors burst open to admit two attendants carrying a stretcher. They emerged minutes later with Lady Daphne. She was swathed in a bright orange blanket, her face partially covered by an oxygen mask. Her hand was held by Prince Teodoro, his face partially obscured by a fedora. The attendants lifted the stretcher into the ambulance. Teodoro climbed into the back with one of the attendants. The other went around and got behind the wheel. Moments later, the ambulance shot off along the roadway, sirens blaring, leaving behind a knot of worried-looking servants mingling with what appeared to be dinner guests in formal attire. With a start Priscilla saw that one of the guests was Gordon Scott. In his tuxedo, he stuck out, noticeably taller than the others.

Percy came up behind her, breathing hard. "What's happening?"

"It's Lady Daphne," Priscilla explained. "They've taken her away." She turned to Percy. "I'm going to follow that ambulance, see where it goes and what I can find out about Lady Daphne's condition."

Percy looked aghast. "How are you going to do that?"

"I've got my car." As though that were the most natural thing in the world.

"Your car? Where is it?"

"It's in that car park near the house."

Percy regarded her with a stunned expression. "Are you mad? You can't go there."

"Yes, I can. I was here before. Who is to say I wasn't invited back tonight? No one will know the difference. There's no time to argue about this, Percy. You get back to your car and head back to London. We'll meet later and compare notes."

Before he could offer more objections, Priscilla started away from the cover afforded by the trees. She crossed the roadway as Wanderworth's guests began to disperse. Gordon Scott, quite handsome in his evening clothes, Priscilla thought, lingered beneath the portico, looking a bit lost. She called to him, "Mr. Scott..."

He turned, surprised, as she approached. "Miss Tempest," he said, the beginnings of a smile animating his tanned face.

"I just arrived," she said, feigning breathlessness, the inappropriately dressed dinner guest running late. "I saw the ambulance leave. Is Lady Daphne all right?"

"I'm not sure," Gordon said. "I was in the dining room when she collapsed. The next thing, everyone's in a panic and calling for an ambulance. I barely got a chance to meet the woman."

"I hope it's not serious," Priscilla said. "But I suppose that's the end of dinner."

"Looks like it. Disappointing." Gordon gave a resigned shrug. "Ah well, back to London."

"You've got a ride?"

"I'm being picked up in a few minutes. A friend of mine wants me to meet him at the Colony Club."

"I've heard of it. It's a gambling establishment, isn't it?"

"If you're inclined that way, you can find a roulette wheel spinning," Gordon acknowledged.

"Are you a gambler?"

"Only when it comes to love," he said. He gave her a look.

She met his gaze. "Do you win or lose?"

"That's the thing about gambling, isn't it? Whether it's for money or love, the gambler always loses in the end."

"Goodness," Priscilla said, feigning a sympathetic pout. "I'm so sorry to hear that."

"What about you?"

"I'm not a gambler, either. At least not where money is concerned."

"What about when it comes to love?"

"Let's say I hedge my bets," Priscilla replied carefully.

Gordon gave a burst of laughter. "Tell you what: If you're coming back to London, why don't you meet me at the Colony Club for a drink?"

She should have automatically said no. Instead, she heard herself say, "Perhaps I will."

"I look forward to seeing you there," Gordon said with evident pleasure.

A Daimler pulled into the drive. "There's my ride," he said.

He gave her one final devastating smile before walking to his waiting car.

CHAPTER SEVENTEEN

Priscilla Investigates

Priscilla clamped down on the Morris Minor's throttle, angry with herself for taking time to talk to—flirt with?—Gordon Scott, and afraid she'd missed her chance to catch up to the ambulance with Lady Daphne on board. But then she spotted distant taillights and hoped against hope that they belonged to the ambulance.

Driving through pitch blackness, she willed herself to stay awake, more tired than she would have expected from her trek through the forest. Not wanting to show weakness in front of Percy, she had pretended to be undaunted by the woodland when in fact she believed no city girl in her right mind would be found—bad analogy perhaps—dead in the woods. Now here she was wasting her time in the dark of night, following an ambulance. *If* she was following an ambulance. She began to wonder about that. Why did she never listen to the voice of her better judgment? But it was such a weak voice. Why, she could barely hear it.

Ahead, the taillights turned off. She approached a gravel roadway, catching a glimpse of the disappearing taillights. She slowed and turned off and saw ahead a nondescript brick building mostly hidden among the trees. If she had any brains, she would turn the Morris Minor around and start back to London, meet Gordon Scott for the drink she shouldn't be having with him, and forget all about this. But she had no brains, at least not when it came to dangerous situations and men—or a combination of both.

She followed the road past a wooden sign that said this was Woburn Rise Health. A single light burned beneath a crumbling portico as Priscilla pulled up. She parked a few yards beyond the portico and got out not far from where the ambulance had been left. There was no sign of anyone.

She climbed broken concrete steps to two formidable oak doors. She pushed at one of them. It made a scraping sound as it opened into an underlit linoleum-floored reception area painted a dull green. A reception desk with a shaded lamp mounted on it was unoccupied. She stood waiting, expecting someone to appear.

But no one did.

From outside she heard the sound of vehicles approaching. Light beams blazed through the windows, throwing patterns of light and darkness across the walls and ceiling. She hurried back to the door and looked out to see black vans on the roadway. Four vehicles pulled in and came to a stop in a semi-circle. As she watched, men in leather jackets began to emerge, caught in the glare of headlights, stretching, lighting cigarettes—and speaking loudly in what sounded like Italian.

Presently, they were joined by Prince Teodoro, draped in black and caught in a combination of bright light and dark shadow. He embraced each man. Then they gathered around him as he spoke. His voice rose so that Priscilla could hear him call out, "*Miei disturbatori!* We come again!" The men answered in unison: "*Veniamo di nuovo!*"

The six new arrivals spent more time embracing Teodoro and each other before the headlights from the vans were extinguished and the prince led them out of sight around the corner.

Priscilla crossed to a hallway off the reception area and made her way along to another pair of doors that opened into a hospital ward, deathly silent and shrouded in darkness. In the distance she heard a door open and close, the murmur of faraway voices. None of the beds was occupied. What was this place? A hospital without patients? Whatever it was, it was not a place where she should hang around. Time to get out of there.

"Miss Tempest!"

Priscilla wheeled around to confront Prince Teodoro, the dim light making him appear especially sinister.

"What are you doing here?" Teodoro demanded.

"I was worried about Lady Daphne," Priscilla stated in a voice she desperately hoped sounded a lot stronger than she felt. "Where is everyone?"

"This is a private hospital, closed to the public." Teodoro stepped closer, a formidable, frightening presence. The charming prince was yet again nowhere in sight.

"Is Lady Daphne all right?" All Priscilla could think of to ask.

"You don't for a moment care about Lady Daphne." Teodoro spoke irately. "I warned you to stay away, yet here you are."

"Yes, here I am," Priscilla said.

"You ignored my warning." Teodoro came toward her. "Do you not remember what I said the last time we encountered one another?"

Priscilla began carefully moving backward. "You know, for the life of me, I can't."

"A reminder then." The silvery blade of a stiletto gleamed.

"A nine-inch blade," Teodoro stated. "Handmade especially for me in Maniago where the old masters still specialize in knives like this."

Cold fear shot down her spine. A prince with a knife made especially for him could inspire such a sensation, she reflected.

"People know where I am," she gurgled, backing away further. "Percy Hoskins... he's doing a story about you, he knows..."

"Nobody cares, Priscilla," Teodoro said, advancing, the stiletto held in such a way as to leave no doubt he'd had plenty of experience using it.

"Yes... they do..." She was having difficulty getting words out.

Teodoro darted forward, the knife raised. Priscilla cried out, sinking back as Teodoro's free hand shot out to clutch the front of her blouse. The tip of the stiletto blade was at her throat.

"No..." was all she could manage.

"Is everything all right?" The nurse in the open doorway wore white, an angel descending out of the darkness. Teodoro loosened his grip on Priscilla. The stiletto quickly disappeared.

"What's going on?" the nurse demanded. "I have a very ill patient in the other room."

Teodoro forced a disarming smile. "A silly disagreement, it's nothing," he said with admirable smoothness.

Priscilla, freed from him, dashed past the startled nurse through the double doors and into the reception area, running for her life, expecting Teodoro hot on her heels.

She burst out into the silent night, passing the parked vans, exhaling loudly, looking frantically around for anyone coming after her. But no one was. She stumbled across the bleak, dark landscape, the moon lost behind clouds. Reaching her car, she got the door open, forced herself behind the wheel and started the engine, all the time frightened that Teodoro would appear.

Only when she was moving down the road away from the hospital did she begin to relax. Ahead, a car approached. She had to pull over to the side to allow it to pass. She wasn't sure but she thought she caught a glimpse of Al Cellini behind the wheel before she started forward again.

Teodoro emerged from the building in time to see Priscilla disappear down the road. He saw Al Cellini turn around and go after her. Somewhat reassured, he went back inside and found the nurse who had interrupted him with Priscilla. An intruder, Teodoro reported. The woman had run off. Everything was all right.

With Priscilla's appearance still nagging at him, he hurried to the hospital room where the doctor and two nurses were attending to Lady Daphne. He asked that they give him a private moment with their patient. They nodded and quickly exited. Such a tiny, vulnerable thing, Teodoro thought as he gazed down at her, all but lost in her hospital bed. She managed a weak smile.

"How are you doing, my love?" Teodoro asked gently.

"Better now," Daphne managed. "I felt so weak suddenly. They want to keep me here for observation. I'm so weak right now, honestly."

"You are strong," Teodoro said encouragingly. "Soon you will be back on your feet."

"Meanwhile, you must lead the group," Lady Daphne said.

"I am honoured, but only until you are rested and feeling recovered. I should tell you our friends from Rome, *miei disturbatori,* the disruptors, have arrived. These are the professionals we discussed. We will soon put them to work across London helping our allies in the National Socialist movement."

"They are idiots," Daphne said disdainfully.

"Idiots we can make use of," Teodoro corrected.

"As I say, you are in charge, you make the decisions." Her expression softened. "Is everything all right? They told me there was some sort of commotion."

"The infuriating young woman from the Savoy," Teodoro said. "A minor irritation that we don't need right now, that's all."

"Miss Tempest." The name emerged weakly from Daphne's thin, dry mouth.

"I'm afraid so."

"She was here? That is hardly minor, Prince Teodoro." Daphne's eyes burned fiercely against the paleness of her face. "What does she know about us?"

"I don't think she knows anything," Teodoro replied. "I can't understand why she keeps showing up."

"I am beginning to wonder if you are attracted to this woman."

"That is not true," Teodoro, thinking to himself that perhaps he was, in a curious way. "I am dedicated to our mission."

"The bitch should have been dealt with before now."

"Unfortunately, she got away," Teodoro admitted. "But as I came outside, I saw Al Cellini. I suspect he has gone after her."

"Excellent," said Daphne, her face brightening. "Cellini is an American thug. Thugs know how to deal with little tramps like Miss Tempest."

CHAPTER EIGHTEEN

The Car Gods Do Not Listen

Percy was lost in the woods, hearing the distant rumble of thunder.

Lost like Little Red Riding Hood, he thought miserably. All he had to do was get back to his car. Simple enough. A child could do it. People who accused him of having no sense of direction, what did they know? He certainly knew the way to his car. Except, well, he didn't. Now night had fallen and the woods, to paraphrase Robert Frost, had become lovely, dark and deep. There was another crash of thunder. Rain threatening. Not so lovely, he amended to himself. Kind of scary, actually. Damn Priscilla, anyway, for leaving him out here on his own.

He came into a meadow lit momentarily by a jagged streak of lightning. He couldn't go on much longer. He would die in this field, his body taken away by wolves so that he would never be found. What an ignominious way to end a brilliant newspaper career, he thought, even more despondent than before. Somewhat brilliant, anyway.

As he stood debating with himself what direction he should take, he heard the sound of a vehicle in the distance. From across the field, he thought. A lonely, echoing sound in the night.

Percy started toward it.

More lightning revealed a line of trees ahead. He picked up speed, jogging across the field. Gasping for breath, he entered more dark woods. In fairy tales, as far as he could recall, nothing good ever happened in dark, haunted woods.

He stumbled and clawed his way through a thicket of trees as it began to rain. He finally broke out onto a strip of roadway. His beloved Bentley was where he left it on the shoulder. Heaving with relief, he ran across the road as the rain started to come down harder. He unlocked the door and got in. Rain thudded against the roof and hood as he inserted his key in the ignition and turned it. A horrible grinding sound rose from the bowels of the Bentley's engine, a sound suggesting the car was not happy at being left alone for so long. It was taking its revenge by refusing to start. Percy tried again. Nothing. The rain struck a tattoo against the hood.

Percy closed his eyes, praying to the gods that made British cars, asking them to forgive his carelessness, begging them to start the car.

The car gods were not listening.

Through the windscreen, headlights suddenly flashed through the pouring rain. A vehicle was coming down the road toward him.

Percy got out, waving his arms as the car approached. He moved to one side so that it could come abreast of him and slide to a stop.

A young woman was at the wheel. She rolled down her window. Percy had a glimpse, in the reflected light from the dashboard, of short, black hair, lovely brown skin and a smile. A wicked smile, Percy observed.

The young woman said in a slightly accented voice, "You look as though you could use a ride, Mr. Hoskins."

CHAPTER NINETEEN

George Raft's Colony

If you were rich enough in London, there existed establishments of sophistication and elegance where, in great comfort, you could lose large amounts of money.

Such were London's private gambling clubs, and such was one of the most popular of those establishments, the Colony Sports Club. Its facade was a bright cube against the Berkeley Square night, a rooftop sign announcing in big neon letters that this was not just anyone's Colony, but *George Raft's* Colony.

The Colony Club's subtly lit Edwardian gaming floor bustled with guests huddled at mahogany roulette wheels and gleaming brass and fine leather baccarat and blackjack tables. A quiet tension permeated the room.

The crowd filling the club tonight, albeit in well-dressed disguise, was pretty rough. The men were older, with hard, tough faces that would have been at home in a waterfront dive. Maybe more so. Their women were invariably much younger, with big, blond hair out of a bottle, cleavages elevated to burst from low-cut gowns and makeup applied with a trowel.

"If this is supposed to be a sports club, where are the sports?" Priscilla asked Gordon Scott as she slid onto the barstool beside him. "This crowd looks as though it doesn't come out until after dark, let alone play any sports."

Driving back to London she had convinced herself repeatedly that she should not go near the Colony Club, that she would go home, recover from the renewed threat of Prince Teodoro and get a good night's sleep.

But then again, she decided as she came into the city, more than anything, she needed a stiff drink.

Gordon gave her a surprised look and then laughed. "I wasn't sure you would come."

"How could I resist?" Priscilla said, thinking that she should absolutely have resisted. But she hadn't. Now here she was—gambling, although perhaps not in a way these patrons of the Colony Club would understand.

"What would you like to drink?" Gordon asked.

A glass of champagne soon arrived for Priscilla. Gordon ordered a Scotch and soda for himself. Yes, she thought to herself as the champagne warmed her, this feels better. She began to relax, putting everything else out of her mind so she could concentrate on this handsome man who appeared to have no inclination whatsoever to murder her.

"I'll introduce you to George Raft when he comes along," Gordon said. "Do you know who he is?"

"The Hollywood actor."

"He's not doing much acting these days. He spends most of his time managing this place. He's one of the club's partners. A real gangster, George."

"George Raft is a gangster?"

"Pretty close. George grew up on the Lower East Side of New York with Owney Madden and Bugsy Siegel. I've never asked him about it, but the story is George was a popular dancer in New York when Owney Madden decided he should be a movie star and sent him out to California."

"Owney Madden and—is it Bugsy Siegel?—are they gangsters?" Priscilla asked.

"Notorious American gangsters. If they wanted a movie star,

they sure got one with George, that is until George made a lot of bad choices that hurt his career. You know he was supposed to do *The Maltese Falcon?*"

"It's one of my favourite movies," Priscilla said. "Humphrey Bogart is in it."

"Just what I like to hear," announced a short, grey-haired man in a tuxedo as he approached Priscilla and Gordon. "A beautiful woman talking about a picture I *didn't* do."

"George," Gordon said. He shook George Raft's hand and said, "I'd like you to meet my friend, Priscilla Tempest."

"Miss Tempest, it's a pleasure," Raft said. If it was a pleasure, Raft did not show it. His face was like a mask, albeit one ravaged by age. The youthful movie star who sauntered without much emotion through dozens of 1940s Warner Bros. films had become creased and jowly. Suspicious eyes peered out from apertures carved into the void of his face. The dark hair of his youth had long since turned white, his baldness camouflaged by a hairpiece.

"Mr. Raft, nice to meet you," Priscilla said, taking his hand. Raft might not show emotion, but even at his advanced age, there was something coiled and dangerous about him, his small mouth curved in a permanent half smile. Without doing anything, he gave the impression of a man you might want to steer clear of. Naturally, Priscilla found that quality irresistible—as, she imagined, a lot of other women did too.

"Miss Tempest," Raft was saying. "You gotta call me George."

"Priscilla is with the Savoy Hotel," put in Gordon. "They don't allow her to address anyone by their first name. She goes through life addressing all men as 'mister.'"

"It's a disease you contract when you work at the Savoy," agreed Priscilla. "It infects everything."

"I'm sorry to hear that," Raft said, those eye slits focused on her. "However, you're not at the Savoy now, so you can call me anything you like."

"Thanks," Priscilla said. "I'll keep that in mind. And I think you would have been great in *The Maltese Falcon*."

"I made a mistake. It made Bogie a star. The luck of the draw." Raft turned to Gordon. "How did it go, Gordie?"

"It didn't," he replied. "Shortly after I got there, our hostess experienced some sort of episode and was taken away by ambulance. There was no chance to meet anyone—except Priscilla here."

"Then the evening wasn't a waste," said Raft.

"I thought you were terrific in *Scarface*," Priscilla said, making sure to mention a movie he was in, in addition to one he wasn't.

"That was a long time ago," Raft said. "Way before your time, Priscilla."

"The trick with the coin," Priscilla said. "I really liked that."

"I picked it up as a kid," Raft said. "Hawks liked it so we used it in the picture. Paul Muni was playing Scarface. He wasn't happy. Thought it took attention away from him—which it did."

"What brings you to London, Mr. Raft?"

Raft gestured in the direction of the busy, smoky gaming hall. "I've discovered that there is more money in gambling than there is in movies. A lot more."

"I'm trying to convince George to play the gangster in *La Dolce Death*," Gordon said.

"Gordie and I are sort of kindred spirits," Raft said. "We both came out of nowhere, with no acting experience, yet we became stars. Gordie doesn't like jumping around half-naked any more—although I gotta admit he looks pretty good that way." He looked at Priscilla. "Don't you think?"

"From what I can gather," Priscilla said noncommittally, not having seen any Tarzan movies.

"I don't like playing gangsters, even with my clothes on," Raft said. "I've had enough of that. I was a gangster for Billy Wilder in *Some Like It Hot*. Marilyn Monroe drove us all crazy. That was enough. No more bad guys."

"What now?" Gordon asked.

Raft shrugged. "Hopefully I'll hear from Al soon. He has access to the people you need to be in touch with."

"I'm looking forward to meeting him," Gordon said.

"Actually, if you're talking about Al Cellini, you met him the other day." The words were out of Priscilla's mouth before she could stop them.

If Raft ever allowed his poker face to flicker with interest, he got close now. "You know Al?" he said to Gordon.

Gordon gave Priscilla a hot look. "What are you talking about?"

"The other day at the Savoy. In the hallway."

"You saw Al at the Savoy?" Raft demanded of Gordon.

"Apparently," Gordon conceded. His face had gone cold. "I didn't know who he was at the time." He aimed another quick, unhappy glance at Priscilla.

"You didn't know." Raft appeared to be sizing up the two of them. "Al at the Savoy," he said quietly. "What the hell was he doing there?" He looked pointedly at Priscilla, as though she should have the answer.

She probably did, but she now knew better than to say anything.

"If you're asking me, I don't know," Priscilla said.

Raft remained silent for a time, considering what he had just been told. Then he jerked his head almost imperceptibly. "Good to see you folks," he said. "Have a pleasant evening."

He strolled away, back into the main hall, leaving a frowning Gordon. "What do you think you're doing?" he demanded of Priscilla.

She looked at him uncomprehendingly. "What do you mean?"

"Why didn't you tell me that character the other day was Al Cellini?" The nice Gordon must have stayed outside the Colony Club, mused Priscilla.

"I barely knew the man's name before you came along," Priscilla sputtered. "And I certainly had no idea you had any association with him."

"George is my ticket out of the sword-and-sandal junk I've been forced to do in Italy," Gordon said angrily. "I'm counting on him and the people he knows. Now, thanks to you, he's pissed."

Priscilla was flummoxed. "Are you serious?"

In response, Gordon threw some pound notes onto the bar. "I have to leave," he said. "I'll talk to you later. Have a good night, Priscilla."

Gordon rose from the barstool and strode away, leaving a dumbfounded Priscilla, her face burning with embarrassment. Her history with men wasn't exactly sterling, but at least until now no one had walked out on her in a huff.

Well, no movie stars had, anyway. Tarzan, she concluded, in addition to being a horse's arse, was a big, spoiled baby.

Priscilla sat eyeing her champagne, any appetite for more of it having evaporated, thinking that maybe Gordon would come back, shamefaced and full of apologies.

But he didn't.

Imagining that the entire casino, the big-haired blonds and their tough-guy escorts, had all witnessed this silly little melodrama, she decided it was time to exit. She lifted herself off the barstool, giving a nod of thanks to the bartender, whose expression had remained—thankfully—neutral. Making her way out, Priscilla chanced a quick glance around. No one was paying the slightest attention; no one seemed to know—or care—that Tarzan had just walked out on her in a huff. When you're losing money, she decided, stood-up dames are the least of your concerns.

It was raining hard as Priscilla emerged onto a deserted Berkeley Square. A cold wind whipped the rain into her face and blew her hair around. Of course, she hadn't thought to bring an umbrella. Attacked by the wind and the rain, she was pre-occupied with feeling very sorry for herself and didn't notice the shape that loomed abruptly in front of her.

She let out a yelp as she caught a glimpse of Al Cellini an instant before he dragged her around the corner and threw her against the wall. The rain hammered down on them, casting Cellini's twisted face in a misty blur. "Bitch!" he snarled before he slapped her across the face. "You were told to stay away! You wouldn't listen!"

His words were all but drowned out by the tumultuous ringing in her ears. The ringing grew in intensity when Cellini struck a blow that knocked her head hard against the wall, adding to the galaxy of stars already exploding around her.

She collapsed to the cold, wet pavement. Cellini kicked her hard in the stomach. She cried out in pain. Cellini was a blurry mass lunging, his foot raised to stomp her.

Dimly, she heard a voice that didn't belong to Cellini.

Three gunshots followed. Cellini staggered away through the rain, clawing at his back. She was aware of a figure fading into the rain. On wobbly legs, still tearing at his back, Cellini lurched into the street, splashing through puddles, his face twisted in anguish. A car appeared and slammed to a halt as Cellini col-lapsed to his knees and then fell forward on the pavement. A gentleman in a bowler hat jumped out, his eyes wide with alarm.

Priscilla, in a miasma of pain, used the wall as a brace so that she could push herself to her feet. She became aware of patrons pouring out of the club. She thought she caught a glimpse of

George Raft but wasn't sure. She could hear sirens growing louder.

What a night, she thought, culminating in a beating in the rain outside a gambling club and now a dead gangster on the street in front of her.

How was she ever going to explain this to Mr. Banville?

CHAPTER TWENTY

Charger Is Suspicious

Priscilla declined the invitation from two ambulance attendants to allow them to transport her to a hospital for observation. They had arrived shortly after police descended to cordon off Berkeley Square. They diagnosed her with a bruised rib or two in addition to the welts on her face and the scrapes on her arms and legs.

Priscilla couldn't face a hospital. Right now, she wanted nothing more than to go home, curl up in her own bed and sleep forever. She was handed a packet of tablets. "Paracetamol should help, luv," suggested the younger of the two attendants. "You can get more at a chemist. But you really should get checked out."

"That's very kind of you," Priscilla said. "But I think I'll be fine."

As soon as the attendants departed, Detective Inspector Robert "Charger" Lightfoot of Scotland Yard escorted Priscilla to a police van and sat with her in the back, notebook on his lap. The dubious expression he usually wore when having to deal with her was firmly etched into his rock-jawed, traditional copper's face.

"Forgive me, Miss Tempest," Lightfoot interrupted after Priscilla had spent some time telling her expurgated version of events.

"You are forgiven, Inspector," assured Priscilla.

"What I fail to understand is how you ended up at the Colony Club in the first place."

Yes, a good question, Priscilla thought through a haze of aching body parts and fatigue. To answer honestly would mean a lot more trouble than she was in now. The trouble would begin with the admission that she had met with a guest of the Savoy, a Mr. Gordon Scott of Tarzan fame, a revelation certain to land them both on the front page of every tabloid in London. She closed her eyes momentarily, gathering the strength it would take to lie through her teeth.

"Miss Tempest!" came the gravelly, no-nonsense bark of Inspector Lightfoot.

"Yes, Inspector." Priscilla made herself focus on her stone-faced interrogator. It was a face that stated firmly that she was not about to receive anything in the way of consideration. A face that would cheerfully lock her up and throw away the key, if she was reading it correctly.

"I ask you again: What were you doing at the Colony Club?"

"I was enjoying a glass of champagne at the bar," Priscilla answered, as though it were the most natural pastime in the world.

"Alone?"

"Yes, alone. I was drinking champagne alone."

"Unusual, don't you think?"

"The next time I decide to have a glass of champagne, I will make certain a male of the species accompanies me. That way, I will be sure to avoid difficulties with police officials such as yourself."

"Very well, Miss Tempest," Lightfoot stated in tired voice. "Let us accept the fact that you were at the Colony, alone. Please continue."

"I had heard about the club and wanted to see it for myself," Priscilla said. "You know, so I might be able to recommend it to guests." Were her teeth rattling as she lied through them? She prayed they weren't.

"It's wonderful that you care so much about the welfare of your guests that you would recommend places where they could so easily lose money." The sarcasm was unmistakable.

"After tonight, I doubt very much I will be making any such recommendation," Priscilla said. No lying necessary there, she thought.

Lightfoot frowned, attempting, Priscilla imagined, to resist the urge to arrest her for the crime of once more complicating his life. From where she sat, she could make out the milling uniformed bobbies and detectives in long coats and fedoras, shifting between light and shadow as they went about the business of investigating a murder. A flashbulb popped, momentarily illuminating the scene, a police photographer manoeuvring his Speed Graphic camera, a pipe jammed in the corner of his mouth, his hat pushed back on his head. He hunched low, taking photos from different angles. The pop and flash from his camera repeated.

The Colony's front-entrance doors opened up and Priscilla saw George Raft emerge, flanked by two bobbies. He stopped to glance at Al Cellini's body in the street, showing no emotion. Then the bobbies ushered him over to one of the police vehicles that crowded the square. Moments later, the car sped off. Naturally, they would question George Raft, Priscilla thought. He could easily contradict what she had told Inspector Lightfoot about her visit to the Colony Club. But would he? Raft struck her as the kind of man who would not give up anything to the police, unless he absolutely had to.

"Miss Tempest, I do need you to concentrate." The intruding voice of Inspector Lightfoot.

"Sorry, Inspector. What were you saying?"

"You had a drink at the bar—alone, as you insist. Then what happened?"

"I finished my champagne, had a peek in the room where people were gambling, and then I left."

"And after that?"

"Simple enough," Priscilla reported. "I was assaulted as I left the club, dragged around the corner by this big, nasty chap. He knocked me to the ground. He kicked me a couple of times..."

"And you have no idea who it was who attacked you?" asked Lightfoot.

"No," said Priscilla. It was a bald-faced lie. She knew full well who it was. Cellini must have followed her into the city after he spotted her driving away from the hospital.

Lightfoot issued another impatient sigh. "Go on," he ordered.

"That's it. I heard three gunshots and the next thing I knew my assailant wasn't hitting me anymore. He staggered away into the square and fell to the ground."

"Who shot him?" Lightfoot demanded.

"I didn't see who shot him, as I told the uniformed officers. I heard gunshots. I caught a glimpse of someone running away."

"You did not get a look at this person?"

"A figure in the night. No more than that. I was barely conscious at that time."

"I see." Lightfoot made it sound as if he didn't see at all. "And just to be clear about the man who attacked you..."

"You mean my assailant who was shot and killed?" Priscilla desperately trying to put off further questions that would force her into more lies.

"Miss Tempest, I ask you again, did you recognize the man who attacked you?" Lightfoot was quickly losing whatever patience he managed to hang on to when having to deal with Priscilla.

"Once again—no." There was nothing else she could say. Admitting that she recognized Cellini only opened lines of questioning that would soon finish her.

"Let me understand this." Lightfoot's impatience was even more apparent. "You decided to visit the Colony Club—alone. You sat at the bar. You drank a glass of champagne. You spoke to no one?"

"I ordered the champagne and to do that, I had to speak to the bartender. He was very pleasant and helpful, I should say."

"Very well. You have your champagne. And then you have a look around. Have I got this right so far?"

"You have, Inspector."

"You then proceed to leave and, out of the blue, a man you don't know attacks you in the street just before he is shot to death by a person you never see."

"You've summed it up very succinctly, Inspector." Verifying her lies was as close to telling the truth as Priscilla would permit herself to get.

"You should know that the man who assaulted you was named Al Cellini. Is that name familiar to you?"

Priscilla dodged answering by asking, "Who is he?"

"Mr. Cellini was one of the owners here at the Colony Club. You mean to tell me that the owner of the club, a man whom you claim not to know, decides to attack you as you step outside and there is no reason for it?"

"I am as baffled as you are, Inspector." Which wasn't true at all.

"Miss Tempest, in my previous dealings with you, I have discovered that if you do not outright lie, you are certainly adept at discovering any number of ways to dodge the truth. Put plainly, I suspect that the story you have been telling me and the other officers is nowhere near the truth."

"You asked me what happened, Inspector," Priscilla protested. "I'm telling you to the best of my limited knowledge."

"I ask you again: the name Al Cellini means nothing to you?"

Priscilla found herself having trouble swallowing, a sure sign that she was about to be hoisted by her own petard. If she said she didn't know Cellini, it was only a matter of time before Lightfoot discovered otherwise. If she acknowledged that she did, well...

"Miss Tempest!" Lightfoot's impatience had finally been replaced with anger. "You must answer these questions."

"Of course I must, and I will, but having been beaten and kicked around and seeing a man murdered in front of me, I am not quite myself. I would like to think you would have some sympathy for my condition, but I should know better, shouldn't I?"

Lightfoot actually seemed offended by her allegation. "I have every sympathy in the world for you," he said in a starched voice that failed at sympathy. "When you are being honest with me," he added. "So here is an opportunity to display that honesty and thus earn my sympathy: Did you know Al Cellini?"

Priscilla cleared her throat before she said, "I did not *know* Mr. Cellini as such," she explained carefully. "But now that you have identified him to me, I do recall meeting Mr. Cellini briefly when he visited the Savoy." Priscilla regarded her interrogator with what she hoped was an expression of pure innocence.

"For God's sake," Lightfoot exploded, abandoning all pretense of compassion. "Are you now telling me that you did know the person who attacked you?"

"I *am* telling you I *didn't* know," responded Priscilla. The more upset Lightfoot became, the calmer she felt. He had that effect on her. "It was dark," she continued, "this man came out of nowhere and surprised me. I never got a good look at him."

Lightfoot issued a loud exhalation that jolted him back so that he hit his head against the side of the van.

"Are you hurt, Inspector?" asked Priscilla, genuinely concerned.

"I would be much better, Miss Tempest," answered the inspector, holding the back of his head, "if you would tell me something that at least approached the truth."

"You should take into consideration that I *am* telling you the truth," Priscilla responded with indignation, choosing words that hinted she *might* in fact be truthful, without having to make an outright denial.

"I don't believe you," Lightfoot stated flatly as he closed the notebook he had been writing in. "And because you are resolutely failing to tell me the truth of what happened here, I will work exceedingly hard to discover the truth you are not telling me. I warn you, Miss Tempest, I am very good at that, at finding truths. I have been doing so for a long time. When I do find it, I will also discover your lies. I must tell you now, you will very much regret them."

Priscilla did her best not to react to the implications of what Lightfoot was threatening. Keeping her voice at a level tone, she said, "Let me ask you this. Beyond making all sorts of wild accusations against me, do you have any idea who might have shot Mr. Cellini?"

Lightfoot shook his head. "Considering the kind of reprehensible character Cellini was, there are many candidates. I have to say, though, whoever did this did you and the world a favour."

Keeping his head low, Lightfoot struggled down from the police van. He turned to Priscilla, taking on a kinder expression. "I know you have been through a lot this evening, and I do believe you had nothing to do with this man Cellini's death, but you know more than you're telling me. It's not too late to change that, Miss Tempest. Any information you have that would lead us to discovering who committed this murder would put you in a much better light with me should such a light be required."

Priscilla considered this as Lightfoot stood by. She noted that the gentle expression was evaporating fast.

"There is perhaps one thing."

Immediately, Lightfoot looked more attentive. "And what is that, Miss Tempest?"

"If I tell you, it must be in the strictest confidence. I could get into a great deal of trouble with my employer otherwise."

"One might go so far as to suggest you are already in a great deal of trouble, but putting that aside, anything you tell me tonight will be in confidence."

"I don't know if it means anything, but I met Mr. Cellini because he was with Prince Teodoro of Italy, currently a guest at the hotel. The two gentlemen seemed to be associates."

Lightfoot had his notebook open again. "Teodoro, you say?"

"He's the Duke of Vento."

"Yes. Carry on."

"If I told you I've reason to believe Prince Teodoro may be here as part of a conspiracy to overthrow the British government..."

Lightfoot was tapping the fountain pen he was using against the edge of his notebook, shaking his head in disbelief. "Really, Miss Tempest, do you take me for a perfect fool?"

"You asked me for more information, Inspector," Priscilla answered. "I'm afraid that's the best I can do."

"If Italian princes and American gangsters out to overthrow the government are the best you can do... well, I suppose I would have thought you a better liar." He folded his notebook, shoved his pen into an inside pocket. He nodded curtly to Priscilla. "Good night, Miss Tempest. You can be assured I am not finished with you. Not by a long shot."

Felicity

"How do you know who I am?" Percy was twisted in the passenger seat so he could keep an eye on his good Samaritan as she drove. A very attractive Samaritan, Percy had already surmised, attired, he now saw, in a black leather jacket and jeans. In profile, Percy took in the perfect coffee-coloured smoothness of her skin, how nicely upturned the dark eyes were that shot a glance that caught him looking. Her full lips permitted the beginnings of an ironic smile.

"I write for *The Sunday Times*. Your name gets mentioned every so often in the newsroom." Now the smile was full—and full of irony.

"Why should anyone be talking about me in the *Sunday Times* newsroom?"

"Mostly it's everyone wondering how a reporter who started out with such promise never quite lived up to that promise."

"What?" Percy asked, startled. He had taken a few blows lately, but this one, thrown by a woman he didn't even know, who claimed to be a reporter, landed hardest.

"Well, you asked."

"Who are you, anyway?"

"Don't worry your head about me, Percy. I'm a nobody."

"Even so, you must have a name," Percy insisted.

"It's Felicity Khan if that helps."

"Well, Felicity Khan, *Sunday Times* reporter who doesn't think I fulfilled my early promise—"

"I didn't say *I* thought that," Felicity protested. "I'm saying that's what I heard in the newsroom."

"What are you doing out here at this time of night?"

"I suppose it's fair to say that we are both pursuing the same story."

"What story are you talking about?"

"Lady Daphne and the Wanderworth Group."

"Is that why you're here?" Percy failed to keep the disbelief out of his voice.

"That's why *you're* here, is it not?"

"I don't like to talk about the stories I'm working on, particularly with a reporter from a rival newspaper."

"The *Evening Standard* is hardly any competition for *The Sunday Times*," Felicity said in a scoffing voice.

"How the devil did you get to be so arrogant so young?" Percy shot back.

"Also, for your information, I will beat you to the story," Felicity added confidently.

"Is that so? I don't know what you've heard, but let me fill you in. No one beats *me* on a story, let alone someone who says she works for *The Sunday Times*."

"The someone who picked you up off the side of the road."

"Even so, I'm way ahead of you." Percy did his best to sound more confident than he was feeling. He was dead tired, his head hurt, his car wouldn't start and now he was beholden to this overconfident youngster. Taken together, he wasn't really feeling ahead of much of anything.

"Then you know about Spearpoint," Felicity was saying.

He forced himself to concentrate on that perfect profile— not hard to do, he had to concede. "I'm sorry, what were you saying?"

"You're way ahead of me, so that means you know."

"Yeah," he said uncertainly. What in God's name was Spear-point? he thought.

She shot him another quick glance as she drove. "You don't have any idea what I'm talking about," she declared.

"You know what? I'm too old and too tired to be playing these games."

The lights of London began to flicker in the distance. All he wanted was to get home and get into his bed. To hell with this far-too-attractive and overconfident young woman. To hell with everything—at least until he got a good night's sleep and his head stopped hurting. And maybe a drink or two might help the healing. Except he wasn't drinking. But then considering what he had been through tonight, who could blame a man for taking a medicinal nip?

"Let's assume that although I'm way ahead of you on this story," Percy ventured, "I want to make certain you have your facts right. Why don't you fill me in on what you've got? I'd be happy to correct any mistakes that you've made."

"You don't *know!*" Felicity pronounced gleefully.

"You're mistaken," he responded feebly.

"Yeah, right. Tell you what, Mr. Percy Hoskins. You hang on to your facts and I'll hang on to mine and we'll see how far that gets each of us. What do you think about that?"

"If you want to be that way about it, fine with me," Percy said more huffily than he intended. "You can let me off at the first tube station you see."

"You're a mess to be travelling on the tube at this time of night," Felicity said. "The least I can do is get you home safely."

"You don't have to do that," Percy said, relieved that he didn't have to sit on the tube wet from head to foot.

"I don't, but I will," Felicity said with a grin that Percy noted was, in the reflected half-light of the automobile's interior, impish. And highly attractive, he thought to himself, although that was not what he wanted to be thinking.

He directed her through sparse traffic and twenty minutes later she stopped on the street in front of his flat. In the shifting shadows, Felicity's face took on a particularly lovely sheen. Her eyes were bright and inquisitive. She said, "So this is where you live."

"I suppose I should thank you," he said.

"For rescuing your ass, I think you should," she said.

"Is that what you did?"

"What would you call it?"

"I would call it somewhat suspicious. A rival reporter shows up on a dark road out of nowhere, you have to wonder..."

"What?"

"If that rival reporter wasn't following me."

"Don't kid yourself. Why would I ever follow you?"

"I don't know. Perhaps because you..."

"Because you're so irresistible?"

"It's a possibility."

"Don't kid yourself, Mr. Percy Hoskins." She leaned across and kissed him on the lips. He pushed her gently away, admiring the way her eyes brightened. Tempted. And yet...

"Then I *am* irresistible," he said.

"Or maybe it's just that I've always wanted to kiss a legendary reporter."

"How was it?"

She shrugged and then kissed him again. This time she was the one who pulled away. "Goodnight, Mr. Percy Hoskins."

"Felicity Khan," he said.

"Yes?"

"I'm not quite sure what I'm supposed to make of you."

"Good," she smiled. "That's the way I like it."

He gave her one last searching look and then opened the passenger door and got out. She leaned over and rolled down the window. "Spearpoint," she said. "That's what this is about. That's the key to what you're after."

And then she drove off, leaving Percy standing on the street, thoroughly confused—and intrigued.

Major O'Hara's New Job

The gunshot death of Al Cellini outside the Colony Sports Club, to Priscilla's immense relief, had occurred too late for the early editions of the tabloids. Still, it would make the afternoon papers, so it would not be long before the story exploded, Priscilla reminded herself as she stiffly crossed the Front Hall the next morning, very much feeling the aches and pains from the blows received the night before.

Yes, Cellini had been kicking her around in the street at the time of his death, but surely that was peripheral to the bigger news of a gangland-style assassination outside a gambling club run by an American movie star with his name on the roof. There was no reason why she would have to be associated with such a shocking incident, Priscilla told herself as she entered 205. She half-expected Susie to be at her desk, upset as usual, apologizing profusely for being so ridiculous as to ever think she could leave her job to chase after a scoundrel like Lord Snowdon.

Except Susie wasn't there.

Instead, Major Jack O'Hara, in a bespoke blue-striped suit, complete with regimental tie, frowned up at her from what was ordinarily Susie's desk.

"There you are, Miss Tempest," the major announced sternly. "You are late."

"Major O'Hara," she gulped. "What are you doing here?"

"Seeing as how Miss Gore-Langton has left the employ of the hotel, it has been decided that you require a replacement for her position—someone who could actually get the job done."

"I'm sorry," said Priscilla, trying to hold back her bewilderment and rising panic, "but who decided you were going to take Susie's place? As far as I know, she has not officially left the Savoy."

"This comes from Mr. Banville himself," Major O'Hara stated. "As for myself, I felt it was time I sought a new role here at the hotel, given recent events in my life, and Mr. Banville agreed."

"You agreed to work as *my* assistant?"

That drew a scowl from Major O'Hara. "That is not *quite* the way Mr. Banville framed it."

"How did Mr. Banville frame it?"

"I have been led to understand that I am to take on more of a partnership role here in the press office."

"I must speak to Mr. Banville," Priscilla said. "He has not said a thing to me about this."

"Very well, Miss Tempest. In the meantime, however..." Major O'Hara kept his disdainful mien in place as he glanced at the telephone messages arranged on the desk. "A Mr. Gordon called and would like you to call him back. Also, I've been talking to Prince Constantino, Italian, I understand. He says he is a regular, valued guest at this hotel and cannot understand why you have not yet arranged a press conference for him. He also would like you to call him."

"I assume you mean Gordon Scott," Priscilla said pointedly.

"He said Mr. Gordon," retorted Major O'Hara peevishly.

"Well, it must have been Gordon Scott. Mr. Scott is a movie star."

Major O'Hara shrugged. "These celebrities, they think they own the world. Well, they don't. And neither do these so-called princes. Foreign fraudsters, the lot of them."

"At this hotel, guests such as Mr. Scott may not run the world, but they do demand the best from us, and rightly so," Priscilla said. "As do the members of royalty who stay with us. That means taking their names down accurately. It's a prerequisite of this job, Major. You must learn that and learn it quickly."

"Do not think for a moment you may speak to me in that tone of voice, Miss Tempest." Major O'Hara spat out the words. "You do not decree what I learn or do not learn."

"That's quite evident, Major, since you appear to have learned nothing."

Priscilla trooped out of the office. She entered the lady's bathroom to have a look at herself. A bit worse for wear this morning, she decided, despite the makeup artfully applied earlier at her flat. Major O'Hara had never taken orders from anyone who did not have a superior rank, a moustache and a membership at a private club. How could he possibly replace Susie? Unthinkable! She continued to stare into the mirror, willing herself to look better than she felt. Something had to be done, and done quickly, she decided. Ordinarily, she awaited a summons to Mr. Banville's office, and given his unhappiness with her, she usually did not have to wait long.

Not today, though. Today, she was not waiting, she was taking action—storming the Place of Execution. She would not—could not!—hide her fury at what had transpired without her consent.

"I must see him," Priscilla declared as soon as she presented herself in front of El Sid, perched like a spectacled buzzard in Banville's outer office. Behind those round, gold-rimmed glasses, his usually scornful eyes looked a bit disconcerted. "What happened to you?"

God, she thought, did she look that bad? "Nothing happened," she answered, rallying. "I need to see Mr. Banville—now."

"He hasn't called for you." Priscilla's unannounced arrival appeared to have had the unexpected effect of actually throwing El Sid into a state bordering on confusion. His day was carefully organized so that there were no surprises for him or for his boss. Here was a surprise.

Priscilla shook her head. "*Now*, Sidney."

He cleared his throat, noting the fierceness in Priscilla's face, hesitated a moment or two longer, then picked up the phone. "Let me see if he's available," he said quietly.

There was a long pause before Banville came on the line. "Sir, Miss Tempest is here and she wishes to see you. I told—what's that?" Sidney's face fell as he listened. "Very good, sir."

Sidney hung up the phone, his expression a mixture of mystification and disappointment. "You are to go straight in," he said sullenly. Priscilla took a moment to savour her small victory. El Sid huffily ignored her. She drew a deep breath before opening the door to the Place of Execution.

"Good, you're here, Miss Tempest." Banville, seated behind his massive desk, actually perked up when she entered. "I was just about to call you."

"Well, sir—"

"I've just heard the news," Banville plowed on.

"Yes, of course—" Her stomach sank. The bloody afternoon papers. Trouble!

"This chap Cellini who was shot outside that notorious gambling club last night—wasn't he with Prince Teodoro the other day in this very office?"

"I believe he was, sir," Priscilla answered. "The same gentleman."

144

"Damn!" said Banville. Now he was frowning. Never a good thing when the boss was frowning. "Cellini wasn't a guest here, though. Correct?"

"No, sir, but of course Prince Teodoro is still with us."

"Never should have gotten involved with that blighter," Banville said reflectively. "Never should have listened to Bertie."

It was all Priscilla could do to stop herself from reminding Banville that she had tried to warn him about Teodoro. For now, there was a much more pressing matter.

"If I may, sir—" Priscilla started again.

"I know what you're about to say, Miss Tempest," Banville interrupted. "You're about to tell me that you'll be working to ensure that the Savoy's name is not connected in any way with this deplorable incident outside the Colony Club."

"Exactly, sir. But there is one thing—"

"Excellent! That's what I like to hear from the press office. Working to protect the good name of this establishment."

"That's what we're doing, each and every day," Priscilla concurred. "However, there is a subject I wish to discuss with you this morning, if I may."

"Subject?" Banville looked baffled. "What subject?"

"Major O'Hara, sir."

Banville immediately brightened. "Ah, Major O'Hara. Yes! Rather clever on my part, don't you think?"

"Sir?" Priscilla did her best to tamp down her growing horror. The parachuting of Major O'Hara into the press office was possibly the least clever thing she'd ever heard.

"Having received word that Miss Gore-Langton has left us—not the worst thing that has happened to this hotel, I must say—and knowing that our colleague, Major O'Hara, was having second thoughts about his role here as head of security—going through something of a crisis brought on by his troubled brother,

I daresay—I thought it might be a nice change for him, as well as fill in a hole in our staffing. I must say I was pleased when Major O'Hara readily agreed to the idea as soon as I brought it up with him."

"The thing is, sir," Priscilla said, moving forward carefully, "I was not consulted or informed about your decision."

"Didn't I tell you?" Banville paused as though to rummage through his memory. "I was sure we discussed it."

"We did not, sir," said Priscilla firmly. "I do have my doubts as to whether Major O'Hara is best suited for the job. Furthermore, I'm not sure Miss Gore-Langton has officially left our employ. She has said nothing to me."

"Be that as it may, Miss Tempest," Banville said, "I disagree with your appraisal of the major. Let's face it, how difficult can it be to toddy up to the odd celebrity? Not difficult at all, I would wager. And I am sure you will make the best of the situation." Banville's face took on the emotional quality of a rock. His voice turned to ice. "In fact, I am certain you will make the best of it."

"Of course, sir." Priscilla saw the path ahead strewn with the eggs she was about to walk on. She swallowed hard and girded herself to ask, "Then, sir, who now is in charge of the press office?"

"Why, you are both in charge," Banville responded quickly, enthusiastically. "I see it as a partnership. Two equals working together."

Priscilla felt as though her smile had been stuck in place with a screwdriver. "A partnership," were the only two words she could get out safely.

Banville was already looking at his watch. "I think that's all for now, Miss Tempest."

"Very good, sir," replied Priscilla with forced courteousness. She retreated toward the door.

"Oh, and Miss Tempest..." Banville called.

Priscilla's heart leapt. Had Banville changed his mind? She turned back to him. "Sir?"

"I almost forgot. Lord Snowdon's assignment has been completed. Our contract with him is at an end."

Once again, Priscilla was caught off-guard. "I didn't realize he had taken all his pictures."

"Not that I'm very happy with the work he turned in. Cooks in tall hats standing over steaming pots. Noël Coward in the American Bar. You'd think the man lived here."

"I believe he does, sir, when he is not at his home in Jamaica."

Banville didn't appear to have heard her. "A bit of a waste of time, if you ask me." He was lost in thought. Then he seemed to realize Priscilla remained poised in front of his desk and quickly cleared his throat.

"Anything else, Miss Tempest? If not, I must get back to work. Life at the Savoy must go on, you know."

Leaving her life in ruins, Priscilla thought as she left Banville's office.

The Reporter from The Times

On the long march from Banville's office to 205, a furious Priscilla wrote and then rewrote in her mind the letter of resignation she would submit immediately.

She was, after all, a strong, independent woman who would not allow herself to be pushed around and undermined by the thoughtless male guardians of the establishment. Banville had been out to get her almost as soon as she had walked through the Savoy's door. He had not hired her, and that had upset him from the beginning. Now he had finally found the way to sideline her: to insert his own man into the press office.

Enough was finally enough.

Entering the outer office, she stopped dead at the sight of Major O'Hara grappling with a young woman. He was trying to hold the woman's arms against her body but as Priscilla watched, stunned, the woman broke free and rather adroitly elbowed the major in the stomach. "Get away from me you bugger," shouted the young woman fiercely.

Gasping for air, O'Hara sank back across his desk, sending papers scattering.

"Major O'Hara!" Priscilla shouted. "Enough! Stand down immediately." As close as Priscilla could get to an imitation of the drill sergeant O'Hara might listen to.

"A damned fraud!" the major cried, pointing a shaky finger at the young woman.

"You can go straight to hell!" the young woman cried right back.

Priscilla stepped decisively between the two combatants. "What's going on here?"

"This... this *girl* pushed her way in here claiming to be a reporter for *The Sunday Times*," O'Hara managed between gasps of breath. "Naturally, I had no alternative but to throw her out."

"I *am* a reporter for *The Sunday Times*, you nit!" shouted the young woman.

Priscilla turned to Major O'Hara. "What makes you certain she is not a reporter from *The Times*, Major?"

"Because she is a *woman*!" O'Hara called out with the absolute certainty of his status in life. "Everyone knows *The Times* would not have a woman on staff. And it certainly would not have a bl—"

"Major O'Hara!" cried Priscilla.

"This is an imposter, I tell you—"

Priscilla spoke calmly to the young woman. "I'm sorry, what is your name?"

"Felicity Khan," she announced defiantly. "Parents emigrated from Mumbai, for your information. Born and raised right here in London. And I *am* a reporter for *The Sunday Times*."

"I'm Priscilla Tempest, Miss Khan." Priscilla held out her hand. "Parents living outside Toronto, Canada, where I was born and raised. I'm supposedly in charge around here, although I'm beginning to wonder. Would you mind stepping into my office?"

"Don't mind at all," said Felicity.

"This way, please." Priscilla opened the door to her office and then stepped aside so that Felicity could pass by. Priscilla threw O'Hara an accusatory look. O'Hara, meantime, was busy straightening himself, ensuring that his regimental tie was properly adjusted—and trying, without great success, to maintain his usual expression of infinite superiority.

Priscilla followed Felicity and closed the door, thoughts of a resignation letter for now set aside. "Would you like something to drink?"

"Is that how you buy off the press?" Felicity asked sarcastically. "By offering free drinks? Well, it won't work with me."

Priscilla managed a smile. "If only it were that easy. No, we offer all our visitors something to drink."

"Thank you for asking, but I'm fine, despite being assaulted."

"I apologize for Major O'Hara. He is—or was—the hotel's head of security. He is overzealous on occasion."

"Or a racist bugger. That might be a better description."

Priscilla managed to keep her smile in place. "You must tell me why you're here."

"I'm working on a piece for my newspaper about the Wanderworth Group, and I'm hoping you can be of some help to me."

Priscilla felt her smile slipping. "If your story doesn't pertain to this hotel—and it doesn't sound as though that's the case— I'm not sure how I would be able to help."

"Let's find out, shall we?" Felicity was extracting a notebook from her handbag as she spoke, a warning sign, in Priscilla's estimation. She was exactly what she said she was—a reporter, and thus dangerous. "You attended Wanderworth House not long ago in the company of Italy's Prince Teodoro. Isn't that a fact?"

"I did not *accompany* the prince, as you put it," Priscilla replied cautiously. "He happened to be at the same function I was."

"That would have been a meeting of the Wanderworth Group, yes?" asked Felicity.

"Why are you asking these questions?" In addition to being worried about where this was headed, Priscilla found herself curious.

"You said you doubted you could help me with my story, and yet here you are, already helping me with my story. Are you a member of the group?"

"I don't know of any such group," Priscilla maintained. "Are you doing some sort of story on Wanderworth House? Is that what this is about?"

"It's not a Sunday layout on the history of the house and its gardens, if that's what you're suggesting."

"Why would I be suggesting anything else?" Priscilla asked, all innocence.

"If you are not a member of the Wanderworth Group, perhaps you could explain to me what you were doing there," Felicity said in a formal, professional voice.

"How did you know I was even at Wanderworth?"

"Let's say I have it on good authority. Would you mind answering my question?"

How to answer? Priscilla thought quickly. Aloud, she said, "I was curious about the house, that's all. There was no more to it than that. As I said, I don't know about any group, and I wasn't aware any sort of function was in progress. I must say I was surprised to find Prince Teodoro among the guests." Even to Priscilla's ears, those explanations sounded rather feeble. She comforted herself with the knowledge that they were not total lies. She had, in fact, no idea, originally, what she was getting herself into. In fact, she never knew what she was getting herself into before it was too late to get herself out again.

"You left London, drove for an hour and just happened to stop at that house?" Felicity obviously wasn't buying it.

"That's correct," Priscilla answered.

Felicity was writing in her notebook as she asked, "Did you happen to meet Lady Daphne Wanderworth?"

"As a matter of fact, I did. Briefly." Priscilla allowed a frown.

"You know she heads the Wanderworth Group," Felicity said pointedly.

"Really, Miss Khan, I have no idea where you are going with this, but it's a busy morning. I do apologize for the way my colleague treated you, but I really must get on with the rest of the day."

"What about the name Spearpoint?" Felicity had stopped writing to focus unblinking eyes on Priscilla.

Priscilla knotted a puzzled eyebrow. "I'm not sure I understand."

"No?" Felicity didn't look convinced.

"I have no idea what Spearpoint is."

"That name means nothing to you?"

"It doesn't. And I'm not sure why it should."

"No reason, I suppose," Felicity replied enigmatically. She was on her feet, closing her notebook. "Thank you for your time, Miss Tempest. It has been most helpful. And thank you for coming to my rescue this morning."

"It should never have happened. Again, many apologies."

"I will be in touch," Felicity said. Priscilla could not decide if the reporter was issuing a warning—or a threat.

No sooner was Felicity out the door than Priscilla looked up to discover her friend Noël Coward poised on the threshold. "Is it safe to enter?" he asked merrily.

"Barely," said Priscilla with more seriousness than she intended. She quickly perked up. "But seeing as how you are Britain's most famous playwright—"

"And a performer of unparalleled genius," Noël added.

"Not to mention a long-running and much-loved guest at the Savoy. Naturally you are welcome at any time, Noël. Please, come in."

"I hope I'm not intruding. I'm just back and thought I'd pop by." Noël ventured further into Priscilla's office. The sophisticate was faultlessly turned out, dress shirt snow white against a polka-dotted bow tie, a complement to the smartly tailored dove-grey suit that somehow managed not to clash with his brown suede shoes. His balding head was nut brown from the Jamaican sun.

He employed the walking stick he carried with him to bang at the chair in front of her desk, as though to test its safety. Satisfied that it could take his weight, he seated himself. "You look frazzled, my dear," he declared after inspecting Priscilla with hooded eyes, leaning forward on his walking stick. "Is everything all right?"

"I'm not sure," Priscilla said. "That was a reporter from *The Sunday Times* who just left."

"From *The Times* you say?" Noël raised and lowered his eyebrows. "Don't tell me that paper has actually entered the twentieth century and hired a woman? Why, next thing, the internal combustion engine will replace horses."

"Miss Felicity Khan," Priscilla said. "She wanted to know about Lady Daphne Wanderworth."

"Lady Daphne, my Lord." Noël's eyebrows once again arched in surprise. "Dragged straight out of her place at the bubbling cauldron if you'd like my opinion. A fascist, unrepentant, through and through."

"Then you know her?"

Noël made a face. "Encountered Lady Daphne before the war. Didn't like her at all, lurking about in the ancient, crumbling pile that is Wanderworth House. But how have you managed to get yourself drawn into that old bat's nasty web?"

Finally in the company of the one person she felt she could trust to keep her secrets, Priscilla eagerly spilled out her experiences at Wanderworth House with Lady Daphne and Prince Teodoro. She told him about the dead body she thought was Colin Ashbury, Prince Teodoro's threats and Al Cellini's unprovoked attack outside the Colony Club that ended with him being shot to death. Lastly, she confided her growing suspicion that she had accidentally uncovered some sort of conspiracy organized by Lady Daphne and Teodoro.

"My goodness gracious," exclaimed Noël quietly, his eyebrows working overtime as he digested Priscilla's story. "The trouble you manage to attract as soon as I leave town. Quite extraordinary, young lady."

"Needless to say, I'm afraid no one will believe any of this, and in the meantime, I will lose my job here. Now this woman shows up, trying to connect me with what's going on at Wanderworth House. Yet another complication I don't need."

"From what you have told me, *something* wicked almost certainly is unfolding," Noël opined. "What you're alleging should be taken very seriously indeed."

"What do you think I should do?"

Before Noël could answer, her office door opened and Major O'Hara appeared, scowling, as usual. "I have returned from lunch," he announced.

"Wonderful," Priscilla said gloomily.

He glanced suspiciously at Noël. "Anything I should be brought up to speed on?"

"Not at the moment, thank you, Major."

O'Hara tossed out more suspicious looks before reluctantly closing the door.

Noël stared at Priscilla in mystification. "What is that supercilious buffoon doing here?"

"Replacing Susie, if you can believe it."

"Where is wondrous Susie?"

"Supposedly, she has left," Priscilla said. "Although I'm not so sure about that."

"Left? Left where?"

"I shouldn't say anything, but as far as I know, she is with Lord Snowdon."

"Lord Snowdon, my God that is not good," Noël said, scowling.

"I've tried to talk to her," Priscilla said. "But she won't listen to me—or anyone else."

"If I were you, I would confirm that what she has told you is in fact the case," Noël said slowly, choosing his words carefully.

"What do you mean?"

"Just do as I suggest," Noël continued. "I could be wrong, but I know Snowdon. Don't trust him. Don't like him. Please be sure to check on Susie."

"I'm sure she's all right."

"I do hope so," Noël replied enigmatically. He used his walking stick to boost himself to his feet. "I will do this discreetly, naturally, and without naming any names, but let me check with my sources at MI5 and Special Branch, find out if they know anything about what Lady Daphne and Prince Teodoro might be cooking up. I knew Colin Ashbury a bit, but I can't remember much about him. Had no idea he was involved with the likes of Lady Daphne. I'll check into him as well."

"I would be most grateful, Noël," Priscilla said. She rose and came around the desk to embrace him. He kissed her on the cheek and then looked her straight in the eye. "Please, until I can get more information, be very careful. These people are playing for keeps."

One of the three telephones on Priscilla's desk began to ring. "I'd better take that," she said with a grimace. "Probably more trouble."

Noël went out the door as she picked up the receiver.
"We've got to meet," Percy Hoskins said.
"Where are you? I've been worried."
"The usual place. In an hour."

Under Arthur Sullivan

A dreary mist had descended upon the Sir Arthur Sullivan Memorial. It swirled around the bench where two weary warriors sat contemplating each other's injuries. A scratched-up Percy, lacking sleep, the victim of attacking tree branches in the dead of night, no longer much resembled the cleaned-up version on display the last time they had met here. Priscilla wasn't exactly feeling fresh as a daisy herself. Her aching ribs caused her to walk stiffly and that slightly puffy face, its bruises artfully camouflaged with makeup to pass muster with both Banville and Major O'Hara, remained. Not that those two would notice anything, anyway, Priscilla thought. Percy, however, was a different story.

"You look a bit rough at the edges, if you don't mind my saying."

"I do mind you saying," Priscilla said defensively. "You're not supposed to notice."

"Put it this way," Percy said. "You look better than I do."

Priscilla quickly filled him in on what had happened to her after they split up.

"Whatever were you doing at the Colony Club?" Percy demanded when she had finished.

"I decided to go for a drink," Priscilla said as breezily as she could manage. "After what I had been through, I thought I needed one."

"You went to the Colony Club—alone?"

"What's wrong with that?"

"A little curious, don't you think?"

"You sound just like the police, unable to imagine a woman having a drink alone," Priscilla said peevishly. No need to mention that, briefly, Gordon Scott had been there. After all, she did arrive by herself and left the same way, and therefore she was telling the truth. More or less.

"Any trouble after I left you?" Priscilla asked. "Were you able to find your car?"

"It wouldn't start in the rain," Percy said miserably. "I'm having it towed."

"How did you get back to London?"

"A passing motorist," Percy said quickly.

"Lucky you," Priscilla said.

The gloom of the day matched their moods as they slumped together, eyeing the bronzed back of Sir Arthur's most fervent and ever-lasting female admirer.

Finally, Priscilla said, "Does Spearpoint mean anything to you?"

"What?" Percy had perked up a bit. "How do you know about Spearpoint?"

"A reporter from *The Sunday Times* came to my office this morning."

Percy's face fell. "Was her name Felicity Khan?"

"You *know* her?"

"She was the motorist who picked me up."

"I see." Priscilla gave him a sideways glance. "Quite an attractive motorist, I would say."

"What's that supposed to mean?" Percy was in full defence mode.

"She's lovely."

"I hadn't really noticed," Percy said.

"More importantly," Priscilla continued, "it appears she's doing a story about Lady Daphne and the Wanderworth Group, perhaps linked to whatever Spearpoint is."

"Damn!" Percy exploded. He was sitting up, no longer slumped over.

"What's the matter?" Priscilla asked.

It was Percy's turn to cast a sidelong glance. "Tell me something: Do you think I'm washed up? Past my prime?"

"What?" Priscilla couldn't believe what she was hearing.

"Is that what you think?" Percy pressed, eyeing her fiercely.

"Who says you're washed up?" It hadn't crossed Priscilla's mind, mainly because Percy was always so quick to remind her that he was London's finest reporter.

"That reporter. Felicity." He paused and then added, "She told me she was beating me on the story..."

"When did she do that?"

"In the car on the way back to London. Just before she kissed me."

"She *kissed* you?"

"Why is that so surprising?" Percy, irked.

"She says you're washed up, she's going to beat you on the story and then she *kisses* you?"

"Something like that, yeah," Percy admitted reluctantly.

"A bit surprising, wouldn't you say?"

"You haven't answered my question." Percy had straightened, keeping his eyes on her.

"Remind me what the question was. The news of kissing reporters has thrown me off the track."

"About being washed up. Finished."

"Uh, no," Priscilla said.

"You hesitated when you said it." Percy's tone was snappish.

"No, I didn't," Priscilla protested.

"Yes. You did." Percy, petulant.

"I don't think you are washed up or finished," Priscilla said with all the authority she could muster. "I think you're annoying a good deal of the time—most of the time, in fact—but you never give me the impression that you're washed up. Just the opposite in fact."

"No, I don't, do I?" Percy's voice was growing in confidence.

"And what's this about allowing this woman to kiss you?"

"I wouldn't use the word *allowed* exactly. It just happened before I could stop her."

"It doesn't sound as though you tried very hard to fight her off."

"It happened so fast," he repeated feebly.

"If you care to know what I think—I think this Felicity Khan is playing games with your head."

"You don't think there's a possibility she finds me attractive?" Percy sounded peeved all over again.

"Let's change the subject," Priscilla said impatiently. "This is getting us nowhere."

"You're the one who seems to be jealous that an attractive young woman kissed me."

"I'm not jealous," Priscilla argued. "However, I am amazed that you, the hard-bitten Fleet Street reporter, is such a pushover."

"Far from it," countered Percy. "This is all part of my strategy, you see."

It was all Priscilla could do to stop herself breaking into laughter, which would only hurt her bruised ribs. She swallowed hard and said, "Pray tell, exactly what is your strategy?"

"To make this woman believe I'm quite taken with her while at the same time extracting information I might find useful."

"Like what for instance?"

Percy did not appear to have heard her. "If you want my thoughts on the matter," he said formally, "I do believe she kissed me because she finds me attractive."

"Percy, let's talk about something else," Priscilla said, fed up.

"You can tell that sort of thing by the quality of the kiss," Percy persisted.

"Percy!"

"Fine." Percy settled back against the bench, folding his arms and tucking in, as though to protect himself against any critical assessment of his attractiveness.

They fell silent. The mist had mostly cleared. A group of uniformed schoolchildren marched noisily past along the wide pathway.

"She's not going to beat me, I can tell you that much," Percy pronounced.

"She's playing games with you, Percy," admonished Priscilla. "If you don't want her to beat you to this story, stay away from her."

"Aha!" Percy declared triumphantly. "You *are* jealous."

CHAPTER TWENTY-FIVE

Complete Bastard

Given the ambiguousness of Noël's warning about Antony Armstrong-Jones, Priscilla didn't know what she would encounter on her return to 20 Pimlico Road. But her concern about Susie's safety was more than enough to chance her friend's renewed anger or anything else she might encounter.

As she knocked on the door, she questioned whether any amount of talk could persuade Susie to return. Perhaps framing it as an act of charity that would spare Priscilla from having to further endure the starched superciliousness of Major O'Hara would do the trick.

Receiving no answer, she knocked again. This time the door opened to reveal a winsome young thing—a winsome young thing who, most definitely, was not Susie.

"Yes? Can I help you?" the young thing asked eagerly.

"I'm sorry, but who are you?" inquired a confused Priscilla.

"I'm Tiffany," the young thing announced, as though keen to let the world know. "I'm Lord Snowdon's assistant. He's out at the moment, but I'll be glad to help you if I can."

"I'm looking for a friend of mine," Priscilla said. "Susie Gore-Langton? Is she here?"

Tiffany looked puzzled. "There's no one by that name. Do you have the right address?"

"I certainly do," Priscilla said. "Are you sure Lord Snowdon isn't in?"

Tony, in shirtsleeves, his tie undone, flushed and somewhat out of breath, grinned and said, "There you are, Priscilla. Come in. Sorry. I was in the darkroom."

His hand touched Tiffany's shoulder "It's all right, Tiffany. Priscilla is a dear friend."

The keenness was slowly dissolving off Tiffany's impressively smooth complexion. "Of course, Tony. I thought that you didn't wish to be disturbed."

"Why don't you run off and do that shopping we talked about?" Armstrong-Jones suggested, opening the door further so Priscilla could come in.

Tiffany looked uncertain.

"I'd like to speak to Priscilla alone if you don't mind."

"Certainly, Tony. I'll be back in a few minutes."

Armstrong-Jones kissed her gently on the forehead. Tiffany, crestfallen now, went out. Armstrong-Jones closed the door behind her and said, "It's so good to see you, Priscilla. I've been wondering how you're doing."

A camera was set up on a tripod in front of a large, white screen. There was a bed, unmade, in an alcove to Priscilla's right that she didn't like the look of. A spiral staircase wound up to a second floor. A bottle of white wine was set into an ice bucket on a counter beside two wine glasses.

"Where's Susie?" Priscilla asked immediately.

"Would you like some wine?" she heard Armstrong-Jones saying.

"You haven't answered me, Lord Snowdon."

"There's no need for formality now, Priscilla. I'm finished with the Savoy. It's all right to call me Tony."

"Please answer me."

"It's cheap plonk, nothing fancy," he said moving over to the counter to lift the wine out of the ice bucket. "I'm a cheap plonk, nothing-fancy kind of fellow."

"Lord Snowdon, please." Priscilla was glancing around, her eyes insisting on straying to that damnable bed.

"I'm afraid I haven't seen Susie lately," Armstrong-Jones said vaguely.

"What's happened to her?"

"Susie's fine. These things have their moment and then they pass. I am a married man after all."

"You're also a liar and a right bastard."

"I'm afraid so," Tony said agreeably. "You understand that. Susie, I'm afraid to say, doesn't. Here." He handed her a glass.

She sipped at the wine and had to work on not making a face. It tasted awful.

"What do you think?"

"About?"

He nodded at her glass. "The wine."

"It's—"

"Dreadful, right?"

"Like you," Priscilla amended.

Tony laughed. "I do find you so charming, Priscilla, I really do."

"You haven't told me where Susie is."

"No, I haven't."

He pressed himself against her, his hands slipping around her waist. "I also find you very attractive. But I believe you know that." His lips began to nuzzle her neck.

"Don't," Priscilla warned.

"Don't what?" With Tony's lips against her neck, his voice was muffled.

"Don't do that." Priscilla pulled away from him and slapped him across the face.

Armstrong-Jones reddened and backed away, holding his face. "Well, there's a first."

"I can't believe I'm the first woman who ever slapped you," Priscilla said.

"Put it this way, you're the first woman who ever slapped me twice. If you'll remember, you also struck me the first time we met. Thus, you will go down in history."

"Where is Susie?" Priscilla repeated, out of breath.

Before Armstrong-Jones could respond, the door opened and Tiffany stepped hesitantly in. "I'm sorry," she said nervously. "I forgot my wallet."

Did she? Priscilla wondered. Or was she suspicious of what her new lover might be up to alone with another woman? She need not have worried, Priscilla thought.

"It's all right, Tiffany," Armstrong-Jones said. "Priscilla was about to leave."

"Not before you tell me where Susie is," Priscilla pushed back angrily.

"As far as I know, she's with her parents," Armstrong-Jones stated.

Priscilla started for the door. Tiffany stood nearby, pale and rigid. "Get out," Priscilla whispered to her. "Don't listen to anything he tells you. It's all lies. Leave as soon as you can. You'll thank me."

Tiffany just looked at her blankly.

Outside No. 20, Priscilla paused to regain her composure.

What a complete bastard Armstrong-Jones is, she thought as she walked to her car. But then she knew that—knew it from the beginning, in fact. After all, he made little effort to hide his bastardness. An attractive bastard, she had to concede, but a complete bastard nonetheless.

Susie should have been wise enough to see that for herself. But then again, if Priscilla had shown any wisdom at all when it came to the bastards in her own life—well, she hadn't. If there was any consolation to be had, she was perhaps wiser. Not nearly wise enough, though.

Lost in thought, Priscilla failed to notice the black sedan pull up beside her. It quickly moved ahead to slide into an empty parking space. It was not until the two big louts got out that she began to suspect something was wrong. The two sported cloth caps, tilted at an angle over their eyes. They wore identical badly fitting checkered orange suits. Priscilla wondered if they had gotten a two-for-one deal on them.

One of the louts grabbed her arm. The other held the rear passenger door open. Before she could cry out an objection, she was hustled into the back of the car. The lout who had grabbed her muscled his way in next to her, not smiling but growling, "Keep your mouth shut."

She was about to point out that she had not had a chance to open her mouth, but by then the other lout was behind the wheel and a few seconds later the black sedan was whizzing off along Pimlico Road. Priscilla wrinkled her nose, inhaling a combination of cheap cigarette smoke and unpleasant aftershave coming off the lout in the back seat.

"You might tell me what this is about," Priscilla said as calmly as she could.

"Just keep your mouth shut," replied the driver-lout without turning his head. "You'll find out soon enough."

They drove through thick traffic along Grosvenor Place, past Westminster Cathedral to Hyde Park Corner and the Wellington Arch. The driver-lout turned right onto Park Lane and entered Mayfair. Priscilla felt curiously reassured. How much harm could come to her in posh Mayfair? A right onto Hertford Street and then into a laneway running behind a line of buildings. The driver-lout brought the sedan to a stop at the end. The back-seat lout immediately opened his door, issuing another snarl: "Out."

Yes, right, she thought. An articulate lout. Was there any other kind?

The driver-lout led the way as his pal propelled her forward. They went through a rear door into a big, silent kitchen. Through the kitchen, along a corridor that opened into a familiar interior—the Colony Club's gaming room. George Raft, wearing a dark suit, sat at one of the roulette tables. He appeared to be closely studying his hands, folded on the green baize near what looked to be a soapstone sculpture of a black bird.

Raft looked up as Priscilla approached. As usual, his face revealed nothing. "There you are, Priscilla," he said. "I've been waiting for you."

CHAPTER TWENTY-SIX

Lucky Lady

"Come and sit down." Raft indicated a chair close to him at the roulette table. Wisps of smoke drifted around him from the cigarette in the ashtray at his elbow. The uncertain overhead light darkened the hollows of his face, giving him a ghoulish cast.

Gingerly, Priscilla went around the table and took the seat. The two louts faded into the dimness of the gaming room. Without the murmur of gamblers at tense play, the room was eerily quiet. Raft had not taken his eyes off her, making her feel more uncomfortable than ever—and determined not to show it.

"You know, Mr. Raft, if you wanted to see me, you could drop around to my office at the Savoy or give me a call—the way normal people tend to do."

"Yeah, normal. That's not a word I'm usually associated with."

"What do you want with me? Why are you doing this?"

Raft deflected the question by asking, "Can I get you something, Priscilla? Tea? Everyone here drinks tea."

"I don't like tea," Priscilla said. She eyed the black bird sculpture.

"I see you're looking at my Maltese falcon," Raft said.

"Is that what it is?" Priscilla said. "From the movie?"

"I thought you might enjoy seeing it," Raft said, moving a hand to touch the sculpture's base. "It's the one they actually used in the John Huston movie."

"But you weren't in *The Maltese Falcon*," Priscilla said.

"No." Raft gave a wane smile. "I keep the bird around to remind me from time to time."

"Remind you of what?" Priscilla asked.

"That I make mistakes," Raft said. "That I pay a price when I make mistakes."

"Then you try not to make mistakes, I suppose."

"Something like that," Raft conceded. He moved his hand away from the falcon. "Did I make a mistake coming to London? I don't know, but after last night, I do wonder."

One of his small, soft hands now moved away from the falcon and drifted over the roulette wheel in front of him.

"Are you familiar with roulette?"

"I'm afraid I'm not a gambler."

"This is a European wheel, slightly different from the American model. The numbers laid out on the table here are mostly the same whether you're in London or Vegas. Looking at this, you think how complicated it must be. But roulette is actually the simplest of games. You put your money on a number. The wheel spins. If your number comes up, you win. Simple. I like it. I like things that way. Simple. Uncomplicated. You win. Or you lose."

"I don't see what any of this has to do with me..." Priscilla began.

"I'll tell you what I don't like, Priscilla: I don't like complications. I don't like my business partner being gunned down outside the club that has my name on the roof. That's a complication. That's a big complication. It starts me thinking I've made a mistake. Maybe a big mistake." He allowed his hand to stroke the surface of the sculpture. "That's when I bring out the black bird. That's when I start worrying."

"Whatever you may be thinking," Priscilla pointed out in a tight voice, "I didn't shoot Mr. Cellini."

"Like I said, big complications," Raft went on, ignoring

Priscilla's remark. He removed his hand from the black bird. "Two things I try to avoid in life: cops and questions. Today, I've got cops all over the place. Why we had to bring you in the back way. Cops forcing me to close this place. Then there are the questions I don't like. Questions like what was Al doing attacking a young woman as she left my establishment?"

"If you're referring to me," Priscilla said, "I'm as much in the dark as you are."

"I hear what you are telling me," Raft said. "Now I want to hear what you're not telling me."

"I don't know what to tell you."

"Try telling me why Al jumped you."

"I told you. I don't know."

"You don't know why Al jumped you?"

"I have no idea." Not nearly true. But Raft didn't have to know that.

"Then who is protecting you?"

"What makes you think anyone is protecting me?" Priscilla asked.

"Someone must have been watching you—keeping you safe. That's why Al got taken out."

"That's ridiculous," Priscilla insisted, genuinely baffled. "Mr. Cellini was a gangster, was he not? Don't gangsters know gangsters who don't like them? Don't gangsters who don't like other gangsters shoot them?"

Raft drummed his fingers against the green baize as though debating with himself what to do—or say—next. "In this town, people don't like one another, that's true, same as in towns all over the world," he said finally. "The difference is, in this town, people who don't like each other stop talking to one another or they don't do business together. It's my experience that people in this town don't shoot each other."

Raft stopped drumming his fingers. "You're not coming clean with me, Priscilla."

"I *am* coming clean, as you say." Great, she thought, in addition to lying to police, she was now lying to an American gangster.

Raft once again ignored her protests. "This time around, Priscilla, it's a courtesy call, me giving you a chance to help me out with no consequences on either side—simple, the way I like things." He got to his feet, reminding her just how short he was, how his height did nothing to tamp down the sense of menace that he gave off. A composed, controlled bad guy and all the more threatening because of those qualities.

She found her voice. "I thought you were helping Gordon Scott make a movie."

"Yeah, we're trying to put some financing together for him. What's the point?"

"The point is, Mr. Scott was at a place called Wanderworth House where he was supposed to meet with possible financiers. That meeting was set up by Mr. Cellini, was it not?"

"It was." Raft was watching her carefully.

"Maybe Mr. Cellini became involved with people who didn't simply stop talking when they decided they didn't like him. Maybe the answer to who murdered your partner is out there at Wanderworth House."

"That still doesn't explain why he attacked you." Raft was once again wearing his suspicious mask.

"Maybe to keep me quiet about what's going on at Wanderworth House." A suggestion, she decided, that could be all too close to the truth.

"Do you need to be kept quiet?"

"I wouldn't have thought so, but perhaps Mr. Cellini had a different idea."

Raft didn't say anything for a time, keeping his eyes on the Maltese falcon, as if the bird could help him decide what to say next. "Here's how you can square things with me," he said finally.

"Do I have to 'square' things with you?" Priscilla asked.

"Yeah, you do." The words came out edged with threat. "You've got contacts at this Wanderworth House. I don't. Get me information on what Al was up to with the people out there. He was a nasty son of a bitch when he wanted to be. Maybe he got someone out there upset enough to kill him. Find out what you can and then get back to me."

"I don't think that's such a good idea," Priscilla ventured in a tense voice, groaning inwardly. What was it about the men she attracted who first frightened the wits out her with dire threats, and then sent her out to get information she had no business getting?

"It's a very good idea," Raft demurred. "Simple. Clean. You help me. I help you." Raft appeared pleased with the notion.

"How do you help me, Mr. Raft?" asked Priscilla anxiously.

"I stay happy, and that keeps you safe," Raft said. "Believe me, in this town, the best thing is to have me as a friend. Makes you a very lucky lady. Who knows? Sooner or later, you may need my help."

"I'm not so sure about that," Priscilla ventured.

"Oh, you can be sure," Raft said. "You don't have any choice but to be sure about it."

The cloth-capped louts insisted on driving her back to the Savoy, even though her car was where she left it on Pimlico Road. Priscilla didn't argue, but she made sure they dropped her off on the Strand. She was in enough hot water without a couple of badly dressed hoods in the forecourt.

Entering 205, she found Major O'Hara behind the desk that should have been occupied by Susie. He looked more like a potentate on his throne than an assistant helping with press inquiries, happy to pour champagne and arrange tickets for visiting celebrities.

He aimed a piercing gaze at Priscilla. "Mr. Gordon has called twice," he announced in an irked voice, as though someone named Gordon should never have had the audacity to bother him.

"Once again, I believe you mean Gordon Scott," Priscilla asserted with forced courtesy. "As I told you previously, Major, he is a movie star, a guest at the hotel."

"I know of no film personage named Scott. I know only that a Mr. Gordon called twice."

Priscilla took a deep calming breath before she thanked him and went into her office and closed the door. She slumped onto the sofa. Her ribcage was aching and her head throbbing. The weight of the world—and George Raft—threatened to crush her. The shrill ringing of the telephone, the clarion call signalling more trouble, made her groan aloud.

Struggling up from the sofa, Priscilla arrived at her desk, closing her eyes momentarily, gathering the strength needed to pick up the receiver.

Immediately she was sorry.

"What about my press conference?" The aggrieved voice of Prince Constantino. Yes, she thought to herself, rubbing her temple with her free hand. Where *is* his press conference?

"Your Highness," she said, quickly adopting her best professional voice. "I have been meaning to get back to you."

"What you have been meaning to do, Miss Tempest, and what you have done are two very different things, I must point out," Constantino said. "I am at the end of my wits. It is most urgent. I beg you, Miss Tempest. The time is running out. I *must* have my press conference."

"Excuse me, but do you mind telling me why time is running out?"

"Teodoro leaves shortly."

"I apologize for the delay. Let me get something organized. Would the day after tomorrow be suitable?"

"Yes, yes, that would be most appropriate. I look forward to hearing from you."

Priscilla shook her head in despair as she hung up.

In the outer office, Major O'Hara, occupied with the important business of filing his nails, barely noticed Priscilla's arrival. Priscilla steeled herself, waiting in stoic silence until he finally gave up on his nails and lifted his head enough to glare up at her. "Yes? What is it?"

"Major," she said slowly, measuring her words, "I would like you to reserve the Pinafore Room for a press conference that Prince Constantino, the Prince of Parma, wishes to schedule for the day after tomorrow at 2 p.m. Once you have done that, I want you to phone the major London papers, as well as the BBC and ITV, and invite them to the prince's press conference. If they ask what it is about, you can tell them the prince is to make a major announcement. No more than that."

O'Hara delivered his I-hate-Priscilla glare before returning to the business of filing his nails.

"Major." Priscilla practically spat out the word.

"I cannot do that." O'Hara continued to calmly file his nails.

"Why not?" Priscilla demanded.

"That is simply not what I do." As though that was known to all and should not be questioned.

Priscilla leaned forward, placing her hands carefully on the desk so that her face was inches from O'Hara's insolent visage.

"Major O'Hara, this is *exactly* what you do. Not only will you do it, but you will do it *now*. If you do not, I will march straight to Mr. Banville's office and inform him that you are refusing to come to the aid of one of the Savoy's valued guests. In this clash of wills between the two of us, he is on your side, I have no doubt. But he will not be on your side when it comes to the care and consideration of the Savoy's guests. As you well know, Major, all guests here at the Savoy are valued, even the princes."

Major O'Hara dropped his nail file and sat back. His face softened, as did his voice. "Naturally, I will be happy to book the Pinafore Room. I do note that Miss Gore-Langton has left behind a list of newspapers, their representatives and telephone numbers. I will get on that now."

Priscilla nodded curtly and said, "Thank you, Major." She turned on her heel and entered her office before O'Hara rallied to offer further objections.

Meet the Parents

The street where Susie's parents lived, Windmill Hill, was little more than a pretty country lane meandering around the stone walls and dense foliage that hid the fine houses on either side. Eleven Windmill Hill was impressive enough that it didn't need to hide. It rose defiantly against a grey sky, a seventeenth-century merchant house with an ornate portico.

Priscilla parked beside a gleaming vintage Rolls-Royce. She crossed the paved drive, imagining Susie tooling about in that Rolls. Actually, she could imagine it quite easily. If anyone was born to look good in a Rolls-Royce, it was Susan Gore-Langton.

As Priscilla came along the walkway, the front door opened. On the threshold stood the personification of the aged, liveried butler with heavy jowls, sleepy eyes and a neutral expression one would expect in a stately old home occupied by a family named Gore-Langton. The butler drawled, "Madam?" in a questioning manner, full of doubt that the likes of Priscilla should even be at the door, then added, "You are expected."

Not welcome—expected. Well, she had phoned and left word that she would be dropping around.

The butler moved with solemn majesty along a passage into a drawing room where a grand piano and a stone hearth fought for space. On either side of the hearth was an olive-green armchair, and occupying them was a couple in their sixties, sitting portraits of casual elegance. The gentleman's fine head of hair was artfully streaked with grey at the temples. The cravat he wore went well with his houndstooth jacket. The lady of the house was in a denim shirt tucked into jodhpurs shoved into shiny leather riding boots. Her silky hair tumbled gently to a point just above her shoulders, a petite, still-fine beauty who had to be Susie's mother.

"Hullo," said the gentleman, rising from his green armchair. "We've been expecting you, Miss Tempest. I'm Derek Gore-Langton. This is my wife, Mrs. Sylvia Gore-Langton."

That was the cue for Mrs. Gore-Langton to lift herself up regally, offering a slim hand to Priscilla, who wasn't certain if she should kiss it or shake it. She shook it.

"It is a pleasure to meet a friend of Susie's." Sylvia spoke with the sort of upper-class inflection that, if one is not careful, can set everyone else's teeth on edge. Mrs. Gore-Langton was not careful.

"Won't you take a seat?" Derek's manicured hand swept over a third green armchair parked behind the his-and-hers armchairs.

"That's very kind of you," Priscilla said politely. "But as I stated when I called, I'd like to see Susie. Is she about?"

The Gore-Langtons traded uncomfortable looks.

"Yes, well, I suppose we should have called to head you off at the pass, so to speak." Mrs. Gore-Langton cleared her throat nervously. "As you know, Susan has not been herself lately."

"No," said Priscilla, taken aback by this declaration. "I have to say I wasn't aware of that."

"I'm afraid she's suffered a bit of a breakdown," piped up Derek Gore-Langton, employing the authoritative tone of a man used to entering a room and immediately capturing everyone's attention. "She's not saying too much but we believe it has to do with a relationship that didn't work out quite the way she had hoped. A broken heart, that sort of thing."

"A heart that needs mending," added Sylvia.

"As all hearts do from time to time," said Derek, perhaps seeking to put an end to further discussion about the state of Susie's heart.

"I am so sorry to hear this," Priscilla said. "I hadn't heard anything from her and I've been worried."

"That is most kind of you," Derek said solicitously. "But for the time being, Mrs. Gore-Langton and I think it best that Susan not see anyone…"

"For now," chimed in Sylvia.

"Well, I am here," Priscilla countered with careful delicacy. "I would only stay for a few minutes."

"I do hate to say no," Sylvia said, a rope of steel added suddenly to her upper-class drawl.

Out of the corner of her eye, Priscilla saw the butler reappear. "There you are, Jeffrey." Derek made it sound as though a long-lost friend had turned up. "Miss Tempest was just leaving. Would you be so good as to show her out?"

"We will be in touch as soon as Susan is feeling better," Sylvia promised.

Priscilla was at a loss for words. The last thing she expected was to be booted out of Susie's parents' house after barely setting foot in the door. Jeffrey the butler was already headed out of the drawing room, assuming Priscilla would dutifully follow.

"Would you be so kind as to tell her I was here?" Priscilla said with forced politeness.

"She will be so glad," Sylvia said.

"Tell her to give me a call if she's up to it."

"Yes, we will," said Derek.

Priscilla started after the butler, but then stopped and turned back to the parents. "I almost forgot to tell you I was at Lady

Daphne's the other night." The words tumbled out of Priscilla's mouth quickly.

The Gore-Langtons looked mutually surprised. "You know Lady Daphne?" asked Derek.

"As it happens, yes. I met her at her lovely Wanderworth estate with Prince Teodoro."

The surprise was even more evident on the handsome faces of the Gore-Langtons. "The prince is a friend?"

"More like a friendly acquaintance."

"A lovely man," piped up Derek. "A credit to his country, I would say."

"Yes, he is," Priscilla agreed.

"Working damned hard to better the terrible political climate that is like a disease across Europe," Derek said enthusiastically. "'We come again'—that's his mantra, and I for one—"

"Derek, that's enough," Sylvia cut in sharply, flashing a glance filled with daggers at her husband. "My goodness, I do thank you for dropping in, Miss Tempest," she said peremptorily. "We will be in touch."

Behind Sylvia, Derek wheeled around to the hearth as though to warm his hands. Except there was no fire. With Sylvia glaring after her, Priscilla followed Jeffrey the butler out. He kept looking back, as if expecting her to make a run for it.

Jeffrey reached the front door, opened it and then stepped aside so that Priscilla could go out. He did not look at her. He did not say goodbye. He firmly shut the door behind her.

As Priscilla started for her car, she glanced up at the house's brick facade. A hand waved at a second-floor window. She peered more closely. The afternoon sun glinted off the windows, but after a moment, she could see the hand wave again. And again, more frantically this time.

Then the hand disappeared.

CHAPTER TWENTY-EIGHT

The Seduction of Percy Hoskins

Percy Hoskins had fallen off his wagon.

The tumble was not dramatic: a libation to end the day, nothing more than that. Medicinal, he liked to think, considering what he had been through lately. And if a reporter in London was going to fall off any wagon, then the best place for a soft landing among friendly faces flushed with drink was within the confines of the El Vino wine bar. Any member of the fourth estate worth the ink in his veins could be found there, and Percy saw no reason why he should be left out by an inconsequential decision like the one he had made about abstinence.

Nothing wrong with a gin and tonic or two—or three—he had decided, leaning an elbow against the bar, listening to the war stories the El Vino regulars never tired of repeating.

Norman, the ancient bartender who had been serving the press mob since the invention of movable type, plunked down another gin. "Drinks on me, lads," Percy cried.

"To Percy," announced Harry Simms, crime reporter at the *Daily Express*, always willing to raise a glass to the man buying. "Welcome back to the fray, my lad. You've been missed."

"Percy!" cried all present, raising their glasses, happy to have a deserter returned to the boozy fold.

In the warm glow of drink and comradery, Percy planned to say something very witty to mark his return to the El Vino, but before he could get his mouth open, he noticed that an uneasy silence now pervaded. Percy was confused, uncertain what had happened. He turned to cast red-rimmed eyes, not seeing as sharp as they would ordinarily, on a hazy figure in a double-breasted suit topped by a grey fedora pulled down over gorgeous dark eyes. Rather fetching, he thought. The suit fit agreeably into the young lad's curves.

Wait just a minute, though.

He shouldn't be thinking like this, he thought, not even when fuelled by gin. He blinked and looked again as those around him began to make gruff, shocked noises. A *woman*! That's who this was. Not a lad at all, thank goodness. A woman in a suit. A woman wearing a fedora. Most disturbing of all a... *woman* inside El Vino. Unheard of! *Not on!*

"Felicity?" Percy achieved a garbled version of her name. The men around him had begun to stir uncomfortably.

Felicity Khan, catlike grin firmly in place, sashayed over to Percy as the aghast group made way for her.

"There you are, Percy," Felicity said merrily.

"I'm sorry, madam," announced Norman calmly from behind the bar. "You cannot be in here. Women are *not* allowed."

"Is that so?" said Felicity keeping eyes on Percy. "You mean, despite the fact I am dressed exactly as a man would dress, my friend Mr. Hoskins cannot buy me a drink?"

"That is so, madam," reiterated Norman. "You must leave immediately."

Percy, befuddled by a mixture of strong drink and embarrassment, was left speechless. My gawd, he thought through his boozy haze, she is beautiful...

Felicity leaned closer to whisper in his ear: "You're a drunken fool, Percy, losing out on the big story."

She pulled away, grinning insouciantly. "That's the end of it, gentlemen. So sorry, but I can't stay. I'm running late and must be off."

Percy was trying to get his head around what she had said to him. Drunken fool? He was celebrating, that's all. Nothing wrong with that...

Felicity was on her way out. He called to her, then followed.

The coolness of the night air had the effect of sobering Percy somewhat as he stumbled out of El Vino. Felicity wasn't far away, leaning against the hood of her Ford Escort. She held the fedora she had been wearing, looking much more like a—well, what could he say in his inebriated state, peering through bleary eyes? A woman. A gorgeous woman. The vision of her struck him like a blow.

"Is this what it takes to get a drunken reporter out of El Vino?" she said with a knowing grin.

Percy took deep breaths of the night air, hoping to clear his head. "You're not going to beat me. Okay?"

"Then maybe you should get off your fat arse to do some real reporting instead of boozing at El Vino."

"I don't think my ass is fat," declared Percy.

"That's because you can't see it." Felicity turned to her car and opened the passenger door. "Get in."

Percy watched her warily, trying to figure her. Unable to do it. "How fat is it?"

"I'll tell you later. Get in."

He got into her car.

Percy fumbled repeatedly with his latch key, fighting to insert it into the lock of his flat. Eventually, Felicity plucked the key from him, slipped it into the lock—*Eureka!*—they were in. The place was surprisingly neat and orderly, Felicity thought as she closed the door. An alcove with a small desk and an

Underwood typewriter, papers and notebooks piled around it, caught her eye.

As soon as Percy tumbled onto a well-used chesterfield, Felicity came to him, moving sinuously, opening her suit jacket and loosening her tie. She noted with satisfaction that his eyes had cleared and become bright with anticipation as he watched her.

She leaned over so that she could kiss him on his mouth. He tasted of gin. Not bad, she thought. She kissed him some more.

"What are you doing?" he mumbled.

She pulled away with an amused expression. "What does it look like I'm doing, you fool? You don't seem to be able to get your act together so I've had to take over and do the job for you."

"Don't... understand," he said.

"I'm trying to seduce you, if I have to come right out and say it." The fedora had already been removed and now she shrugged out of her suit jacket and pulled off her tie. The white blouse she wore underneath was undone just enough to capture Percy's attention.

"Why?"

"Why not?" Felicity removed her blouse. She wore nothing beneath it. She kicked off the boots she had been wearing and then dropped her trousers to the floor. She knelt to him and began to unbutton his shirt. "I'm not sure..." he said.

"Yes, you are," she said firmly.

She undid his trousers and pulled them down. It did not take long for him to become a lot more certain.

She raised her head. "Where is your bedroom?"

An hour or so later, Felicity slipped naked out of Percy's comfortable double bed—clean sheets, she had noticed earlier with relief. Percy lay sound asleep on his side, not snoring, thankfully. Not bad, all things considered, she thought as she tiptoed across the parquet floor. In her limited experience, she had found that drunken sods of reporters were hopeless in bed. Percy, bless him, had actually risen to the occasion, so to speak.

She went into the sitting room. They had left the lights on in their haste—or, more accurately, her haste—to reach the bedroom. She stood taking in her surroundings before retrieving the shoulder bag she had dropped on the floor beside the chesterfield. Carrying her bag, she entered the alcove he had transformed into a home office. She sat at his typewriter and ran her fingers over its well-worn keys. What was Percy writing? The Great British Novel? Was there a Fleet Street hack who didn't long to be the next Graham Greene? If only they would close all the pubs and transport each hack off to a lovely, affordable Spanish villa overlooking the sea where he could write his masterwork in peace.

Wire-bound notebooks were piled beside the typewriter. She picked the top one off the pile and began to flip through its pages. Percy made careful notes, she had to give him that—and in a legible hand as well. Beneath the underlined heading "Priscilla Tempest Intel" were notes about Prince Teodoro visiting Lady Daphne. A feud between the prince and his cousin Prince Constantino...

A separate line was dedicated to "A dead body." That was followed by "Wanderworth" and then, on the line below, a name: "Colin Ashbury."

Dead body? That was a surprise. But from what she could see, Percy didn't have enough to write anything about this Ashbury, or even go to the police.

Continuing to flip through Percy's notebook, she could find nothing else. Still, he knew more than she might have imagined. It would be a mistake to underestimate him, either in bed or chasing a story.

She reached for the desk phone, listening for any sound emanating from the bedroom. Satisfied Percy remained sound asleep, she carefully dialled. The operator at the Savoy Hotel's switchboard came on the line almost immediately. In a low voice she asked to be connected to Prince Constantino's suite.

"Constantino here." The prince sounded wide awake.

"I'm with Percy Hoskins," she reported, her voice barely above a whisper.

"You're saying what?" the prince asked.

"With Hoskins. I can't talk for long."

"What have you found out?"

"He knows, but he doesn't know—more than I would have thought, however."

"It's of no consequence," Constantino said. "He will not have the story. You will have it because you have me—the scoop as you call it here."

"When, Your Highness? How much longer?"

"There is a press conference at the hotel tomorrow. The beginning of the end. Will you be there?"

"Better if I'm not."

"Shortly after that, my cousin will lose his claim to Vento and I will take over and you will be able to expose him for what he is."

"Are you sure about this?" Felicity was having difficulty hiding her misgivings.

"There is no doubt. My voices are clear, my vision is within reach," Constantino said confidently. "Soon, as it has been ordained, I will become the Duke of Vento. Then I will make good on my promise, and you will become my princess."

"I've got to go," Felicity said, thankfully hearing stirring from the bedroom so that she wouldn't have to spend time ducking Constantino's nonsense about making her a princess. As if that was ever going to happen.

"We will talk soon," Constantino said.

She quickly hung up the phone.

Dusty streaks of a bright dawn were seeping through the flat's tall windows. She returned the notebook to the pile where she had found it, and then returned her shoulder bag to the floor where she had dropped it.

Felicity started back for the bedroom, refusing to allow herself to dwell on Constantino and her increasing conviction that, with his visions and the voices he swore he heard, he was out of his mind. She wanted the story, that's all that counted. She could put up with the rest, including his promises of marital bliss.

Right now, she was anxious to discover if Percy might be even better in the morning than he was at night.

CHAPTER TWENTY-NINE

The Press Conference

Prince Constantino's press conference had been scheduled for 2 p.m. in the Pinafore Room. Major O'Hara, to his credit, over the past two days had meticulously phoned the relevant newspapers as well as the BBC and ITV. However, only two reporters showed up at the appointed hour.

As she surveyed rows of empty chairs, Priscilla tried to hide her disappointment and told herself that two reporters was better than no reporters at all. The two were from weekly papers that Priscilla was only vaguely aware of. She was surprised—and impressed—that Major O'Hara had even bothered to contact those publications. One of the reporters was plump and middle-aged with thinning grey hair, the stubble that his razor had missed displayed on his two chins, suffering, Priscilla was sure, from a good-sized hangover. The other attendee was a skin-and-bones young fellow with a Beatles haircut, horn-rimmed glasses, facial acne and a sports jacket that hung like a shroud from his thin shoulders.

"I'm afraid we haven't attracted much of a crowd," Major O'Hara observed. Prince Constantino had yet to make an appearance.

"You've done your best," Priscilla said. Much to her surprise, he had. "I'm afraid we can only let the press know of an event at the hotel. We can't force them to actually attend."

"More's the pity," mumbled the major.

"The world, at least the world as perceived by Fleet Street, apparently could care less who is or who is not the Duke of Vento," Priscilla said.

"Comes to that, I suppose I can't blame the blighters."

Prince Constantino made his entrance, moving so lightly that once more he seemed to Priscilla to float. He wore the black suit that made one think of an intense priest arriving with his chin up, shoulders back, preparing to convert any sinners he encountered. There were, alas, few sinners present.

"Where is everyone?" he asked in a voice full of disbelief as he gazed about the empty room.

"I'm so sorry to report, Your Highness, there has not been the response to your press conference we would have liked."

"There must be some terrible mistake," the prince said, his fierce eyes darting about.

"There are a couple of reporters here," Priscilla plunged bravely on. "Perhaps you would like to speak to them."

Constantino faced Priscilla. His eyes burned with anger. "You have failed to properly do your job, Miss Tempest," he said, his voice taut. "I must hold you responsible for this."

"I say, old chap," chimed in Major O'Hara, "Miss Tempest and myself have done everything in our power to attract the press. The point is, and you must come to terms with it: no one gives a damn about bloody Italian princes and their feuds."

Priscilla would have opted for more diplomacy, but it was too late for that. Constantino responded to the major's words with a shake of his head. "That is where you are mistaken." He cleared his throat and appeared to straighten his shoulders in an effort to pull himself together. "There are other methods at my disposal. The time has come to use them." He gave a quick nod. "You will hear from me again."

He fled from the room, brushing past the plump reporter who, Priscilla saw, marked the prince's passing with a look of disgust. A curious reaction, Priscilla thought fleetingly.

"He's a harmless fool," remarked Major O'Hara as Constantino disappeared out the door.

Was he? Priscilla silently wondered. A harmless fool who thought he should have his cousin's duchy because of a vision? Or a dangerous prince making a threat that he might well make good on?

The plump reporter, having reclaimed an amused expression, trundled over to Priscilla and the major, adjusting his badly knotted tie, somehow mismatched with the ill-fitting corduroy jacket he wore. "Most unfortunate, that," he growled in a deep Scottish-accented voice cured by many years and many, many whiskies. "Not going to ask what the blazes went on."

"As well that you don't," Priscilla said.

"I should introduce myself," he said. "Name's Mackenzie, Rupert Mackenzie. You are, I must assume, Miss Priscilla Tempest." He thrust a pudgy hand at her.

"A pleasure, Mr. Mackenzie." Priscilla took his hand in hers. "I apologize for Prince Constantino."

"Not at all, Miss Tempest," Rupert said. "I must say I don't get invited to the Savoy all that often—don't get invited at all, usually. It's a bit of a treat for me."

"You must thank my associate, Major Jack O'Hara," Priscilla said, nodding in the major's direction.

Major O'Hara did his best not to appear pleased, but it was evident that he was. "Glad you could be here," he said brusquely.

"If you don't mind my saying," Rupert went on, "I am led to understand that the press office at the Savoy is famous for its generosity when it comes to providing a drink or two for the visiting press. Anything to that?"

"Notorious is probably more accurate," suggested Priscilla. She took him by the arm. "Come along, Mr. Mackenzie. The least we can do is pour you a drink." She glanced at Major O'Hara. "What do you say, Major? Shall we make a strategic retreat to 205?"

"If you don't mind, I'll leave the two of you to it. I've a few errands to run. If that's all right with you, Miss Tempest?"

"Of course, Major." Was it her imagination or was she actually starting to, well, not like him, but more or less tolerate the major? Must be her imagination. She could not possibly like Major Jack O'Hara, could she? Endure him, maybe.

But still, he did seem to be coming around a bit.

She stopped to invite the young reporter with the Beatles haircut, but he said he didn't drink, and it was all a waste of his time, before quickly departing. Back in her office, Rupert fussed a bit with his tie and straightened his jacket as he occupied the sofa, while Priscilla at her desk pressed the magical waiter button. Karl Steiner soon appeared in his crisp, white jacket, bristling with Old World formality, to take Rupert's order. Whisky straight for him—"make it a double, will you, old boy?"—and the usual champagne for Priscilla.

"Tell me, Mr. Mackenzie, have you always worked for this London weekly?" Priscilla asked when Karl had left.

"Used to play on a much bigger field, I have to admit." Rupert gave up on his tie and dropped his voice to a low, sad growl. "Parliamentary correspondent for *The Scotsman*, a novel, no sales, but well received. Alas, I fell on hard times. Strong drink may have had something to do with it. *The Scotsman* let me go. There never was a second novel. Reduced circumstances brought me to this little weekly and thus here I am, your servant with no qualms about accepting a whisky— or two."

"What I don't quite understand," she went on, "is why you would come to this press conference when no one else was interested."

"Silly, really, but I did want to hear what the cousin of the evil Prince Teodoro might have to say for himself—and about Teodoro."

"When you say Prince Teodoro is evil, do you mean that literally?" asked Priscilla, intrigued.

"You see, I was with British intelligence, stationed in Rome shortly after the war," Rupert explained. "We were tracking down various fascist terrorists who were trying to undermine the government at the time. We suspected that Prince Teodoro, a well-known friend of Mussolini, was behind what was going on through a group called Punta di Lancia—Spearpoint."

"Spearpoint, you say?" Priscilla put in.

"You've heard of it?"

"Vaguely," said Priscilla, carefully.

Rupert raised surprised eyebrows. "Well, if you have, my dear, you're in a small minority. Mostly Spearpoint has been lost to the mists of time, and the willingness of so many to simply forget. But in its heyday, Spearpoint was behind all sorts of bombings and assassinations in Italy—anyone they deemed to be a communist. Or who they plain didn't like."

"But you obviously didn't forget, Mr. Mackenzie."

"Not me, no. Teodoro always stuck in my craw. One of our Italian agents was a lovely young woman named Maria. I was quite taken with her. There were suspicions that she had become a double agent, working for the communists. No evidence, mind you, but that made no difference. One night, members of Spearpoint stopped the car in which she was travelling. They pulled her out, put her on her knees and shot her in the head. I can't be sure but I suspect Teodoro pulled the trigger."

"I'm sorry, Mr. Mackenzie."

"It was a long time ago. And Maria wasn't his only victim. There were others. Yet today he swaggers around, still spouting his fascist ideology, free as a bird."

"I gather from seeing you at the press conference that you don't think much of his cousin Constantino, either."

"Constantino is a bit delusional from what I hear. Claims he's hearing voices and receiving visions that tell him he, and not his cousin, should be the duke. It would have been interesting today to hear what he has to say for himself, to understand his rationale for going after his cousin. But it doesn't look as though that will happen."

Karl arrived with drinks. Rupert all but finished his in a couple of gulps. He literally licked his lips in appreciation. "That's more like it," he announced. He looked at Karl. "Don't suppose you could do this again?"

"Certainly, sir," said Karl, the picture of courtesy.

"What do you know about a woman named Lady Daphne Wanderworth?" Priscilla asked.

"Ah, yes... her. I know of her from before the war, and her pro-Nazi sentiments that were so popular with the upper classes. But then there was the war, and that silenced Lady Daphne and her acolytes, although I'm not so sure it changed their views. I have no idea if she is still around. Why do you ask?"

"No particular reason," Priscilla answered quickly. "Her name came up in discussions about Prince Constantino and his cousin. I have been led to believe they may be linked—Teodoro and Lady Daphne."

"News to me," Rupert said with a shrug. "But then what I know goes back to just after the war. My regret is that we never brought Teodoro and his Spearpoint lot to justice at the time."

Priscilla leaned forward and asked, "What about Colin Ashbury? Is that name familiar to you, Mr. Mackenzie?"

"Ashbury, you say?" Rupert made a show of stroking his stubble as he appeared to dredge through his memories. Karl returned with more whisky. Rupert stopped stroking to accept the glass. "Many thanks, old man. Many thanks."

This time around, Rupert satisfied himself with a couple of sips. "Colin Ashbury," he repeated. He put his glass aside and looked at Priscilla. "I'm afraid I'm fogging a bit. Was he with MI6?"

"Could have been," Priscilla agreed.

"The name certainly sounds familiar. Can't quite place it—but yes, familiar."

He finished the remainder of his drink. His cheeks were flushed now. He licked his lips again and then set the empty glass carefully to one side. "If you'd like, I can rummage through my memory—and my notes from that time—and see what I can come up with."

"I'd be most thankful if you could," Priscilla said.

"Let me see what I can do," Rupert said, standing. "I will give you a call, if I may."

"Of course, any time. Would you like something else?"

"No, no, my dear," Rupert responded. "You've both been very hospitable to an old reprobate such as myself, but I don't want to take advantage, and so I toddle off."

"Take care of yourself," Priscilla said, standing.

"I will indeed—and thank you."

He started for the door, and then stopped, his head bowed. "I loved her, you see. Loved her very much."

"Maria?"

"Never quite forgiven myself for her death." His voice was ragged. "Still haunts me... after all this time..." He raised his head showing infinitely sad eyes. "So sorry..."

"It's all right, Mr. Mackenzie, really. I understand."

"It's the drink," he said. "Does funny things to me sometimes..."

"Please call," Priscilla said.

He gave a quick nod and then slumped out the door, leaving Priscilla feeling deeply sorry for him—love lost so long ago yet never forgotten. What about her lost loves? Just as soon forgotten, the sooner the better, she decided as her phone started to ring.

She picked up the receiver.

"Priscilla." The scared, breathless voice of Susie Gore-Langton.

"Susie, I've been trying to reach you. Are you all right?"

"I've only got a couple of minutes before they discover I'm on the phone." She spoke slowly in a frightened voice, as though trying to carefully articulate every word. "Priscilla, my parents are holding me prisoner. I came to visit, to tell them about Tony... the next thing I woke up, locked in my bedroom. They keep giving me pills that make me dopey... don't know what to do... Desperate to get to Tony. I'm sure he doesn't know what's happened... he must be frantic with worry."

Priscilla doubted Antony Armstrong-Jones was frantic with anything, let alone worry about Susie. But now was not the time to say so. Aloud she said, "What would you like me to do?"

"Save me!" she gasped. "Get me out of here!"

"Yes," Priscilla said without having the slightest idea of what she would do to help her friend. "But I can't imagine your parents will continue to hold you." Let alone why they imprisoned her in the first place, she thought.

"Please, please, please, come up with something," Susie said in a pleading voice. "You are my only hope—"

"Susan!" Priscilla heard a female voice call out.

"Oh God," Susie cried.

The call ended abruptly.

Priscilla dropped the receiver onto its cradle feeling numb and helpless. Rescue Susie? From her own parents? How was she supposed to do that? Who could possibly help her?

A thought crossed her mind. Madness, but the more she thought about it the more she knew there was one person who might be able to help.

If she could just work up the nerve it would take to approach him.

CHAPTER THIRTY

Dame in Distress

They agreed to meet by a phone box outside King's Cross Station at 8 p.m.—under the comforting cover of darkness.

Priscilla waited on the street a few yards from the phone box. Behind her, the railway station's giant arched windows were like monster eyes. She shivered with anticipation, feeling curiously alive—and frightened too! What was it that made her want to put herself in jeopardy—break into someone's hotel suite, for example—in ways that she would never consider if she had a whit of common sense?

No explaining that now for here was the black sedan pulling up to the curb. The louts in the cloth caps and bad suits presumably had the night off. Filling in this evening was a character the size of a refrigerator. He squeezed out of the sedan, motioned her forward as he opened the rear passenger door. She ducked inside, assailed by the strong woodsy scent of cologne, the movie star–gangster smell of George Raft. He sat expressionless in the shifting shadows of the light from passing traffic. It struck Priscilla, as the door closed, that Raft always seemed to set himself in a place somewhere between darkness and light.

"What have you got for me?" No back-seat chitchat, Priscilla thought. Cutting straight to the chase.

"First of all, as I told you on the phone, I need assurance that you will help me." Out of the corner of her eye she could see the refrigerator slide into the front beside a second refrigerator at the wheel, if anything even bigger than his companion.

"Yeah, your friend who needs rescuing," Raft said. "I must be out of my mind, given my current situation, the cops, the government breathing down my neck. It probably means I've lost my marbles, but yeah, I'm willing to give you a hand. But you've got to talk to me, Priscilla. Give me something."

"The people I told you about before, the Wanderworth Group."

"You said Al was involved with them?"

"That's right. They were very pro-German before the war."

"I'm a Kraut myself." Raft looked impatient. "What's that got to do with anything?"

"Are you really German?"

"My real name is Ranft. My mother emigrated to the States from Germany. My father's parents came from Germany. Is that German enough for you?"

"I suspect the Wanderworth Group and its autocratic beliefs have been resurrected by Lady Daphne Wanderworth and Prince Teodoro. Al Cellini was also part of it."

"Al working with a bunch of Nazis? I don't believe it." Raft's face in the uncertain light left little doubt that he was not happy with what he was hearing.

"For whatever reason, he was. These are the people I believe are responsible for the death of Mr. Cellini."

Raft looked at her blankly. The flickering shadows made him look more ominous than ever.

"That's what you want, isn't it?" Priscilla ventured. "Mr. Cellini's killer?"

"Yeah," he said with a slight nod. "But why do I suspect you're making this up as you go along? You don't really know what the hell you're talking about."

Maybe she didn't, Priscilla admitted to herself. Best not to say that to George Raft, however. "Look, right now you don't have anything, do you?"

Raft didn't react.

"And I'm willing to bet the police don't either."

"I don't talk to cops." Raft said it like a line out of one of his Warner Bros. movies.

Priscilla continued quickly. "You knew Mr. Cellini's friends. Ask around, see if they know anything about the Wanderworth Group. Meanwhile, I'll continue to find out more."

Raft said nothing for a time. "Okay," he said finally. "What are we doing?"

"Like I told you on the phone—a friend of mine is being held against her will. She needs to be rescued. Given your background, you are perfect to help with that."

Raft produced a mirthless snort of laughter. "My background? What? You think I've had a lot of experience rescuing dames? That's movie stuff. It's not real life."

"Fine," Priscilla conceded. "But at the same time, I suspect you know about tight situations and how to get out of them safely."

"You say this dame is being held by her parents?"

Priscilla nodded. "They are friends of Lady Daphne's."

Raft shook his head. "Anyone ever tell you that you're a pain in the ass?"

"It's been said," agreed Priscilla.

"But a pain with a certain irresistible quality, I have to say."

"Will you help me, Mr. Raft?"

"Let's see what we can do," he said. "Eleven Windmill Hill. That's the address you gave me, right?"

"That's where my friend is being held," Priscilla confirmed.

Raft addressed the two men in the front. "You hear that, Jimmy? And you too, Rourke. Eleven Windmill Hill. You know it?"

"I can get us there, boss." Jimmy the driver spoke at the rearview mirror. "What's up?"

"Nothing much, boys," Raft said. "Just another night in London putting our asses on the line to rescue a dame in distress."

It had grown dark by the time Jimmy parked down the way from the Gore-Langton house. No sooner had he pulled to the curb than headlights flashed behind them. Raft nodded with satisfaction as he opened the back door.

"Is anything wrong?" asked Priscilla, worried about the rear vehicle.

"Let's see," Raft said enigmatically.

Priscilla followed him out of the car as two shadowy figures came forward, caught in the glare of the second car's headlights.

One of the figures was a fireplug of a man, his grey hair pushed back from a high forehead. He wore a suit that probably would have looked better on just about any other body than his. With him was a taller, younger man, also in a suit, his thin, pale face set in a permanent expression of anger.

"Gentlemen, good, right on time," Raft said by way of a greeting.

"Not a lot of notice," said the fireplug.

"Priscilla, this short fellow is Bernard 'Ace' Stoker," explained Raft with a nod at the fireplug. "Ace is a former Scotland Yard detective who gives me a hand every so often."

"More helpful when I have a little more advance warning, George," Ace said.

"I'll do better next time, Ace." George turned to the taller man. "Mick Seymour. Mick is young and tough, a good guy to have around if it comes down to the type of tight situation you were talking about."

"Glad to be here, Mr. Raft," Mick said.

"What's the plan, George?" asked Ace, past complaining, his voice now full of businesslike authority.

"According to my friend Miss Tempest, in that lovely house over there is a woman being held against her will. Our job is to get her out."

Raft jabbed a finger at Ace Stoker. "Ace, you're back to your old job. Scotland Yard has heard there's a problem involving a young woman. You and Mick, backed up by Jimmy and Rourke, distract the couple while Priscilla makes her entrance."

Raft addressed Priscilla. "Any idea where your friend is located in the house?"

"The second floor, I believe," Priscilla said. "But the door to her room may be locked."

"That's okay," Raft said calmly. "Jimmy will be right behind you. Any heavy lifting, he's your man. The door hasn't been built that he can't knock down. That right, Jimmy?"

"You got it, Mr. Raft," Jimmy replied.

"Okay, fellas, that's the play, in and out quick as we can," Raft said. "Let's get to it."

"Showtime," said Ace Stoker with satisfaction. He started back along the street, Mick Seymour trailing after him. Priscilla followed with Jimmy and Rourke. Glancing over her shoulder, she saw Raft, leaning against the car, lighting a cigarette.

The ground floor of the Gore-Langton house was lit, but the rest of the house stood in darkness. The group reached the front entrance, and Ace Stoker wasted no time pounding authoritatively on the front door. When no one answered, he pounded harder. This time the door opened. A dull-eyed Derek Gore-Langton, tumbler in hand, peered out at his visitors. "Yes?" he inquired in a haughty, whisky-soaked voice.

"Mr. Gore-Langton," the detective said, flashing what must have been an old warrant card. "Inspector Bernard Stoker, Scotland Yard."

"What?" Derek inquired blurrily, scrutinizing the proffered warrant card.

"This is my associate, Detective Mick Seymour."

"Pleased to meet you, governor," Mick said.

"Sir," said Ace, his voice deepening with even more authority, "we have reason to believe, based on information received, that a young woman is being held in this domicile against her will."

Derek looked shocked. "That is preposterous."

"Nonetheless, sir, we have authorization to search the premises. Please move aside."

Before Derek had a chance to object, Ace pushed past him into the vestibule where he was confronted by Sylvia Gore-Langton. Dressed in a blue silk robe, her hair back in a bun, she looked even shakier than her husband, Priscilla thought.

"Bernard Stoker, Scotland Yard," Ace announced gruffly to Sylvia, who gaped at him for an instant before retreating toward the sitting room.

As Priscilla headed for the staircase, Jimmy in tow, she could hear Derek mounting his high horse: "What is the damned meaning of this?"

She charged up to the second floor. A series of closed doors faced her along a beautifully carpeted hallway. She ran down the hall, trying each door, until she reached the end. The door was locked. She rapped. "Susie? Are you in there? It's Priscilla."

From the other side came a low, anguished moan. She had only to glance at Jimmy before he was slamming into the door, shoulder first. He smashed into it a second time. It splintered and burst open. Priscilla following, he hurled himself into a dark bedroom. Susie, fully dressed, lay on a queen-size bed, struggling to sit up. "Priscilla?" she asked groggily.

"Susie, are you all right?"

"They gave me something... so sleepy..."

Priscilla sat on the bed and embraced her friend. "We're going to get you out of here," she announced.

"They won't let me," Susie mumbled. "They make me stay."

"I've got some people with me," Priscilla said comfortingly. "They're going to make sure you're safe."

"So sleepy..."

Priscilla shook her gently. "Susie, stay awake, okay? You must stay awake."

Susie nodded, eyes fluttering.

Priscilla turned to Jimmy. "Can you pick her up?"

He nodded curtly and moved to the bed, bent down and gathered her into his arms as if—well, as if he regularly carried around drugged women. For all she knew he did, Priscilla speculated as she followed them out of the room.

In the hallway, focused on making as fast an escape as possible, Priscilla missed the arrival of Sylvia in her floor-length silk robe, her expression fiercely determined—and a Luger pistol gripped in her tiny hands.

Pointed straight at Priscilla.

Sleeping Beauty

"Put my daughter down!" cried Sylvia melodramatically. "Put her down. Or I will shoot!"

Priscilla could see that she would be the target if Sylvia pulled the trigger.

"Did you hear me?" Sylvia's voice had become a high shriek. Her eyes had grown small and nasty as they focused on Priscilla. "They said they would take care of you," she practically hissed. "Why are you still here?"

In that instant, Priscilla was convinced that she was about to get shot. Her heart was pounding. She had trouble breathing.

George Raft seemed to come out of nowhere.

With a graceful smoothness—which seemed to be the only way he did anything—Raft plucked the gun from Sylvia's grasping fingers just as it went off with a loud bang. A bullet whizzed past Priscilla's ear. Sylvia cried out in alarm as Raft, holding the Luger in one hand, used his other to force her against the wall.

"Now, I have never in my life hit a lady." Raft spoke quietly. "So please don't make me start now."

Breathing hard, Sylvia was like a trapped animal showing its fangs. "Susan is my daughter—my daughter!"

"All the more reason not to keep her drugged in a locked room," Raft countered.

He motioned for Priscilla and Jimmy to move. Jimmy promptly whisked the comatose Susie down the staircase. Priscilla hurried to keep up. She was aware, as they passed, that Ace Stoker, Mick and Rourke had created a barrier of sorts, behind which Derek shouted furiously, "Bastards! I'm calling the police!"

Then they were outside. A misty rain had begun to fall. Jimmy continued down the street with Susie. Priscilla turned to see Raft's three men come down the steps, followed shortly after by Raft with the Luger.

By the time she reached the car, Jimmy had Susie laid out in the back. Everyone gathered around Raft. "Jimmy, you're driving," Raft ordered. "I'll ride in front with you. Priscilla, you're in the back with your friend." He looked at Ace Stoker. "Ace, you drive Rourke and Mick. Got that?"

"Done," pronounced Ace, immediately turning to the second car. Priscilla got into the back of the first car, cradling Susie's head in her lap. Raft slipped into the front, closing the door as Jimmy started the engine and then roared off into the rain.

Raft swung around to face Priscilla. "Okay, we've got her. Now what? What's your plan?"

Plan? thought Priscilla. She wasn't certain they would actually rescue Susie. Now, what to do with her? "She shouldn't stay at her own flat right now," Priscilla said. "I guess the best thing is to take her to my place."

Raft frowned. "If they come looking for her, which they're liable to do, they're likely to knock on your door."

"What do you suggest?" asked Priscilla.

"I've got an apartment—or flat, as you call it here—just off Berkeley Square, not far from the Colony. Let's take her there until you can get things straightened out. She'll be safe and you can stay the night with her. How does that sound?"

Raft was right, thought Priscilla. Her flat was not safe for herself or Susie. Priscilla nodded agreement. "Yes, that sounds good."

Raft turned back to Jimmy. "Okay, let's head for the apartment—or flat. Or whatever the hell you call it in this strange place."

A strange place? Yes, it was, Priscilla thought. And lately she had never felt more like a stranger.

Jimmy parked in front of a terraced house near Berkeley Square. The rain had stopped, leaving the silent street wrapped in fog, its residents sound asleep, spared the sight of Jimmy carrying a semiconscious woman up the steps to where an aging tough guy was unlocking the door.

Directed by Raft, Jimmy, with more tenderness and efficiency, transported Susie into a back bedroom, laying her with great care onto the bed. She stirred and moaned, then rolled onto her side. A sleeping angel, Priscilla thought, aglow with innocence, at least when she was unconscious. The angel with a heart broken by the deceitful Earl of Snowdon; the angel drugged and held hostage by fascist parents, rescued by a movie star. You couldn't make this stuff up, Priscilla thought as she left the bedroom.

The flat offered no sign that it served as a hideout for gamblers working around the corner at the Colony Club. In the sitting room, a painting of a three-masted schooner riding in rough seas hung over the hearth. Hunting prints adorned the walls above a wine-red sofa. An eighteenth-century nobleman wearing silk and brocade posed in a gilt frame. There were embroidered regency chairs scattered about, so delicate that they gave one pause when it came to actually sitting on them. Raft perched on the edge of an armchair, lighting a cigarette. He studied Priscilla through a cloud of grey smoke. Jimmy was nowhere in sight.

"How is she?" Raft inquired.

"She's sleeping. They've been drugging her, but I think she'll be fine."

Raft stood up, holding his cigarette. "I'll leave you with her then," he said. "The place is well stocked. There's orange juice in the fridge, some fruit, a selection of ladies' sleepwear in the bedroom closet. I'll check in on you in the morning. Hopefully, Susie's awake and the two of you can decide what comes next."

"Do you mind if I ask you a question?" Priscilla said.

Raft produced one of his enigmatic half-smiles. Reading him was nearly impossible. Did George Raft ever have real emotions? If he did, he hid them masterfully.

"Shoot," he said.

"I'm still not sure why you've done this."

"That's not a question." He regarded her with those aperture eyes for a couple of moments. "I help people because at some time I will want something in return. With you, it's finding Al's killer."

Raft paused. "Or, it could be something as simple as I like you, Priscilla. I like your spunk. Your willingness to take a risk. You say you don't gamble. I disagree. You gamble big time, lady. I've never seen anything quite like it away from a roulette wheel."

"I'm not sure whether that's a compliment," Priscilla said. "But whatever it is, Mr. Raft, I owe you a debt of thanks. Susie, too."

"Don't get me wrong," Raft added. "You're not off the hook with me."

"No?"

"Get me more info on this Daphne dame. I need answers. It's like the detective says in that movie I didn't do: when someone kills your partner, you've got to do something about it. Doesn't matter what you think of him, you have to do something. Because he was your partner. That's Al, okay? He was my partner. I gotta do something."

"I understand." Yes, she did, and she did have answers—some answers, anyway. But if she told Raft or just about anyone else what she knew—or thought she knew—well, she wasn't prepared for that. Not yet.

"For now, get some sleep," Raft said.

"Thank you again," Priscilla said.

He touched two fingers against his forehead in a kind of salute and then disappeared out the door, trailing cigarette smoke.

Priscilla went into the bedroom to check on Susie. She remained a soundly sleeping beauty, except now she had turned onto her back, arms at her side, like a lovely corpse awaiting the mourners. Priscilla shook off that particular image and went to the closet where she found a blanket she could use to cover her.

Back in the sitting room, Priscilla decided she was too tired to go looking for the sleeping garments George Raft might have on hand for his overnight female guests. That somehow seemed a little much. Instead, she stretched out on the wine-red sofa—marvelling all over again at the incongruity of this formal room as a gangster's love nest. She closed her eyes and almost immediately fell asleep.

Visions of Lady Daphne dipping her into a boiling cauldron crowded her dreams.

CHAPTER THIRTY-TWO

Susie in the Morning

Priscilla awoke with a start, cast in shafts of the pale light inching through the draped windows. An exhausted-looking Susie, wrapped in a blanket, sat on the edge of one of the regency chairs you might think twice about sitting on. She viewed Priscilla with sleepy, mascara-smudged eyes.

"Where am I?" she asked in a lost-little-girl voice.

Priscilla sat up slowly, shaking off her sleepiness.

"And how did I get here?" Susie added.

"How are you feeling?" Priscilla countered.

"Like someone hit me with a brick," said Susie. "But please answer me, Priscilla. What happened? How did I end up here?"

"Your parents drugged you," Priscilla explained quietly. "I came around last night to get you away from them."

"How did you do that?"

"I had help from gentlemen friends concerned about your safety."

Susie held her head in her hands. "I can't believe any of this has happened."

"It must have been done in order to keep you away from Lord Snowdon," Priscilla offered. "But what I don't understand is why your parents would behave like this."

"I'm sure it was that awful Commander Blood," Susie said insistently. "At one point, when I was a bit more lucid, I heard Mum and Dad talking about the Walsinghams and what they were demanding. I don't know for sure, but I think they supplied the drugs my parents used to knock me out. No idea how they would have gotten them otherwise."

"That would explain a lot," said Priscilla, recalling Commander Peter Trueblood's visit to her office and the icy warning he delivered. "I'm afraid you may be right."

Susie dropped her hands away and sat up, shaking her head. "What a bloody fool I've been."

"You're hardly alone when it comes to foolish behaviour where men are concerned," Priscilla said supportively. She rose to her feet, signalling that she was about to enter her take-charge mode. "Here's what I think we should do..."

"Good," said a reassured Susie, "because at this point I have absolutely no idea."

"You're in a flat just off Berkeley Square. I'd like you to stay put until the dust clears a bit and I can talk to Commander Blood, and assure him that if you ever were, you are no longer a threat to royalty."

"Priscilla, how am I ever going to thank you?"

"By getting back to work as soon as you can."

"You want me back?" Susie asked with a combination of relief and amazement.

"The fact that Major Jack O'Hara is filling in as your replacement will tell you everything you need to know about just how badly I want you," Priscilla said.

"Major O'Hara has my job?" Susie stared. "I don't believe it."

"Actually, to be fair to the major, he's starting to come around a bit. But he's no Susie Gore-Langton, that's for certain."

The doorbell sounded, causing Susie to jump in fear. "Who's that?"

"Let me see." Priscilla went through the archway into the vestibule and peered out through the spyhole in the front door.

George Raft was a concave image standing impatiently on the other side.

Priscilla opened the door to allow him in. As usual, he was impeccable, this time in a light grey suit with a matching grey tie and a white shirt with long collar tips. He even smelled good.

"How's everything?" he inquired, glancing around as though half-expecting someone with a gun to appear. Priscilla could hardly blame him.

"Susie's awake, tired, but seems to be recovering. Come along and meet her."

"A little more formally than last night," Raft added.

He entered the sitting room. Susie, wrapped in a blanket, was shrouded in morning light, tendrils of blond hair floating around her—a golden angel. Slightly smudged, granted, but if Raft's reaction was any indication, an angel nonetheless. He didn't quite stop in his tracks, but it was awfully close, Priscilla thought. What's more, as much as his natural expression would ever allow an onlooker to use the word smitten, George Raft was smitten.

Priscilla could hardly believe what she was witnessing. "Mr. Raft," she said, finding her voice, "this is Susie Gore-Langton. Susie, Mr. George Raft is the man who came to your rescue last night."

Susie was on her feet, holding the blanket close, presenting her hand for the shaking. "Mr. Raft, is it?"

"A pleasure to meet you, Susie," Raft said. "Please, call me George."

"George." Susie said his name like a purr.

"Are you feeling better?" Raft asked, the picture of the courtly gentleman caller.

"I'm feeling much safer, that's for certain," Susie said. "I have you to thank... George."

"Glad I could help," Raft said. He glanced around at Priscilla, who was beginning to feel very much like a third wheel.

"I've got to get to work," Priscilla said.

Raft retrained his eyes on Susie. "I was about to have breakfast, Susie. Are you hungry?"

"Starved," Susie said eagerly.

"Well, why don't I take you?" Raft aimed a quick glance at Priscilla. "You're invited too, Priscilla." He sounded a lot less enthusiastic at the prospect of Priscilla accompanying them.

"Thanks, but I'd better show my face at the hotel," Priscilla said.

"Jimmy is outside with the car," Raft said. "He'll drive you."

Priscilla addressed Susie. "Are you going to be all right?"

Susie was smiling at Raft when she said, "I think I'm going to be fine."

The last thing Priscilla saw as she left the apartment was something she had not seen before: George Raft, beaming.

CHAPTER THIRTY-THREE

Place of Execution Redux

Priscilla was late arriving at the Savoy after showering in her flat and then spending time in front of the mirror dealing with the lingering effects of Al Cellini's attack. She dressed in a light blue wool suit with an above-the-knee straight skirt and a collarless short jacket. She once again studied herself in a mirror. Yes, she decided, she was more or less presentable for her day job—the one that didn't include breaking into castles to rescue damsels in distress.

Arriving at the hotel, she was looking forward to Karl with life-saving coffee. However, as soon as she entered 205 and saw Major O'Hara at Susie's desk, unexpectedly pale, she suspected the coffee would not be forthcoming any time soon.

"Thank goodness you're here," Major O'Hara said. He actually looked relieved.

"Problems?" Priscilla asked, as if she didn't know better. At 205, there were always problems.

"Mr. Banville has been phoning. He wants to speak to us—he *demands* us," O'Hara reported tensely.

"Us?"

"You and me, Miss Tempest," answered O'Hara unhappily. He rose to his feet. "Incidentally, that Rupert chappie called a few minutes ago."

"Rupert Mackenzie? The reporter?"

"Said he has new information for you. I left his number on your desk."

"Much appreciated, Major."

"All part of the job, right?"

Yes, thought Priscilla, and so was what followed: the inevitable walk to the Place of Execution. Final words from the condemned. A last cigarette. The waving away of the blindfold.

As it always did at these moments, Priscilla's stomach tightened. Her breath was not coming quite so easily as it had minutes before. Major O'Hara marched ahead like an officer at his court martial, head held high, shoulders back, accepting his fate.

Perhaps because she was accompanied by Major O'Hara, El Sid passed on the usual snide remarks. He ushered them straight into Banville's office. The man himself stayed seated behind his desk, resplendent in the morning suit that marked his vaunted status at the Savoy.

"Finally." Banville pronounced the word like a death sentence.

"My apologies, sir," Priscilla said quickly. "It was my fault. Not Major O'Hara's."

"Major O'Hara is *always* on time," Banville said. "You, Miss Tempest, are *never* on time."

"I'm afraid this morning, sir, I would have to agree." Spoken with head humbly lowered, hands clasped demurely in front of her, the remorseful employee.

"Let me get to the reason I have called you both here," Banville continued, shifting personas from the lecturing boss, into the concerned guardian of all things Savoy. "I've had a call from Prince Teodoro." Priscilla felt her stomach drop even more—if it was possible to drop any further.

"Miss Tempest, Prince Teodoro is making serious accusations. He claims you visited him in his suite." Banville had taken on the prosecutorial tone of a barrister at the Old Bailey. Major O'Hara shot a swift, sharp glance at her.

"I beg your pardon, sir?" Priscilla wasn't sure what she was expecting. But not this.

"You heard me. Did you visit Prince Teodoro in his suite?"

"You asked me to go to him and update him as to the press situation."

Banville nervously cleared his throat. "He claims you gave him very little information and made inappropriate advances while you were with him."

"He claimed *what?*" Priscilla stared in astonishment. The man had assaulted her, for God's sake.

"You heard me, Miss Tempest." Banville looked even more nervous. Major O'Hara kept his eyes resolutely away.

"His allegations are simply not true," Priscilla said weakly.

"Why would he make such a claim?"

"I have no idea," Priscilla said.

"You should know that he has asked that I remove you from your position in the press office."

"This is preposterous," Priscilla sputtered.

"Be that as it may, you have upset one of our most esteemed guests. Also, I have received a phone call from Teodoro's cousin, Prince Constantino. This chap is equally upset. He's very critical of the manner in which the press office organized his press conference."

"If I may, sir," piped up Major O'Hara, "Miss Tempest was good enough to place me in charge of organizing the prince's press conference."

Priscilla could hardly believe what she was hearing. Was this Major O'Hara *defending* her?

The major continued. "I personally phoned around to all the newspapers, including a couple of weeklies—Miss Tempest keeps a very good Rolodex of contacts, I must say. I also called press representatives at the BBC and ITV. I'm sorry to say that none of these outlets was interested enough to send a reporter. If anyone must take responsibility for the disappointing attendance, it is myself. Miss Tempest is blameless."

A *blameless* Miss Tempest? How could that be possible? Alien words never before uttered within the dark confines of Banville's office.

"Yes, I see, very well." Banville seemed at a loss for words in the wake of Major O'Hara's declaration. He quickly recovered.

"One thing further, Miss Tempest," Banville continued, his face ominous.

"Sir?" Priscilla groaned inwardly. Just when she thought she might escape the noose.

"An incident the other night outside a gambling establishment called, I am told, the Colony Sports Club. An American gangster was shot to death. Do you know anything about this?"

"Only what I read in the press." Priscilla could barely get the words out of her mouth.

"I have it on reliable authority that this gangster attacked a woman just before he was killed. Would you happen to know anything about that?"

"No, sir." Priscilla choked out the words.

"One of the higher-ups at Scotland Yard is an old chum," he noted, as though a man of his stature would not be caught without his own Scotland Yard chum—higher-up at that. "I will put in a call to him. I am sure the woman's identity is known over there."

"Yes, sir," said Priscilla quietly.

Banville's eyes were laser-focused on her. "Taken together, none of these claims reflect well on you or the hotel, Miss Tempest. Certainly, they warrant further investigation, particularly the allegations made by Prince Teodoro. For now, I will leave you at your post. But I warn you that you are on probation. Do I make myself clear?"

"Crystal clear, sir," answered Priscilla.

"Then that will be all—for now." Banville's tone succeeded in transforming the dismissal into a warning.

"Thank you, Mr. Banville," declared Major O'Hara as though calling an end to the morning parade. It was all Priscilla could do to stop herself from performing an about-face as they left the office.

Outside, she took deep breaths. "Why do I always feel as though I have dodged a bullet as I leave his office?"

"I'm not sure you have," opined Major O'Hara.

"Just so you know, Major, Prince Teodoro assaulted me."

"Perhaps you should have said something to Mr. Banville."

"I doubt it would have done any good," Priscilla said. "It would be his word against mine, and we both know how that works out."

"I'm afraid that is the reality," Major O'Hara said, looking embarrassed to be having this sort of conversation. He quickly retreated to safer ground as they made their way to the lift. "Don't forget to phone that Rupert chappie."

CHAPTER THIRTY-FOUR

Veniamo di Nuovo!

Life-saving coffee, delivered by the unflappable Karl, arrived soon after Priscilla and the major returned to 205, providing faint hope that she might survive the day. The more she thought about Prince Teodoro, the angrier she became—the bugger! If he couldn't beat her or stab her, he would get her fired.

Pushing aside nasty thoughts of Teodoro for the time being, she called Rupert Mackenzie.

He answered almost immediately, his voice clear and seemingly unimpeded by alcohol. "I've been thinking a great deal about that name you asked me about."

"Colin Ashbury."

"Yes, yes, kept rattling around in my sluggish old head. Familiar, as I said earlier, but I couldn't quite place it. I then went back over the diaries and notes I kept from that time in Rome with MI6. Now I have to say, I wasn't close to the investigation, but at the end, we were all ordered to keep our hands off Prince Teodoro. Colin Ashbury was the superior who ordered us to stay away."

"Why?" asked Priscilla.

"He was part of Punta di Lancia, Spearpoint. It was funded by the CIA."

"Wait a second," Priscilla interrupted. "You mean the Americans were backing Spearpoint?"

"At the time, yes. We ran it, though. The CIA didn't want to get its fingers dirty as Spearpoint spread terror across Europe."

"Then Teodoro and Ashbury must have known each other."

"Thick as thieves back then," Rupert asserted. "*Veniamo di nuovo*—we come again. That was Spearpoint's motto. I lost track of the group after I left Rome in the early 1950s. But as far as I know, it continues to exist—at least remnants of it, including Prince Teodoro. Against all odds, he thrives in this brutal world of ours."

"I can't prove it for certain," Priscilla said, "but I do believe Prince Teodoro or the people around him murdered Colin Ashbury."

Instead of being surprised, Rupert reacted with what to Priscilla seemed like relief. "If that's the case, I'm delighted," he said. "If no one can kill them, then perhaps they can kill themselves."

"Thank you, Mr. Mackenzie. You've been a great help."

"It is a part of my life that haunts me to this day, I must admit. I keep thinking we should have done more at the time, that we should never have let men like Teodoro go. But we did and now we reap the whirlwind."

"Yes, you may be right," Priscilla said.

"I would leave you with one note of caution, if I may."

"Certainly."

"I am not sure what inspires your interest in all this, but I would urge you to be very careful. Although we could never put our hands on either one of those bastards, no one in my group doubted how dangerous those monsters were. Whatever you do, Miss Tempest, you must exercise the greatest caution."

Yes, Priscilla thought. She was already only too aware of the perils of dealing with Prince Teodoro. "Thank you so much, Mr. Mackenzie," Priscilla said into the phone. "Please, if you think of anything else, will you get in touch?"

"I'll continue to go through my notes," Rupert said.

"One more thing, if I may."

"Yes, Miss Tempest?"

"Your novel?"

"*The Devil's Lair* it was called. What about it?"

"Do you still have a copy? I'd like to read it."

"I'm flattered, but it's not much of anything, I'm afraid." Rupert sounded sad—another failure in what Priscilla imagined was a life of failures.

"Still, if you have a copy, you should drop it around."

"I'll see what I can do." Rupert's voice fell to a warning tone. "Take care of yourself, Miss Tempest."

Priscilla dropped the receiver back on its cradle as Major O'Hara popped his head through the door. Priscilla glanced up questioningly. "What is it, Major?"

"About Mr. Scott..."

"Yes, what about him?"

"Mr. Scott would appreciate a word," said Gordon Scott, peering over the major's shoulder, looking appropriately sheepish.

Priscilla was on her feet, trying to ignore a suddenly fast-beating heart. "Very good, Mr. Scott, please come in."

Gordon squeezed past the major, who delivered a scowl to the actor's back before closing the door. Priscilla regained her seat while Gordon stationed himself in front of her desk. He looked as though someone had recently polished him to a fine lustre. Priscilla wondered how he could walk around in that tan suit without creasing it. Wondered further how such a stylish man had ever played the King of the Jungle.

"I really am a jerk," Gordon said softly, his face reddening.

"You are a guest of the Savoy, Mr. Scott." Priscilla had adopted the professional servant-to-guest voice that every good Savoy employee soon mastered. It was also effective— yes, *necessary*—when it came to hiding otherwise troublesome emotions. "There are no jerks, as you say, at the Savoy, only valued guests."

"That's right out of a playbook the Savoy must give to all its employees," Gordon said. "Inside, you're thinking I'm a real jerk."

"Inside, I'm not letting you off that easy," Priscilla conceded.

"I have been trying to get in touch with you," Gordon said.

"I apologize, Mr. Scott," Priscilla replied, keeping everything at a distance. "I've been quite busy. What is it you need? Fresh towels in your suite, perhaps? I'd be glad to ring housekeeping."

"The towels are fine. However, I've been having trouble reaching the head of the press office at the Savoy."

"Well, you have reached her now," Priscilla said.

"I wanted to tell you how sorry I am for the way I acted the other night at the Colony Club. I'm not sure what happened after I left, but George tells me you were attacked. I see in the papers that Al Cellini was shot to death. I feel terrible for leaving you alone."

"I was fine," Priscilla said coldly. "Not to worry." Never mind that if Gordon hadn't gone off in a huff and they had left together, Cellini would never have pounced on her.

"I'm hoping you can find it in your very attractive heart to forgive me."

"There is nothing to forgive." Priscilla made sure to keep the frost on the edge of her voice.

"I'd like to make up for my transgressions," Gordon said. The humble expression he had adopted was particularly attractive, Priscilla couldn't help thinking.

"There is no need," stated Priscilla.

"I'm not sure why it's important to you, but I'm pretty sure it is..." Gordon said.

"I'm afraid I don't know what you're talking about," Priscilla said.

"The dinner that fell apart at Wanderworth House? It's back on. Apparently, Lady Daphne has fully recovered and returned home. I'm invited back. I'd like you to come along as my guest."

A number of conflicting thoughts churned through her mind, foremost among them the risk of returning to the witch's castle.

"I'm sorry," Priscilla stated in her professional voice, "but as I have made clear to you previously, Mr. Scott, employees of the Savoy are not allowed to date guests."

"This isn't a date," Gordon countered. "It's a guest, alone in London, who requires someone to accompany him to a dinner party in the country." He paused and smiled. "I also need a ride."

"We have a Daimler on call twenty-four hours a day for our guests. I would be happy to arrange the car for you."

"I'd very much like you to come with me," Gordon persisted. "Is it not the policy of the Savoy to please its guests? Here is a guest that needs pleasing." This was followed by the sort of impish expression designed to make her melt a bit. It worked— almost.

"I'm sorry, Mr. Scott," Priscilla said firmly. "I have no choice in the matter."

Impishness was replaced by disappointment. "Well, if you change your mind, the dinner is tomorrow evening. Call my suite and leave a message."

"Thanks for dropping by, Mr. Scott," Priscilla said, maintaining her neutral-but-helpful tone. "If there is anything the press office can do to make your stay more enjoyable, please let us know."

Her heart was beating far too fast as Gordon exited her office. Just as well he left when he did, she mused. As much as she hated to admit it, she could not have maintained her carefully orchestrated cold front much longer.

CHAPTER THIRTY-FIVE

The Gossip's Bridle Club

The Gossip's Bridle Club was once again in emergency session at the American Bar. Present at their usual corner table amid the rising hum of surrounding cocktail hour conversation, in an atmosphere best described as cruise-ship modern, were the legendary actor Sir Laurence Olivier, fresh off a couple of movie sets and happy to be away; Sir John Gielgud, also legendary but between engagements at that moment; Miss Priscilla Tempest of the Savoy staff, the newest member, who had called the emergency meeting; and finally, the group leader, Noël Coward, in a particularly rapacious mood.

"I daresay, I almost didn't recognize you out of uniform, Larry," stated Noël laconically, taking the opportunity to lob the first verbal grenade at Laurence Olivier once everyone had settled with their drinks. As he spoke, he casually inserted a cigarette into its ivory holder, not so much so he could smoke it, but to use it for a pointer to emphasize his every bon mot.

"What's that all about?" John Gielgud's instinct for the kill had been aroused.

"Haven't you heard? Sir Larry here is our new commander-in-chief." A waiter hurried over to light the cigarette. Noël took his time infusing the air with a stream of cigarette smoke.

"Haven't a clue what you're talking about, old boy." Olivier was already indicating he would rather be anywhere than on the acid tip of Noël's tongue.

"What has it been, Larry? Not one but two war films," Noël mused. "*Oh! What a Lovely War?*"

"A *cri de cœur* to end all wars," protested Olivier. "Damned proud to be part of it.".

"I have it on good authority that you win the Battle of Britain in *Battle of Britain*," Noël said.

"Congratulations, Larry," said Gielgud with an evil glint in his eye. "I knew you could do it."

"Actually, Larry is not without experience fighting the air war," Noël went on. "I visited him and Vivien at RAF Worthy Down, where I learned that Larry had managed to crash more planes than Ralphie Richardson. Which is saying something."

"You damned bugger," trumpeted Olivier. An onlooker couldn't fail to see the steam coming out of his ears.

"Well, yes, as it happens there is a certain amount of truth to that accusation," Noël agreed amiably. He sat back contentedly, gripping his cigarette holder like a spear, in case Olivier should attack.

Priscilla decided it was time to break up the verbal warfare before someone got hurt. "If I may, gentlemen." She spoke softly, forcing the others to concentrate on her, rather than themselves. "First of all, I wish to thank you, my fellow members of the Gossip's Bridle Club, for agreeing to meet on such short notice."

"Tell us about your emergency, Priscilla," prodded Noël. "As you know, we've had to slightly amend the club's purpose since you were voted in as a member."

"You have?" asked Priscilla.

"Comes as news to me," a glum Olivier added. "I thought the purpose of the club was to find new ways to insult me."

"We certainly don't need a club in order to do that," put in Gielgud.

Noël said, "As you know, Priscilla, the Gossip's Bridle Club was founded so that us three rascals, in addition to assaulting each other with deliciously conceived verbal abuse, could trade the juiciest gossip of the day."

"You are all very good at that," agreed Priscilla.

"We're not bad when it comes to the gossip, either," Gielgud said.

"However," Noël went on insistently, determined not to be drowned out by the others, "since your arrival, we now serve as a sounding board and advisory panel for your latest peccadilloes." He waved his cigarette holder around, creating another jet stream of smoke in the air of the American Bar. "Therefore, I now officially call the meeting to order. That means we must concentrate on Priscilla's latest dilemma and shelve further insults about Larry's war record or his recent film choices until after the meeting."

"What's wrong with my film choices?" demanded a peevish Olivier.

"Sacrifices must be made if it means being of service to Priscilla," Gielgud said with false resolution.

"Oh, shut the hell up, both of you," said a miffed Olivier.

"Noël," Priscilla had turned toward the playwright, "you were going to check with your sources at MI5."

"Which I have done," said Noël. "But I'm afraid I haven't come up with much. Lady Daphne's extreme views are certainly well known, but she is considered a harmless old thing ranting away at her Wanderworth pile. They don't regard her as a security threat to the country."

Disappointed to hear that, Priscilla dropped her voice while taking a quick look around to ensure that she could not be overheard. "Well, they are very wrong," she said insistently. "She is very much a threat, and Teodoro too. I was talking to a man named Rupert Mackenzie. He's a journalist now, but after the war he was working in Rome for MI6."

"God, Rupert Mackenzie, there's a name I haven't heard for an age. Rupert and the man we talked about earlier, Colin Ashbury. They worked together in Rome after the war."

"Rupert told me that his boss at MI6 protected Prince Teodoro and his group of anti-communist thugs and terrorists known as Spearpoint. Do you know anything about it?"

"There is no doubt all sorts of villains received a pass simply by climbing to the highest point on one of Rome's seven hills and yelling at the top of their lungs that they were anti-communists," Noël explained. "Spearpoint was perhaps the most ruthless of those groups." He had laid the cigarette holder across an ashtray. "I wasn't aware of Teodoro—or I'd forgotten all about him until you brought his name up. I don't think I was aware of his involvement in Spearpoint. Colin Ashbury, as far as I have been able to learn, oversaw Spearpoint. I remember him coming across as likeable enough, but I am now told by my sources that he was actually a ruthless bastard. You had to be, in order to deal with that bunch of thugs. So was Rupert Mackenzie for that matter."

"Rupert?" Priscilla was taken by surprise. "What makes you say that?"

"Vague rumours, most of which I can't recall," Noël said. "Lost in time's fog. But there was something about him being very useful with a garrotte when it came to getting rid of the communists Spearpoint didn't happen to like. If I remember correctly, hearing reports from that time, Mackenzie and Ashbury disliked each other intensely."

"I'm not sure I understand what you're both getting at with all this," Gielgud interrupted.

"Despite what my sources tell me, Priscilla believes the fascist

Wanderworth Group has been resurrected and is plotting to end British democracy," Noël explained.

"Oh, well, British democracy," Gielgud said mildly. "That's a tall order, isn't it?"

"There's a dead body involved, and Priscilla has been threatened," Noël explained. "A dangerous situation, I would say."

"Good God," exclaimed Olivier. "And all this is going on out at Wanderworth House?"

Priscilla nodded. "There is a dinner party there tomorrow night. I am invited. I wasn't going to go, but now I'm thinking perhaps I should. That's why I called this meeting. I'm anxious to hear what the three of you think."

"It's quite obvious, given what we have just heard," put in Gielgud. "Don't you dare go anywhere near that place."

"I hate to agree with Johnny on anything," Olivier added. "But in this instance, he is right. It sounds far too dangerous."

Noël had retrieved his empty ivory holder and now twirled it as though it were a magic wand conjuring wise words. "I am not so sure," he stated.

"What?" Olivier looked appalled.

"The point is," Noël continued, "if we tell Priscilla not to go, I am willing to bet she will then go. Knowing what you will do anyway, Priscilla, I would say, go. We can keep an eye on you."

"And just how will we do that?" questioned Olivier.

"We will know where she is. If she doesn't return safely then we can alert the police or people I know in the security services. In truth, I expect all that will happen is that Priscilla will be forced to listen to Lady Daphne and her crazy fascist views all evening."

Priscilla looked at her watch. "I'd better get back to the office." She glanced appreciatively at her fellow club members. "Thank you, gentlemen. I do want you to know how very much I value your advice."

That drew a frown from Larry. "Does that mean you're not paying the least bit of attention to what Johnny and I are advising and you will listen to Noël? Who is absolutely bonkers, incidentally."

"I resent that," said Noël impishly. "A bit mad, perhaps, but certainly not bonkers."

"I don't know what to do," Priscilla responded frankly. "I really don't."

"Don't listen to Noël—*never* listen to Noël—and don't go," pronounced Gielgud. "That's the best advice you will receive tonight, my dear, believe me."

Priscilla started to rise. Noël looked uncustomarily concerned. "What is it, Noël?" Priscilla asked.

"Possibly nothing," he said. "But I was just thinking... Rupert Mackenzie and Colin Ashbury."

"What about them?"

"I'm recalling intelligence reports from Rome at the time. We employed a lovely Italian agent named Maria Pacelli. She and Mackenzie were thought to be lovers. However, it came to light that she was in fact a double agent working for the communists. The next thing, her body washed up in the Tiber River. There was no evidence, at least none that I ever saw, but it was generally believed that the man responsible for her death was Colin Ashbury."

CHAPTER THIRTY-SIX

The Devil's Lair

After the other members of the Gossip's Bridle Club had departed, and the early evening pre-theatre crowd in the American Bar was beginning to thin out, Noël Coward decided that one more Buck's Fizz was not going to change the course of the Empire. And that last cigarette wouldn't hurt anything either. It was one of those rare evenings when he had no social engagements, nothing to do, nowhere in particular to go. He was feeling a bit lonely, if he was being honest with himself—although it was never a good idea, he had long ago learned, to be too honest with one's self.

He thought about Priscilla—a permanent pleasure to the eye, he liked to say. How he adored her, her feistiness, her sense of danger, not unlike himself when he was a young man, the wild streak in her that he recognized so well. Had he given her the right advice about attending the dinner at Wanderworth House with that vile old bat, Lady Daphne? Possibly not, but then, as he observed previously, she would probably go anyway, and it was that throw-caution-to-the-wind aspect of her personality he loved about her. Nonetheless, it did not serve her well, particularly in a sheltered atmosphere like the one at the Savoy—a place for proper young women who had no trouble obeying the strict rules of decorum that had been laid down over the years. Priscilla was not a proper young woman, and she had a great deal of trouble obeying any rules, let alone the ones dealing with decorum.

Still, there was a big difference between flouting stuffy rules inside a great hotel and getting oneself killed. The idea of anything happening to Priscilla filled Noël with dread. He finished his cigarette, swallowed the remains of his Buck's Fizz. His sources at MI5 would be of little help, but there was someone who might respond to the alarm he was about to set off. Resisting the urge to order another drink, he rose and went over to the bar.

"Can I get you something, Mr. Coward?" asked Joe Gilmore, the American Bar's supremely attentive barman.

"A telephone if you please, Joe," said Noël.

"Just the telephone, sir?" Was that a twinkle Noël detected in Joe's eye?

"Ah, Joe, you know me too well," said Noël with a grin. "But I'm exercising Herculean discipline this evening. I have had my last drink and my final cigarette. Now the telephone."

"Coming right up, sir." The telephone was promptly placed on the bar in front of him. Noël picked up the receiver and waited for the operator to come on the line.

"Yes, if you will, please connect me with Buckingham Palace," he said into the receiver.

The Front Hall had grown quiet at the end of the day, save for a porter manhandling a familiar-looking suitcase. Priscilla spoke to the young man. "It's Wilfred, is it not?"

"Yes, it is, ma'am, it is." Wilfred didn't hesitate to show his delight that a senior member of the hotel's staff actually remembered his name.

"Wilfred, can you tell me whose suitcase that is?"

Wilfred the porter regarded her with eager blue eyes. "Prince Constantino's, ma'am," he explained importantly, as though it wasn't every day he got to handle a prince's luggage.

"He's checking out?"

"I believe he has checked out," Wilfred replied.

Curious, Priscilla thought. Why would Constantino leave so suddenly?

She thanked Wilfred and went over to where Mr. Tomberry was manning the reception desk. He gave her his usual doleful look. "What can I do for you, Miss Tempest?"

"I didn't realize Prince Constantino had checked out."

"He was most unhappy, I'm afraid." Tomberry might just as well have added, "With you, Miss Tempest."

"I'm sorry to hear that," Priscilla said, thinking how curious this was since, despite Constantino's anger, he had given no indication he was leaving.

"An unhappy guest making an early exit, most unfortunate." Mr. Tomberry's voice dripped with implied criticism.

"But he didn't take his suitcase with him," Priscilla noted.

"He's asked us to ship it back to Italy," answered Mr. Tomberry.

"One suitcase. Did he say why?"

"He told me when I spoke to him that he had an important engagement in the country and wanted to make sure his luggage was sent on."

"Unusual, wouldn't you say?"

"Yes, I suppose it is," Mr. Tomberry said with a sigh. "But that's our job here, isn't it? Dealing with the curious. Doing our best to make an unhappy guest happy."

"He didn't happen to say where in the country he was going."

Tomberry shook his patrician head. "Why would you be interested?"

"Curiosity, that's all," Priscilla hastened to say. More than curiosity though—concern. Constantino was headed for the country. Wanderworth House was in the country.

Mr. Tomberry's tiny chin lifted high in preparation for the lecture he could not resist giving. "A little more curiosity, or perhaps the word is *effort*, on your part, Miss Tempest," he said frostily, "and we might have had a happier guest who stayed longer."

"Thank you for your assistance, Mr. Tomberry," Priscilla said with forced courtesy. "Let me ask you one more question, if I may. Is Prince Teodoro still with us?"

"I have not seen him lately, but yes." He looked pointedly at Priscilla and then added: "For the time being."

"Again, many thanks."

"Anything I can do to help, Miss Tempest." Tomberry spoke as if he would rather be poking at his eye with a fork.

Confused about Constantino, and not sure what she should do, Priscilla escaped back to the comparative safety and quiet of 205.

Major O'Hara must have gone for the day. That probably accounted for how Rupert Mackenzie ended up on the sofa in the outer office, a glass of whisky in hand. "That very nice chap, Karl, I believe, offered it to me," Rupert explained as he lifted up the evidence of what Karl had provided. "Such a delightful place, yes. All one has to do is walk in and you are offered a libation. How could I say no? I hope you'll forgive me, Miss Tempest."

"No problem at all, Mr. Mackenzie. It's good to see you," Priscilla said, putting into place the welcoming front that hid the fact that given what was happening, Rupert was not someone she wanted to deal with right now.

"I was in the neighbourhood and thought I'd drop around with a copy of my book. You expressed some interest in it." He pulled a thin volume with a black cover from the worn leather bag he was carrying. He handed it to Priscilla.

"*The Devil's Lair.*" Priscilla read out the title with enthusiasm. "This is most kind of you, Mr. Mackenzie. I'm anxious to read it."

"A love story, if you can believe an old fart like me is capable of a love story. Based on those terrible years in Rome. Written from the heart—but like I told you, never amounting to much."

Priscilla wondered if the love story had to do with an Italian agent named Maria Pacelli. She almost said something, then thought better of it. "Lovely photograph of you," she said, eyeing the back cover showing a younger, thinner Rupert with the Trevi Fountain in the background.

"Your interest in all this, my novel, I'm afraid you've rather got me obsessing about the past," Rupert said.

"I'm not sure if that's a good thing or a bad thing," offered Priscilla.

"I'm not sure, either. It was a terrible time that I've done my best to obliterate, possibly with too much strong drink," Rupert said. "I truly hated those people, the way they were able to get away with the most outrageous acts."

"How did they get away, do you think?" Priscilla asked.

"Like I said earlier, they had Colin Ashbury in their pocket, methinks because he was being paid off by Prince Teodoro."

"Are you sure about that?"

"Pretty damned sure. Teodoro was bribing anyone who he thought could help him."

"What about you?"

Rupert shook his head sadly. "Alas, I was probably too damned honest for my own good. Not sure whether I would have taken the lucre—like to think I wouldn't have. But it was a moot point since I was never offered anything."

Rupert finished off his drink. "Well, there you have it. Final thoughts from an angry old man about those awful days."

He was a trifle uncertain regaining his feet. It struck Priscilla that the whisky might not have been his first whisky of the day. "Are you all right, Mr. Mackenzie?"

"Oh, yes. Good as gold. Never better."

"I was just talking to Noël Coward," Priscilla said, rising to stand with him. "He remembered you from the war." Not in a good way, Priscilla thought.

"Ah, dear Noël," Rupert said with a sad shake of his head. "Some of us climb to the heights. Others... well, others can't quite get out of the gutter." He made a throwaway gesture with his hand. "But there you have it. Pleased he remembered me."

"Thanks for coming by, Mr. Mackenzie. I appreciate it."

"Take care of yourself, Miss Tempest."

"You too."

She wanted to say more, but say what? And by the time she gave it thought, he was gone. She glanced at the book. A love story, Rupert said. A dead lover, a man ruined for life...

Priscilla went into her office and sat at her desk, enjoying the rare silence and feeling slightly buzzy from the champagne in the American Bar.

She stared at the phone for a time, running through the pros and cons of what she should not have been considering. The small voice of reason that was so often so hard for her to hear quietly urged her not to pick up that receiver. A much louder voice, that maverick voice of carelessness and impetuousness that had dominated her life, cried out for her to do so.

"Shite," she said to the silent room.

She lifted up the receiver. The operator promptly came on the line. "Yes, Miss Tempest? What can I do for you?"

"Good evening," Priscilla said to the operator. "Would you please connect me to Mr. Gordon Scott's suite?"

CHAPTER THIRTY-SEVEN

At Your Service

"It's a lovely old inn," Felicity was saying as she drove out of London. "I think you'll like it. Oliver Cromwell once stayed there."

"Even though he was one of England's greatest soldiers and statesmen, Oliver Cromwell was so much better known for his taste in inns," Percy said. He still wasn't sure what he was supposed to make of Felicity's invitation for the weekend. Where Felicity was concerned, uncertainty was becoming the order of the day.

"You sound surprised," Felicity said.

"Do I? I don't think I'm at all surprised by Oliver Cromwell."

"You know what I mean."

"Am I surprised that out of nowhere you invite me for a weekend at a country inn in Buckinghamshire, not far from Wanderworth House? Not surprised so much as suspicious."

"You might consider this," Felicity said. "I'm crazy about you and therefore want to spend time with you."

"What made you decide that?" asked Percy, skeptical, but nonetheless flattered. His ego would not allow him to summarily dismiss the possibility that Felicity was in fact crazy about him.

"It could have something to do with the fact I shagged you the other night and wouldn't mind doing it again."

"In the country," Percy said.

"What's the matter? Don't you like country shagging?"

Felicity was flawlessly dressed for said country in a hounds-tooth jacket, form-fitting jeans and knee-high leather boots. Yes, Percy thought, he had no objection to shagging in the country.

"If that's all there is to it," Percy said carefully. "Not so long ago, I was your washed-up rival who you were determined to beat."

She darted a sly look at him as she drove. "What makes you so sure anything has changed?"

Percy had no comeback for that. Why did he feel as though he was constantly running to catch up to this woman—to most of the women in his life, come to think of it? The hard-to-fathom-or-catch Priscilla Tempest came to mind immediately.

He had no reason to feel this way, but he had to admit he was experiencing a bit of guilt when it came to Priscilla. He hadn't been in touch. She didn't know about his involvement with Felicity, although using the word *involvement* was probably too much. He was being used, he suspected, an all-too-willing victim of Felicity's sheer seductive force, her youthful confidence. But then what was he being used for, other than maybe sex?

There was his ego again, working overtime.

The Chiltern Hills loomed in the dusky distance. Whatever his doubts, here they were headed back to Wanderworth.

Putting aside her gnawing trepidation that Wanderworth House was a place of malignant evil, Priscilla could understand why someone seeing it brightly lit in the deepening, dusky gloom might mistake it for a magnificent piece of English history sur-viving with elegance and majesty above the Chiltern Hills of Buckinghamshire. But Priscilla knew better, knew it to be occu-pied by a witch, visited by an evil prince.

Her violet empire-waisted evening dress—set off by dan-gling amethyst earrings—was hiked to her thighs so she could manage the pedals of the Morris Minor as she drove. Beside her, Gordon Scott's six-foot-plus tuxedo-clad frame was jammed uncomfortably into the passenger seat.

Priscilla couldn't decide if Gordon was more interested in her or in making some sort of movie deal for *La Dolce Death* to change his image. She, of course, leaned toward his interest in her. The movie sounded terrible and besides, she was pretty certain the people at Wanderworth, anxious to upend democracy, would not be much interested in film financing. But Gordon didn't have to know that.

Not that she had to be concerned about romance this evening, she thought as she swung past the familiar marble nymph still occupying her perch on the cockleshell and went along the gravel drive toward the house. Romance was the least of her problems. She parked away from the ranks of gleaming automobiles already in the car park—in case a fast getaway might be necessary.

It was a cool, breezy night, the stars twinkling picturesquely above Wanderworth as Priscilla straightened her gown, and then took Gordon's arm for the walk to the main entrance. She felt quite comfortable holding on to him, the soothing strength of Tarzan. No matter what the reaction to her arrival, she told herself, they would think twice about knocking off Tarzan, and, by extension, at least for tonight, his Jane. Wouldn't they?

"You seem nervous," Gordon observed as they arrived at the entrance.

"Do I?"

"You do."

"I'm always a bit nervous at these affairs," Priscilla said.

Gordon burst out laughing. "Come on," he said. "You? Priscilla, you must attend these things all the time."

"Or it could be that it's the unknown—what's going to happen tonight?" Would she emerge from Wanderworth House on her feet? Or—and she did not want to even think about this—in a body bag?

"I believe I have some idea." Gordon interrupted her dark train of thought.

"Do you?" she asked.

"Nothing. That's what will happen, in all likelihood. People will ask me about playing Tarzan. I will give them the stock answers I always provide. As soon as I start talking about investing in a movie that doesn't have me in a loincloth, either as Tarzan or Hercules, eyes will glaze over. We will end up totally bored and sorry we ever came, and I will start thinking about a flight back to Rome where another loincloth awaits."

"I hope you're right—about the boredom," Priscilla said.

"You sound doubtful," Gordon said.

"Whatever happens," Priscilla asserted, "I doubt you will be bored."

The dread beginning to bubble up inside her, she took Gordon's hand, gripping it hard.

Oak beams propped up the slanted roof in their room. Percy eyed the big brass bed while Felicity used the bathroom. She was naked except for the leather boots when she emerged looking somewhat surprised. "What are you doing with your clothes on?"

Okay, he thought. No messing around or wasting time. On with it.

Later, they dressed and went down to the dark wood-panelled pub that was attached to the inn. They sat facing a glittering wall of spirits. A dozen middle-aged couples, self-consciously staring at their beer glasses, were seated at round tables. The small room filled with the murmur of stilted conversations. What was it with this stiff-collared formality? Percy wondered. The English idea of having fun, he guessed.

Percy was feeling relaxed, finally, following their lovemaking. Perhaps this really was a weekend getaway with an attractive, willing young woman. Maybe there was no more to it than that. Maybe—just maybe—she really was crazy about him.

Felicity ordered red wine. Percy had one of the local beers on tap.

"I wonder, did Oliver Cromwell drink here?" asked Percy.

"Oh, shut up," Felicity said.

"I hope he enjoyed himself while he was here," Percy said. "I'm afraid it didn't end well for poor Oliver."

"You don't say," Felicity said in a disinterested voice.

"After his death, they dug him up again, cut off his head and stuck it on a pike."

"Not at this inn, I hope."

"The Palace of Westminster, I believe." Percy gave her a sideways glance. "I'll bet the other lovers you brought here knew nothing of Cromwell."

"They peppered me with sweet nothings instead," replied Felicity.

They fell silent, concentrating on their drinks, Percy thinking about his feelings for this beautiful young woman seated beside him. Did he have feelings? He was considering that, despite himself, he might, when someone brushed against his shoulder.

A small man, bristling with repressed energy, wearing a dinner jacket almost as white as his intense face, seated himself next to Percy. The reporter had a momentary thought that the fellow looked familiar. Couldn't quite place him, so out of place in a dinner jacket in a country pub.

"Is this then the inimitable Mr. Percy Hoskins?" said the small man in an Italian-accented voice that verged on the contemptuous.

"I beg your pardon?" said Percy.

"I must tell you, my first impression is that there is so little to him." The small man talked past Percy to Felicity. "I would have expected more."

Percy must have misheard this bloke. He didn't know him from Adam. Did he?

"Percy," Felicity was saying, "I'd like to introduce my friend Prince Constantino, the future Duke of Vento. Constantino wanted to meet you."

"It has been my honour to be of help to Felicity in pursuit of this story," Constantino said. "At the same time, I have been following your career with interest, Mr. Hoskins."

"Apparently, I disappoint you," Percy said.

"Let's say I was expecting, I don't know, perhaps a more authoritative figure."

"I could say the same about you," Percy retorted, determined not to allow this little prince to get under his skin. "If I'm to be honest, I would not have mistaken you for a prince or a duke."

Constantino permitted himself a weak smile. "If everything goes as I have planned, we will both emerge from this evening much different people. You will believe I am a duke."

"And what will you believe?"

"I might mistake you for a reporter who has witnessed a great story," replied Constantino.

Percy addressed Felicity. "Not a weekend in the country then."

"I'm sorry, Percy. The prince was adamant that this was the best way to do it."

Percy didn't like any of it. Nothing felt right. He had had the wool pulled over his eyes, and, most devastatingly, his ego punctured.

"It would perhaps be best if we continue this discussion outside," Constantino said.

"And why would I want to do that?" Percy was doing his best to keep his voice equally conversational.

Constantino said, "You don't wish to go to dinner?"

"I don't understand." Percy's suspicions were aroused now. He was feeling increasingly uncomfortable.

"Dinner at Wanderworth. We are expected."

"You're kidding." Percy looked at Felicity. She appeared as surprised as he was. "Did you know about this?"

She shook her head and then turned to the prince. "What are you doing, Constantino?"

"Shall we go out? We don't want to be late." Constantino reached into his pocket, withdrew some pound notes and placed them on the bar. "Let me get your drinks."

Percy and Felicity traded quick glances. Felicity was impossible to read. "Did you know that Oliver Cromwell once slept at this inn?" Percy asked Constantino.

"Who is this Oliver Cromwell?" Constantino looked vaguely mystified.

Percy smiled knowingly. "All right, sure," he said, "why don't we go outside?" He rose from the barstool. "I'll follow you," he said to Constantino.

"No, my friend, please, you first."

The three of them filed out into the car park, an uneasy Percy in the lead, Constantino and Felicity following. A robin's-egg-blue Bristol 408 sedan was at the side of the inn. Percy gave it an admiring look. "Posh car," he said.

"I am here as a result of what I consider to be a higher

calling—to make right the injustices that my cousin has been responsible for."

"Those who called you decided you needed a luxury car, did they?" Percy asked with a sneer.

"My single indulgence," Constantino said. "After all, I am soon to become Duke of Vento, and such a vehicle will fit my position."

"Your cousin might have something to say about that," Percy said. "No matter who called you or what kind of car you're driving."

"Please." Constantino spoke politely. "Open the Bristol's boot for me."

"Why would I want to do that?" Percy asked.

"Open it." Constantino's expression hardened. He withdrew a gun from under his jacket.

Percy frowned at the gun and then looked at Felicity. She had gone pale.

"I will not ask you again, Mr. Hoskins." Constantino lifted his gun to emphasize the point.

Percy stepped to the rear of the Bristol and twisted the handle that released the lid. It popped up to reveal an empty cavity.

"Felicity, please get in," Constantino said.

"I will not," Felicity protested in a high, tight voice. "This is absolutely crazy. What are you doing?"

"What is necessary. What I have been called to do," Constantino asserted.

"Well, I'm sorry, but I haven't been called to get into any car boots," Felicity said.

"I have received a vision. This is a necessary part of my vision." Constantino's eyes were burning a brilliant blue. He pointed the gun at Percy's head. "Get in or I will shoot your lover, Mr. Hoskins. Believe me, I have nothing to lose. I will do it."

"No." Felicity was shaking her head more, beginning to tremble. Her voice was a choked whisper. "You can't do this—"

"Come on, Constantino, no matter what vision you think you're seeing, this is not the way to become the Duke of Vento," Percy said, mounting what was as close as he could get under the circumstances to a reasonable argument. "Let's go inside where we can talk. Tell us your story, describe your visions. We can finally expose your cousin for what he is. That will be much more effective than anything you've got planned."

"It is far too late." Constantino pressed the gun harder against Percy. "Get in, Felicity. I will not harm either of you if you co-operate, I promise. But I will not tell you again."

Tears running down her cheeks, trying to maintain a brave front, Felicity crawled into the boot's cavity.

"Lie down, please," ordered Constantino. As soon as she complied, he turned to Percy. "Now close the lid."

"You're mad, you know," Percy said as he lowered the lid.

"Yes I am, Mr. Hoskins," Constantino said. "But we are wasting time calling each other names. We will be late for dinner."

CHAPTER THIRTY-EIGHT

Wanderworth

Unless Priscilla was mistaken, the six men in brown leather jackets stationed around Wanderworth's portico were the same ones she had seen being embraced by Teodoro. What was it she heard Teodoro calling them? *Miei disturbatori?* Yes, that was it. She turned to Gordon. "You speak Italian, don't you?"

"As a matter of fact, I do."

"Translate *Miei disturbatori* for me."

"Disturbers or disrupters. Why do you ask?"

"Those fellows over there." Priscilla indicated the men who now scrutinized them closely. They were young, dark-haired, with trimmed beards and tough-guy demeanours. "Don't they look like disturbers to you?"

"I suppose they do," Gordon said noncommittally. "If we misbehave, they can throw us out."

Or worse, Priscilla thought as she and Gordon entered the hall and made their way along to the great room. It was unchanged from her last visit: the crimson sofas, the same elderly men, this time with their elderly women, everyone formally dressed, the uncertain light muted by the fringed lampshades. The conversation dropped to a hum as Gordon and Priscilla appeared.

Gordon towered over the other guests. Priscilla imagined that he dominated any space he occupied, radiating a self-confidence that she could only envy. Even if he thought the evening would be a waste of time, he seemed determined to give it his best and most charming shot.

"Good evening, folks," he announced, projecting a voice Priscilla thought would work fine for the Tarzan yell. "I'm Gordon Scott and I'd like to introduce you to my friend, Miss Priscilla Tempest."

Amid subdued greetings, Lady Daphne, the Wanderworth witch herself, prune-like face scrunched in disapproval, bore down on them. No wheelchair this evening, Priscilla noticed. Instead, she leaned hard on a cane. Daphne threw out her hand and announced melodramatically, "Mr. Gordon Scott, so delighted you could be with us finally."

"It's a pleasure to be here." Gordon's smile held steadfast. He turned to Priscilla. "I believe you've already met Miss Priscilla Tempest."

Lady Daphne scowled as if about to cast a dark spell on Priscilla right then and there. Her eyes widened for an instant, nostrils flaring in—what? Alarm? "Miss Tempest," she said in a voice dripping with icicles. Nothing about it being good to see her again. Hardly surprising, Priscilla thought.

Behind Lady Daphne trundled a scrawny little man in formal dress and a slightly taller pale scarecrow of a woman in a crimson evening dress, her jet-black hair pulled back severely in a bun.

"Mr. Scott, allow me to introduce the Duke and Duchess of Windsor, dear friends who to my absolute delight have arrived unexpectedly this evening."

The duchess produced an icy smile as Gordon allowed himself a slight bow, taking her hand. "A fellow American," said the duchess. "Expats lost in the wilds of Buckinghamshire."

The duke grinned inanely, as though someone had just hit him on the side of the head. "The wife tells me you are some sort of actor."

"Dear, remember that I told you Mr. Scott played Tarzan in the movies." She shot an appreciative glance at Gordon. "Is that not correct, Mr. Scott?"

"Yes, it is," Gordon responded. He pushed Priscilla gently forward as though to place a barrier between himself and more Tarzan questions. "This is a friend of mine, Miss Priscilla Tempest."

"Enchanted." The duke's eyes gleamed—lustily? Yes, unless Priscilla missed her guess. The duke took her hand and kissed it.

"Are you an actress as well, Miss Tempest?" he asked.

"Priscilla is far too clever for that," Gordon cut in. "She is employed at the Savoy."

"The Savoy!" gasped the duke as though that was the most exciting news he'd ever heard.

"We *love* the Savoy," enthused the duchess. "Clive Banville is a dear friend." She turned to the duke. "Right, darling?"

The duke looked at her blankly.

The duchess made an impatient face and then returned to Priscilla. "What do you do there, Miss Tempest?"

Priscilla wanted to say she changed the bedsheets. Instead, she said, "I work in the press office."

"The press." It was as if a fly had just flown into the duchess's heavily rouged mouth and she was trying not to spit it out. "We don't like the press, do we Bertie?"

"The press? What about the press?" The duke looked confused.

"As something of an interesting sideline," Gordon went on, "Miss Tempest also manages to get herself into a great deal of trouble."

The duchess looked intrigued. "Do you? How do you do that?"

"I'm not sure," Priscilla answered. "Let's see how it plays out this evening."

An awkward silence ensued. The duke seemed to have arrived from another planet and was in a muddle as to where he had landed. The duchess had had enough of Priscilla and was concentrating on Gordon. "I particularly liked you in *Tarzan's Greatest Adventure*," she said enthusiastically.

"You saw *that*?" Gordon couldn't hide his amazement.

"Of course," replied the duchess with surprising seductiveness. "I cannot resist movies featuring handsome, well-muscled, scantily clad young men swinging from vines. You are still making those movies, I trust."

"Not for a while," Gordon said. "These days I'm Hercules, but," he added reassuringly, "still scantily clad."

"No swinging from vines?"

"I push over big pillars instead," Gordon said.

It was plain from the look on her face that Lady Daphne did not like the direction the conversation had taken. She tossed her hand into the air and announced, "They are calling us for dinner"—even though Priscilla hadn't heard anything.

The duke's face lit with excitement. "Dinner! Oh, jolly good! I must say I'm famished." He addressed Lady Daphne. "Will Teodoro be joining us this evening?"

"Perhaps later." Lady Daphne's face had gone rigid.

The duke grinned inanely. "Well, I am famished. Or did I already say that?"

"You did, darling," said the duchess. "But then you are always famished."

If the Duke and Duchess of Windsor were part of some nefarious plot, Priscilla thought, it had not affected the duke's appetite.

"You said we wouldn't be bored," Gordon whispered in Priscilla's ear.

"Are you bored?"

"Aren't you?"

"The night isn't over," Priscilla said glumly.

Lady Daphne hobbled along using her cane, shepherding her guests into a pale-blue dining room overhung by a trio of chandeliers above a linen-covered table the length of a country road. Silver candelabra, each holding six flickering candles, were positioned at intervals along the table. Not far away, tall windows were heavily draped. Beyond the dining table a painting of a woodland nymph hung above a dominating stone hearth. It was possibly the only display of innocence in the house, Priscilla thought.

Red-jacketed attendants escorted guests to their seats. Priscilla was gently removed from Gordon and seated in a purgatory at the far end of the table. There was an empty chair beside her. Gordon, on the other hand, was seated between the Duke and Duchess of Windsor. A place of honour, Priscilla supposed, except the two of them made unlikely film financiers. Gordon spotted her, grinned and waved, the movie star in his glory.

With her guests seated, Lady Daphne rose at the head of the table and with a quick chopping movement summoned quiet. "Thank you all for being here tonight," she said in her high, brittle drawl. "As many of you know, our last get-together had to be cancelled due to my unexpected illness. I'm fine now, in good health." A sprinkling of applause greeted her assertion, promptly cut off by another chopping movement from Lady Daphne's hand.

"In addition to having you all here this evening supporting a better Britain," she continued, "I am so pleased that my good friends, Edward, the Duke of Windsor, and his lovely wife, Wallis, the Duchess of Windsor, have joined us. Nothing says more about the importance of our work than their presence and support. Welcome, Bertie and Wallis!"

CHAPTER THIRTY-EIGHT

The duke and duchess acknowledged with thankful smiles the applause that rippled along the table. Priscilla was so busy watching them that it was a moment before she realized an arriving guest had slipped quietly into the empty seat beside her.

"My cruel Princess of the Savoy," breathed Prince Teodoro. He pressed the snout of his pistol against Priscilla's still-sore ribs.

"Ouch," she said.

CHAPTER THIRTY-NINE

Standoff!

The steady buzz of conversation rising from the guests, their faces glowing in the candlelight, failed to distract Priscilla from the sinking realization that, once again, she was at the mercy of Prince Teodoro.

"You are poking a gun in my ribs," Priscilla whispered indignantly. "In this country we don't do that at dinner parties."

"It is my way of making clear what will happen should you choose to make a scene," Teodoro replied, keeping the gun against her.

"What sort of scene are you talking about?" Priscilla could see waiters at the far end of the table beginning to serve the guests smoked salmon.

"A scene in which you would make loud and baseless accusations in front of the Duke and Duchess of Windsor."

The waiters were moving with smooth efficiency down the table. Guests leaned into each other to discuss the delights of fascism—managing to do it, presumably, without the necessity of guns.

"You have been a thorn in my side ever since I arrived at the Savoy," Teodoro was saying. "I have spoken to Signor Clive Banville about you. I am seriously considering staying at the Dorchester in the future."

"That's very good news," Priscilla countered. "I would have to say you are not the sort of guest who should be at the Savoy."

The prince eased the pressure slightly on her ribs as servers reached them with the salmon.

"Lady Daphne has a very good kitchen," Teodoro offered. "The smoked salmon comes from Scotland. The main course will be roast crown of lamb with Béarnaise sauce, another favourite of mine. It's a shame you won't be able to stay for it."

"I don't like Béarnaise sauce, anyway."

"I would not miss it for the world," the prince said.

"I thought you might be out tonight with your disruptors—disrupting."

In reaction, Priscilla was sure she could see the light of revealed truth switch on in Teodoro's eyes. "Priscilla, Priscilla, what have you been up to? Why do you know the very things that will get you killed? Why are you so careless?" Teodoro pressed the gun against her harder.

"Perhaps because I don't want you doing what I believe you are planning to do."

"And what is that?"

"Destroy British democracy."

Teodoro let out a loud snort of laughter that jolted nearby diners. At the other end of the table, Lady Daphne's head jerked up from her plate. "Prince Teodoro," she called to him. "I am intrigued that Miss Tempest is managing to keep you so amused."

"She is indeed, Lady Daphne." Teodoro was doing his best to control his mirth. "She keeps me laughing at her ridiculous assertions."

"Oh dear. Miss Tempest has been an outrageous meddler from the moment I set eyes on her. You must tell us what she is up to now," ordered Lady Daphne. "That way we can all enjoy her latest bit of nonsense."

"The prince is so easily amused," Priscilla responded. "I was telling him that I don't like the idea of all of you plotting to overthrow the government. He seemed to get a kick out of that."

Murmurs of confusion came from Priscilla's fellow guests.

"What doesn't she want us to overthrow?" the Duke of Windsor asked of no one in particular.

"The government, darling, the government," responded the duchess impatiently.

"Curious," said Lady Daphne, adopting the scowl she wore whenever Priscilla was around, "I don't find that at all amusing."

The sudden arrival of Prince Constantino, a frazzled-looking Percy Hoskins in tow, brought further debate about overthrowing democracy to an abrupt halt. The two men appeared at the far end of the table, close to where Lady Daphne was seated. Dinner guests panicked upon seeing the gun Constantino held.

"Ladies and gentlemen, if I could have your attention, please." Percy spoke in a piercing, nervous voice.

"Who the devil's that?" demanded the duke.

"Quiet, darling," admonished the duchess.

"Can't hear a deuced thing the fellow's saying," complained the duke.

"Prince Constantino has brought me here tonight in my capacity as a journalist—at gunpoint, I might add—to inform everyone present that not only has he come to denounce his cousin, Prince Teodoro, but also to expose the illegal activities of members of the Wanderworth Group."

"What activities?" loudly demanded the duke, looking more befuddled than ever.

"Hush, darling," said the duchess.

"I am to inform you further that I will be reporting on these events for my paper, the *Evening Standard*." Percy glanced back at Constantino. "That's what you wanted me to say, right?"

"*Bastardo!*" cried Teodoro, leaping to his feet, so that everyone could clearly see the gun in his hand.

Constantino jerked around, glaring at his cousin, and raised his gun. The two princes were frozen at either end of the table, the duelling princes, a standoff with guns.

Priscilla noticed Gordon's perplexed expression, as though he had lost his place in the script and the scene was playing out much differently than he expected. The duke put down his fork and said, "What is happening? Who are these people? Why have they delayed the main course? I am quite famished."

"Bertie," the duchess ordered crossly, "for God's sake, shut up!"

Percy chose that moment to summon courage Priscilla would not have thought he had in him. He shoved a hard elbow into Constantino's stomach, knocking him backward. At the other end of the table, Teodoro raised his arm to shoot, but Priscilla lunged into him, knocking the gun aside as he fired. The bullet hit one of the overhead chandeliers, cutting it loose. It came crashing down onto the dining table, and alarmed guests screamed and scrambled for safety as the table collapsed under its weight, sending dishes and silverware flying. The candelabra tipped over and the candles scattered, setting the tablecloth on fire. Constantino emerged through smoke and flame, gun raised, shouting in Italian. He fired at Teodoro and missed. Teodoro fired back.

Then they both shot at each other simultaneously. Constantino staggered and sank to his knees. Priscilla twisted around to see Teodoro fall back against the wall, dropping his gun.

Plaster from the ruined ceiling rained down. Priscilla could see Gordon Scott stumbling through the chalky mist and smoke, his tux jacket covered in white dust, and Percy, his shocked face visible through the smoke. Gasps and cries rose from dumbfounded dinner guests, and suddenly a keening wail sounded as Lady Daphne fell to her knees. The Duke and Duchess of Windsor, both looking horrified, clung to each other, trembling.

Suddenly, a gaunt wraith cut through the swirling plaster dust. Priscilla recognized Commander Peter Trueblood as he strode into the wreckage to the two royals, quickly guiding them away. They followed meekly as a platoon of young men in smart suits burst in, scattering throughout the dining room.

The Walsinghams had arrived. Not quite in the nick of time, Priscilla thought. Not nearly in the nick of time.

CHAPTER FORTY

Officially Secret

Despite the warmth of the night, Priscilla, seated on a bench in the garden behind the house, couldn't stop shivering. Briefly, she had been allowed into one of the bathrooms to clean away the dust as best she could. She had a recollection of Percy being taken away by the police amid a cacophony of noise and protests from shaken dinner guests. She guessed that Gordon Scott was among them.

Presently, Commander Peter Trueblood materialized out of the darkness. He carried a blanket. Commander Blood did not look happy. But then in Priscilla's experience no one in authority ever looked happy when she was around.

He proceeded to open the blanket and, with surprising gentleness, wrapped it around her. "You will be glad to know that the Duke and Duchess of Windsor have been taken safely away," he reported. "They are shaken up but otherwise unharmed— thank goodness. The duke complains that he hasn't been fed. We will have them back in Paris by morning."

"You do realize, Commander, the duke and duchess you are so eager to protect were probably here to participate in the plot Lady Daphne and Prince Teodoro were cooking up to overthrow the British government."

"You will be glad to know that to that end we have tonight also arrested six Italians, international criminals and thugs hired by Teodoro."

"They are called disruptors," Priscilla said. "I think you will find there were plans to do just that."

"So it appears," Trueblood acknowledged.

"How are Constantino and Teodoro?" Priscilla asked.

"Teodoro has succumbed to the gunshot wound he received," Trueblood said, seating himself beside the blanketed Priscilla. "Constantino has been taken to a local hospital where I understand his condition is critical. There is doubt as to whether he will survive."

"Constantino knew what his cousin was up to," Priscilla said. The blanket had helped her stop shivering. "He came here to stop him."

"He appears to have done so. You should know that thanks to information supplied by Mr. Percy Hoskins, we have rescued Miss Felicity Khan from the boot of Prince Constantino's automobile."

Felicity Khan and Percy, Priscilla thought, fuming. She should have known he wouldn't be able to keep his hands off her. If she ever spoke to him—and she would never, ever speak to him—she would have to pry out the details of how his lover ended up in Constantino's boot. For now, she grudgingly asked, "How is she?"

"A bit traumatized, like everyone else connected to this sorry affair, but otherwise fine. We are in the process of questioning her," Trueblood said. "She was using Constantino as a source for a *Sunday Times* piece she is writing."

"Constantino was her source?" Why was she not surprised—although she was surprised.

"From what I can understand, Miss Khan lured Hoskins out here at the behest of Constantino."

Priscilla doubted it took much luring.

"But tell me, Commander," Priscilla said aloud, "how did you know?"

"Know?" Trueblood raised a questioning brow.

"Know what was going on out here."

"I must say I didn't—until I received an urgent call from your friend Noël Coward. He told me that events were possibly transpiring at Wanderworth House that could result in scandal for the royal family. He suggested strongly that I'd better do something about it. He will never know how right he was."

"No?"

"Nor will anyone else, Miss Tempest. Because of the presence of the Duke and Duchess of Windsor, and the possible conspiracy you describe, it is necessary to keep this entire episode quiet. Therefore, I am invoking the Official Secrets Act. This will prevent Mr. Hoskins and Miss Khan writing about it. And, of course, you talking about it."

"Can you do that?"

Trueblood smiled thinly. "I can do just about anything when it comes to the protection of the royal family—and the Crown in general. I suspect the Italian government will be onto me in the next day or so about keeping the involvement of their princes out of this as well, washed up and troublesome though they may be."

"Then I suppose Mr. Banville does not have to hear about any of it."

"It is imperative no one hears anything, including Clive Banville."

"Supposing Constantino survives," Priscilla asked. "What are you going to do then?"

"We will cross that particular bridge when we come to it." Trueblood rose to his feet. "A dreadful mess, I daresay, and here you are, Miss Tempest, once again up to your ears in the midst of it."

"You can't be blaming me for what's happened," Priscilla said, not bothering to keep the anger out of her voice.

"No, we can't, can we?" Trueblood sounded unconvinced. "I understand you drove here this evening. You'll be released in a few minutes to return to London with this Mr. Scott chap, your date."

"Yes," said Priscilla dully. The last thing she wanted to do was drive back to London.

"I preferred Johnny Weissmuller," Trueblood said.

"What?"

"As Tarzan. I liked Johnny Weissmuller better."

"I'll be sure to tell Mr. Scott," Priscilla said.

He turned to go. She called after him. He swung back expectantly. "Yes, Miss Tempest?"

"I want you to leave Susie alone."

"I beg your pardon?" Trueblood carefully arranged a look of mystification on his pale, skeletal face.

"You put her parents up to abducting their own daughter to keep her away from Lord Snowdon. You probably provided the drugs they used. She's had enough. Leave her alone."

"Lord Snowdon has come to his senses," Trueblood said evenly. "It won't be necessary to bother her further."

"You mean Lord Snowdon has met someone else. What are you going to do, Commander? Drug her too? You may end up having to drug most of the single women in London."

"Goodnight, Miss Tempest. Please drive carefully." He was about to start away and then seemed to have another thought. "Oh yes. Before I forget. Thank you for your service to Britain this evening."

And he was gone.

Yes, Priscilla thought as she sat there, the night wind off the nearby Thames against her face, she had saved England from Lady Daphne and Prince Teodoro. Soon there would be a statue dedicated to her, possibly close by Sir Arthur Sullivan in the

Victoria Embankment Gardens. Passersby would sit on a bench marvelling at her. A statue was the least a grateful nation could do for Priscilla after she nearly got killed.

She closed her eyes, gathering the strength to go in search of Gordon. The night's events should teach him never to invite her to dinner parties, Priscilla thought ruefully.

Something stirred in front of her. She opened her eyes. Lady Daphne, withered and witchy, seemed to float on air toward her. Priscilla thought she was hallucinating—the levitating witch of Wanderworth. Except the tiny gun—a derringer?—in her hand was real enough, a pistol so small she could hide it from the authorities swarming over her estate.

"Bitch," Lady Daphne screeched.

Priscilla's last thought before the gun went off was that she might not be around for the unveiling of her statue.

A pity.

CHAPTER FORTY-ONE

Susie in Love

Gordon Scott guided the Morris Minor into a parking spot not far from Priscilla's flat. He turned off the engine. His dust-streaked face softened. "Home safe and sound," he murmured, palpably relaxing after the tense drive back to London on what for him was very much the wrong side of the road. But then the wrong side of the road, mused Priscilla, was the least of the challenges Gordon had faced on their first—and quite possibly last—date. "Are you going to be okay?"

A good question, Priscilla thought. How was she after tonight? Lady Daphne's aim, thankfully, had been so shaky the bullet only grazed her arm. After discovering she wasn't dead, Priscilla had risen to her feet, walked over to a petrified Lady Daphne and socked her in the jaw. Nearby police officers descended to pull her away. Further questioning soon followed, accompanied by a fair amount of dismayed headshaking on the part of the officers while ambulance attendants patched up Priscilla's arm and placed it in a sling.

"I did say you wouldn't be bored," Priscilla said hesitantly as they sat together in the car's dim interior.

"I think it's more accurate to say you *hoped* I wouldn't be bored," Gordon said.

"And you weren't."

"I should have taken you more seriously."

"I'm a very serious person," Priscilla said.

CHAPTER FORTY-ONE

"I would say it's more like you're totally unpredictable." He paused and looked over at her. "Not to mention quite lovely."

She thought he might kiss her then, and debated briefly how she would respond—the Savoy employee with the guest she was not supposed to kiss.

But he didn't. So she didn't.

Instead, Gordon got out and opened the passenger door so he could help her out. The perfect gentleman, Priscilla thought.

"Come up," she said, putting her usable hand on his arm.

"Are you sure?"

"It's late," she reasoned, although she was at the point where she was beyond reasoning.

He didn't say anything in response but followed her up to her flat. She handed him the latch key and he opened the door. They didn't bother with the lights. By the time he had washed the grime off his face in the kitchen sink, she had discarded the violet gown. The lack of lighting, she thought fleetingly, concealed most of the evidence of the disarray in which she tended to live, although as he caressed her, it was clear he wasn't paying much attention to his surroundings. The mess of her life, she mused, as she gently lifted her arm from its sling so that she could help him undress, impressed by the massiveness of a hairless chest whose smooth contours gleamed in the available light.

In case he should have trouble locating it, she took his hand and led him into her bedroom, thankful that she had at least made the bed the last time she had slept in it. And how many ages ago was that? After, everything became a blur, the pain in her arm, the excitement of a naked man thrusting himself gently into her, the warming pleasure. Not difficult at all for Priscilla to enthusiastically play Jane to his Tarzan. Excelling in the role.

Priscilla was still mulling over that night with Gordon two days later, seated in the salon of the hideaway off Berkeley Square where Susie had been sequestered since being rescued from the clutches of her parents and Commander Trueblood.

"No, I'm doing fine," Priscilla said in answer to George Raft's question. "Frankly, I'm wearing my arm in a sling so I can tell people I broke it."

"I'm just so glad you're all right," Susie said.

Raft was sartorial perfection in a charcoal-grey double-breasted suit with delicate pinstripes. His face was the same inscrutable mask, save for the narrow apertures that were his eyes. They reflected an unusual gleam as he sat next to Susie. The picture of rosy health this morning, she leaned against him, clutching his hand and gazing at him adoringly.

Priscilla said to Raft, "You wanted me to get you information on who killed your associate, Mr. Cellini."

"That's right," Raft acknowledged.

"Unfortunately, I can't say anything."

"No? Why not?" The apertures that were his eyes had narrowed even more.

"Because I am now bound by the Official Secrets Act."

"The Official Secrets Act!" Susie's eyes had become large. "Priscilla, what have you been up to?"

"I would tell you all about it, except that I am bound by—"

"Yeah, the Official Secrets Act." Raft seemed amused by the idea. "Only in this country can you shut everything down with three words. Amazing—but very useful if you're part of the establishment that runs things." He rose to his feet. "I guess at this point, official secrets or not, I know more than enough. If you'll excuse me, you ladies must have things to talk about. I've got a few errands to run before I leave town."

"You're leaving?" Priscilla asked.

"Back to LA for business," Raft said.

"I'm going with him," Susie blurted.

Priscilla's eyes grew large. Her mouth opened in amazement.

"Like I said, you ladies have a few things to discuss." Raft bent down to kiss Susie on the mouth. Susie responded eagerly.

"I'll see you in a couple of hours. Glad you've managed to survive, Priscilla."

When he was gone, Priscilla leaned forward to Susie. "You're not really going with him, are you?"

"Yes," she enthused. "I do believe I'm in love, Priscilla."

"I thought you were in love with Lord Snowdon," Priscilla countered.

"That was a big mistake, and I'm so sorry for what I put you through. But this is real." She moved closer to Priscilla and lowered her voice. "You know what they call George?"

"What?" Although Priscilla wasn't sure she wanted to know.

"The Black Snake! Because of—"

"He *told* you that?" Priscilla couldn't believe it.

"Well, it was evident that something very unusual was happening down there." She dropped her voice to a whisper. "I must tell you, it's the biggest I've ever—"

"That may not be the best reason to go off with someone like Raft," Priscilla cautioned.

"There's so much more to George—"

"Than his...?"

"Yes, oh yes. He's so wise and mature..."

"And so much older than you are," Priscilla added, trying not to think about the size of a guy nicknamed the Black Snake.

"If you know George the way I do, then you'd know that age makes no difference. He's young in so many ways and he's the man I love," said Susie with great certainty.

"It doesn't look as though I can talk you out of this," said Priscilla with a sigh.

"As I said, I so appreciate all you've done, Priscilla. I don't know what would have happened if you hadn't come to my rescue. For one thing, I would never have met George."

Aha, thought Priscilla, so all this was her fault after all.

"But it's my life," Susie concluded. "There's nothing for me here. I'm going to Hollywood with George."

Priscilla stood and awkwardly embraced Susie, being careful of her sore arm. "If you change your mind..."

"I won't," Susie said vehemently.

"If you do, your old job is waiting for you." At least she hoped it was waiting, Priscilla thought.

"Thank you, Priscilla," Susie said with a wounded smile.

A little lost, Priscilla thought as she left. Lost in love.

The Heavy Heart

Entering the Savoy's busy Front Hall, Priscilla was overwhelmed by a renewed sense of comfort and well-being. After what she had been through, returning to this small, well-ordered, tradition-bound universe gave her such a feeling of safety. How she had missed it! How she never again wanted to leave the luxury of its warm embrace!

As Priscilla mused about perfection in an imperfect world, here was Gordon in the light-brown suit that matched his smooth, tanned skin, which in turn accented the blond highlights in his perfectly curly brown hair. That hard-to-resist smile showed off his perfect white teeth as he sauntered over. "I stopped by your office," he said. "That guy with a moustache and an attitude said he didn't know when you were coming in."

"Ah yes, Major O'Hara," Priscilla said.

"I got the impression he's taken over," Gordon said.

"Is that what he told you?"

"I thought maybe you might have decided to take some time off."

"Not as far as I know," Priscilla said with a confidence that she was not feeling. The Front Hall suddenly felt a lot less cozy and safe.

"Anyway," Gordon continued, "I didn't want to go without saying goodbye."

"I wasn't aware you were leaving us," she said formally. And I'm a bit disappointed that you are, she added silently.

"Time to move on," Gordon said. "Now that *La Dolce Death* seems to have evaporated, I'm off to Rome to pick up the sword and put on the toga in something called *Hercules and the Princess of Troy*."

"Are you scantily clad?" Priscilla asked, cheekily.

"Of course. Muscles rippling."

"The Duchess of Windsor will be pleased."

He shrugged. "Can't decide lately if I'm an actor or a nomad. A bit of both, I suppose. You go where you can get the work."

"You sound as though you're tired of it," Priscilla said.

"No, not really," he said. "I was a lifeguard in Las Vegas when they picked me to play Tarzan. Before that, I had no thoughts of acting. Now I suppose I'm hooked on the life. The money is so easy, I travel first class and I meet beautiful people, like you." He gave her a fond look. "What can I say, Priscilla? It's been... exciting? Is that the right word?"

"Yes, that about covers it," she agreed. She marvelled at how two lovers could be so cool with each other. But then they were standing in the midst of the Savoy's Front Hall, agonizingly public. She wanted to say more, but what?

"I suppose a kiss goodbye is out of the question," Gordon said, as though reading her mind. He looked a little sad.

"I don't think that's a good idea... Mr. Scott." She offered her hand. "It's been a pleasure having you as a guest with us. I hope you've enjoyed your stay."

Gordon took her hand. "It has been delightful, Miss Tempest. Thank you for all your help while I've been here."

"Please come back soon and stay with us again."

"I will keep that in mind, Miss Tempest—and believe me, I won't soon forget you."

"And I won't forget you, Mr. Scott."

"But I do have one complaint," Gordon said.

"And what is that?"

"I never did get those flowers."

"I'll make a note for the next time."

"I look forward to it." The final smile he gave her was very nearly irresistible. She felt weak and silly. It was all she could do to resist throwing caution to the wind and kissing him.

But she didn't.

Their eyes met and locked together for much longer than Priscilla intended. Then she shook herself loose and continued across the Front Hall.

Carrying a heavy heart.

CHAPTER FORTY-THREE

Onward, Upward

Determined to put the attractiveness of Gordon Scott out of her mind, Priscilla hurried to 205. Praying that she still had a job.

She found Major O'Hara in her office, seated at her desk. Looking far too comfortable, Priscilla thought.

Clive Banville lounged on the sofa beneath the rogue's gallery of famous guests at the Savoy—guests, Priscilla asserted to herself, who would never have stayed at the hotel had Major O'Hara been in charge of the press office.

Or so she liked to think.

"There you are, Miss Tempest," Banville said as though pleased that he had found an object that had been missing. "We have been waiting for you."

That sounded ominous, thought Priscilla.

"Shut the door if you don't mind."

That sounded worse.

She carefully closed the door and then said, "It's good to see you, Mr. Banville." Lying through her teeth.

"Yes, well it's... good... to have you back, Miss Tempest." Banville looked less pleased and more uncomfortable. Major O'Hara wasn't looking at her, keeping an eye on the far wall in case there should be movement.

"Recently I've had a chance to be filled in on a few particulars by Commander Trueblood at Buckingham Palace, very much on an eyes-only, need-to-know basis," Banville went on. "You

267

should understand that he speaks most highly of you and your efforts to preserve and protect the monarchy."

Commander Blood had invoked the Official Secrets Act, with the promise that no one could know what went on at Wanderworth House, including her employer. Now here was Banville suggesting he knew exactly what had happened because he had heard it from no less a source than Commander Trueblood.

"That's kind of him to say, sir, but as I understood the situation, he was not supposed to say anything."

"Nonsense, Miss Tempest, you mustn't be modest." Banville's smile was as false as his cheeriness. "Commander Trueblood regards you as a bit of a heroine, I must say. In fact, Major O'Hara and I were just discussing that in connection with your situation."

"My situation?" That went beyond ominous. That landed in the middle of territory marked Dire Warning.

"Yes, your situation," Banville confirmed. "Given recent circumstances, Major O'Hara and I have decided that it would be best if we relieved you of some of your duties until you're back on your feet."

"But I *am* back on my feet," Priscilla protested. "I was never off my feet, not as far as my duties at the Savoy are concerned."

Banville did not appear to hear her. "To that end, I've asked Major O'Hara to take over as head of the Savoy's press office for the time being."

"A temporary measure, certainly," put in the major, continuing to be fascinated with what was on the far wall.

"No question about it. Temporary," added Banville. Somehow, the way he said it did not seem at all temporary to Priscilla's ears.

Banville looked at his watch. "There you have it. Must be going." He fired a weak smile in Priscilla's direction. "Again, Miss Tempest, welcome back."

And off he went, leaving in his wake a decidedly edgy Major O'Hara. Priscilla felt as though she had just been hit over the head with a bat.

"Here I was beginning to think you might actually be on my side," Priscilla said, her voice choked.

"I *am* on your side, Miss Tempest, believe me."

"It certainly doesn't feel like it," Priscilla said, desperately holding everything in, resolute about not showing weakness in front of this man.

"I'm afraid you have been betrayed by Commander Trueblood—a bit of a cad in my opinion," Major O'Hara explained. "I'm not sure how much he told Mr. Banville, but enough to start him thinking about dismissing you. I managed to intercede with a solution that allowed you to keep your job."

"Then I suppose I should be thanking you, Major," Priscilla said coolly.

"No thanks needed, Miss Tempest. I gather Miss Gore-Langton is not coming back, so for the time being, I would suggest that even though we are very different people, we do our best to get along and keep this press office running smoothly."

There didn't seem to be any other solution, short of her walking out, which she didn't want to do.

"Very well, Major," Priscilla allowed. "Let's see what we can do."

"That's the spirit, Miss Tempest," said a relieved Major O'Hara. "Onward and upward and all that."

"And all that," Priscilla echoed, doing her best to summon enthusiasm.

"Incidentally, before I forget, that newspaper chappie, Hoskins?"

"Yes? What about him?"

"He called earlier. Said to meet him. 'The usual place, this evening,' he said. "No idea what that's all about. Rendezvous with the enemy, I'd say."

Or maybe with the only friend she had left in the world.

Much had changed since the last time Priscilla visited Sir Arthur Sullivan's memorial. But Sir Arthur remained steady in place, unmoving, implacable. His half-naked muse, as she always had, clung to his pedestal for dear life. Priscilla wondered if her own back had looked nearly as good to Gordon Scott. She immediately pushed aside the thought. She should not be thinking like that, what with Percy rising from their usual meeting bench looking concerned—and quite handsome, she decided, shaved and combed, and wearing a wrinkle-free suit that actually fit him. To her surprise, he immediately embraced her, a firm embrace that failed to consider her sore arm nestled in its sling.

She gave a yelp.

"Sorry, sorry," he said springing away. "I forgot that you've been wounded in action."

"Flesh-wounded," Priscilla amended. She inspected him up and down. "You look pretty good," she said to him. "All things considered."

"What's that supposed to mean?" Percy immediately was on the defensive.

"You know," Priscilla said quickly, "bearing in mind what we've both been through. You could be forgiven for looking a bit worse for wear. But I must say, you don't."

"Well, you're looking good yourself—all things considered," Percy offered.

Priscilla grinned. "Considering all things." She regarded him more solemnly.

"That night, I wanted to find you," Percy said, "but they dragged me away. Grilled me for hours."

"I notice you haven't written anything about what happened," Priscilla said.

"They wouldn't let me do that, either. Maybe something later on about the feuding cousins, depending on what happens to Constantino."

"Have you heard anything?"

"Hanging on by a thread, I understand." He gave her an admiring look. "From what I can gather, you're quite the hero."

"You're something of a hero yourself," Priscilla said. "I wouldn't have thought you had it in you to jump Constantino the way you did."

"Yes, sometimes I even surprise myself." Percy was glowing.

"But never mind all that," Priscilla said, a little more sharply than she intended. "Did you sleep with Felicity Khan?" Sounding a lot more jealous than she intended.

"What would make you ask me that?" The question was accompanied by a wary frown.

"I have it on good authority that the way Constantino was able to get his hands on you was because Felicity lured you to him."

"Lured? Nobody *lured* me anywhere," Percy objected.

"It would not be difficult to conclude that the way in which she would do that was to sleep with you."

"Yeah, well, what about your Tarzan?" Percy asked accusingly.

"I have no idea what you're talking about," Priscilla answered, carefully adopting the innocent expression she always hoped would make her lies more palatable.

"I don't like that look." Percy pounced immediately.

"What's wrong with my look?"

"It's the one you use when you're lying."

"There is no such look—and I am not lying," Priscilla stated obstinately.

"To gain access to that dinner party you would've needed someone who was already invited. Why do I suspect that someone was Tarzan."

"His name is Gordon Scott, incidentally, not Tarzan."

"Okay. How about it? Did you sleep with Gordon Scott?"

Given the ferocity of what transpired between them, someone she didn't recognize had been with Gordon. Not her at all.

"Priscilla?" Percy's strident voice interrupted her train of thought.

"What?"

"Did you sleep with Gordon Scott? A question answered easily enough. Yes or no?"

"Then the answer would have to be no."

The ascending moon discovered a couple rigid with uncertainty on a park bench, watched over by Sir Arthur Sullivan's stern bronze visage. He didn't look happy about the two of them lying to one another. But then what did Sir Arthur know of life and love in a modern world? Sorry, Sir Arthur, she thought, but it's all so complicated.

"Are you going to see her again?"

"Who?"

"Felicity."

"She's not returning my calls." Percy spoke in a soft voice. "Not that it makes any difference, of course."

"Of course not." Priscilla issued a long sigh and said, "Incidentally, I've lost my job."

That brought the slumping Percy into an upright position. "You're joking."

"Not quite lost, demoted, I suppose is the best way to describe it. As of now, Major Jack O'Hara has taken over as the new head of the Savoy Press Office."

"Bloody hell!" exploded Percy. "After what you've been through."

"What I've been through is probably why I'm no longer head of the press office," Priscilla said. "What I've been through is not exactly part of my job description."

"What does this mean?" Percy sat incensed. "Are there going to be big changes?"

"I would not count on a lot of free beer going forward if I were you, but otherwise I'm not sure. We will have to see."

"You could marry me," Percy said. Priscilla looked at him expecting the playful expression that showed he was joking. But Percy looked awfully serious. It struck her that he might not be joking.

"I don't think that's the answer, Percy," Priscilla said gently. "I believe I have mentioned in the past that I don't want to marry anyone."

"Particularly me, I suppose."

"Particularly you," Priscilla said. And she meant it, she told herself. She was certain she meant it. Didn't she?

"I bet you'd marry Tarzan," Percy said with a sneer.

"Mr. Scott has departed. I don't think that's an option."

"You're left with me," Percy said. "The consolation prize." He sounded a trifle bitter when he said it.

"Unless Felicity Khan returns your phone calls."

"I am not holding my breath."

Priscilla stood up and as she did, she knocked her purse off the bench. Some of its contents spilled onto the ground.

"What's that?" Percy asked.

"A book someone lent me," Priscilla said, picking up the copy of Rupert Mackenzie's *The Devil's Lair*. She placed it on the bench while she recovered the other articles that had fallen out. She was feeling very tired. All she wanted to do was go home and sleep forever, forget for a time the world and the men in it. She picked up the book. A love story, he'd said. Based on a woman named Maria, a communist agent the young Rupert loved in Rome? The woman whose murder, according to Noël Coward, had been arranged by Colin Ashbury?

"It looks like we're both right back where we started," Percy was saying, dejectedly. "The place where we always seem to be."

"Which is no place at all," Priscilla added.

"I still think you love me," Percy said.

"Dream on," she threw back at him as she started off with the book.

"You do," he called after her.

She kept walking, unable to stop thinking about *The Devil's Lair*.

The moon, fully risen now, was held captive behind wisps of clouds as Priscilla walked back to the Savoy. Ahead, a lamppost shone down on the man in a fedora standing beneath it, dapper in a black suit and shirt that set off his white tie. Drawing closer, Priscilla recognized George Raft. He was lighting a cigarette as Priscilla came abreast of him. "Hello, Priscilla."

"Mr. Raft," she said. "This is a surprise."

"One of these days, I'm going to convince you to call me George."

"I thought you were going back to America."

"I am," Raft said. "Plane leaves at midnight. I was hoping to catch you before I left so I could say goodbye."

"That's very sweet," said Priscilla. "Where's Susie?"

"That's the thing," Raft said. "She won't be making the trip. I wanted you to know."

"Why isn't she going with you?" asked Priscilla, puzzled.

"She almost had me persuaded," he said. "But then I thought better of it. I guess you don't know I'm already married."

"No, I didn't, and I don't imagine Susie does either."

"Same woman for almost fifty years. But we don't live together, not for a long time. I go my own way. I'm better flying solo. A loner, I guess you'd say. Susie's adorable, but she doesn't fit into the way I live."

"Which is alone," Priscilla said.

"Yeah, that's it," Raft said. "I've heard people say that I'm the loneliest man in Hollywood."

"The way you like it, George," Priscilla offered.

He gave her a speculative look. "You know what?"

"What's that?"

"You called me George." The mask cracked into a triumphant smile.

"Yes, I did."

"You're very special, Priscilla. You won, in case you don't know. You beat all those snobby establishment bastards at their own game. Don't let anybody tell you different."

"I'll try to keep that in mind," Priscilla replied.

"Check at your office," Raft said. "I've left a little something for you—a memento you might say."

"That's kind of you," Priscilla said, baffled as to what sort of memento George Raft would leave her.

Raft dropped what was left of his cigarette. He used the heel of one highly polished shoe to grind it out. "Take care of yourself, Priscilla."

He used two fingers to touch his fedora in salute. She gave him an appreciative nod in return. For a minute or two as he walked on, he was caught in moonlight, a man in black, alone, throwing off a long shadow.

And then George Raft was gone.

Finale

Something unanswered, something unfinished, Priscilla thought as she came into the Front Hall, quiet as a tomb at this time of night. A sleepy night clerk rallied a greeting as she passed. The duty concierge snapped his eyes open, embarrassed to be caught napping when Priscilla stopped and asked to use his phone. For some reason, she thought it best to make the call out here.

Once she had done that, she went along the corridor into her office. On her desk stood the gift Raft had left for her, the soapstone black falcon. The sightless eyes of the falcon seemed to follow her as she picked up the card leaning against the statuette. In a smooth cursive hand, Raft had written: "A memory of an opportunity missed. The black bird is for you, Priscilla, a young woman who won't miss the opportunities. You've got your job back."

Was that true? Had Raft worked some magic and made it so that she did have her job again? Could Raft pull off that kind of miracle? According to his note, he could.

She sat staring at the falcon, tired but strangely exhilarated, her heart beating fast, as she pressed the waiter button. The young man on night duty responded almost immediately, although he too looked sleepy-eyed. She asked him to bring a bottle of Scotch whisky and a couple of glasses. He was back soon, setting the bottle and the glasses on the desk as she directed.

It wasn't long before Rupert Mackenzie showed up at the door, rumpled, his hair askew, cheeks flushed. He played a bit with his tie as he came in, appearing to be wide awake, almost as though he had been awaiting her call.

"I thought you could use a drink," Priscilla said to him.

"The truly wondrous thing about a hotel like the Savoy," Rupert said, moving further into her office. "You can get a drink any time, night or day. Life is made so easy here. All your impossible desires become possible. It's as though you are floating on deliciously scented air in a beautiful dream where the whisky is free." He looked suddenly quite miserable. "A life I will never know, alas. Nose pressed against the window looking in on occasion, but nothing more."

"I will take that as a yes," Priscilla said, pouring whisky into one of the glasses until it was half full.

"Much appreciated," Rupert said. He plunked himself down with a deep sigh, as though relieved. "This is just what I needed."

"I thought as much," Priscilla said.

His face flushed even more as he finished off the glass. His eyes shone brightly. Priscilla placed *The Devil's Lair* on the desk. He regarded it without comment. "You know, from the moment I met you, Miss Tempest, I had this feeling that you were smarter than the rest. That you sensed things, saw things others didn't."

"Noël Coward has told me about Maria Pacelli," Priscilla said softly.

Rupert's eyes widened a bit, then closed down again, perhaps settling in preparation for mounting a defence. "How would he know about Maria?"

"He remembered intelligence reports from Rome saying that although Maria was supposed to be an agent for Spearpoint, she was actually working for the communists."

"That was a lie," Rupert flared. He immediately forced himself to remain calm. "She was set up, no more a communist than I was."

"Yet she was murdered," Priscilla said.

"Yes, she was." Rupert's voice was a haunted whisper.

"Noël thinks Colin Ashbury was responsible for her death."

"Do you suppose I might pour myself another whisky?" Rupert inquired, placing his glass on the desk.

"Help yourself," Priscilla said.

"Noël knows more than I would have imagined."

"He does."

"Ashbury claimed he had nothing to do with Maria's death, but I didn't believe him," Rupert said. "He sent Teodoro to do it and Teodoro gladly obliged. It was all covered up, forgotten, but I never forgot."

"Revenge all these years later," Priscilla offered.

"Justice," Rupert amended. "They all made me very angry then. They make me angry now." He drank more whisky. "You have to admit, though, I did come to your rescue outside the Colony Club."

"That was you," Priscilla said.

"I'd followed you as you returned from Wanderworth to the Colony Club, a little worried about you, I must say. You were upsetting some very dangerous people. When you came out of the club, I was pleased. You were probably headed home. Next thing I saw that bugger viciously attack you. I thought I should do something. You had a better chance to bring down these people than I ever would have had. Without you, I was concerned they would get away. You needed a guardian angel and needed him quickly. I decided to step in and fill the bill."

He continued, "I dislike the gun, actually, but in that particular instance there was no other choice. Otherwise, I prefer more subtle methods." He reached under his jacket to pull out a length of wire, either end attached to short wooden grips. "The garrotte, for example that I used for Colin after he left Wanderworth. Silent, compared to a gunshot. I employed it quite effectively on occasion in Rome."

He laid the garrotte on the desk. Priscilla felt her stomach tighten. Not a good sign. "I'm beginning to think you may not be my guardian angel after all," she said in a small voice.

"Not anymore," he said. "Justice, after all these years, finally done. And British democracy saved from the clutches of dreadful Teodoro, Lady Daphne and her Wanderworth Group."

"I don't know about that," Priscilla said, tensing as Rupert got up, the garrotte in hand. "Saving democracy might be a bit much."

"You are a prize, Miss Tempest, there is no doubting that. But I suppose the price paid for our pleasant chat, the very good whisky, would be a phone call to the police informing them of what you have learned."

"It would be better if you turned yourself in, Rupert," Priscilla said, carefully measuring her words.

"I don't think that's in the cards. Life hasn't been good, but it's much preferable to prison, I must say."

Before Priscilla had a chance to respond, Rupert lunged, knocking her back. She couldn't help but be impressed by the speed with which he moved, the wire of the garrotte stretched taut between his hands. He had her pressed against the wall, the wire digging into her neck, cutting off her breathing. She struggled against him, but given his size and the power of his hands as he pinned her, movement was hopeless.

Only her left hand was free, flailing about desperately, brushing against the cool soapstone surface of the falcon. Everything had begun to blur. She could hear herself choking, feel the warmth of the blood where the wire cut into her throat.

Her hand found the base of the black bird, closed around it. For an instant, Rupert's energy for the kill appeared to desert him and he loosened his hold on the garrotte in an exhaustion of hot whisky breath. That was enough for Priscilla. Gripping the base of the falcon, she lifted it up and smashed it against the back of Rupert's skull. His eyes popped with surprise. The wire was gone from her neck, Rupert crying out, falling away to the floor. Now she held the falcon in both hands and smashed it into Rupert's head. He issued a loud grunt and then stopped moving.

Priscilla dropped the falcon, stumbled over Rupert's body and broke out of 205 into the hallway, blood trickling down her chest onto her dress, straight into the arms of...

"Miss Tempest!" Clive Banville let out a shriek as Priscilla sank against him. "Miss Tempest, you're bleeding," Banville continued in an astonished voice, his noble features locked in an expression of horror.

"So sorry, Mr. Banville," Priscilla said, holding onto him for support.

"Whatever have you been doing?" he demanded.

"Trying to stop a man from killing me," Priscilla replied.

"What?" Banville looked more stunned than ever. "Certainly not here at the Savoy!"

Priscilla, by now feeling terribly weak in the knees, began to drop. Banville held her in his arms, carefully lowering her to the carpet. "Miss Tempest, are you quite all right?"

"I'm afraid I'm not at the moment," Priscilla replied.

"We must get you help," he said.

"Yes, but I have to ask you a question," Priscilla gasped.

"What is it, Miss Tempest?"

"Is it true? Do I have my job back?"

"Good God, Miss Tempest." It was as though she was back in his office and he had just identified yet another of her many shortcomings. "If you must know, I was working late, coming down here to leave you a note. Yes, circumstances have evolved. I am not particularly happy about it but unidentified admirers of yours in high places have come forward, the outcome being that you do have your position back." He added sternly, "With one proviso."

"Yes, Mr. Banville?" asked Priscilla.

"That in the future you resist becoming involved in the sort of difficulties that could get you killed at the Savoy."

"I will do my best, sir."

Priscilla made sure her fingers were crossed as she said it.

EPILOGUE

Guests of the Savoy

Having survived eighteen rocky years of marriage, Antony
Armstrong-Jones, 1st Earl of Snowdon, and HRH Princess
Margaret finally divorced in 1978. Miss Susan Gore-Langton
was just one of many lovers, both female and male, Lord Snowdon was associated with in the late 1960s. The easy explanation
for his lustful escapades was that he suffered from sex addic-
tion. If that was the case, he seemed to have suffered happily.
He remarried in 1978 to Lucy Mary Lindsay-Hogg, but that did
not end his affairs. Most notably, he carried on with journalist Ann Hills for twenty years. Their affair ended when Hills
committed suicide. Ms. Lindsay-Hogg and Lord Snowdon sep-
arated in 2000 after it was revealed he had fathered a son by
another woman. Whether the encroaching years calmed Lord
Snowdon's sexual appetites is not known. Those appetites did
not appear to affect his health, however. He lived to the ripe old
age of eighty-six. He never again contacted Miss Gore-Langton,
although she might have wished he had.

Mr. George Raft no sooner left London—without Miss Susan
Gore-Langton, incidentally—than British authorities labelled
him undesirable and refused to allow him back into the country. Thus ended the European portion of the life of perhaps the
most fascinating character to come out of Hollywood's golden
age in the late 1930s and 1940s. Mr. Raft, as Miss Gore-Langton

discovered, really was known as the Black Snake. In Hollywood, he was said to have made love to a different woman every day. He had affairs with Carole Lombard, Marlene Dietrich and Betty Grable, among others. Unlike his fellow actors at Warner Bros. who merely played gangsters, Mr. Raft *was* a gangster, who became an actor. He grew up in the Hell's Kitchen section of New York where his best pals were two of America's most notorious future hoodlums: Owney Madden and Benjamin "Bugsy" Siegel. As a young man, Raft was a semi-pro baseball player, boxer and, most famously—and incongruously—a taxi dancer who specialized in the tango. Owney Madden persuaded him to try his luck in Hollywood. Director Howard Hawks, knowing a good gangster when he saw one, cast Raft opposite Paul Muni in the 1932 classic *Scarface*. By 1937, Raft had become one of Hollywood's biggest stars—and quite possibly the dumbest. He turned down lead roles in *Dead End, High Sierra* and most notoriously *The Maltese Falcon*—parts that made a little-known Warner Bros. contract player named Humphrey Bogart a star. Mr. Raft said later he also turned down *Casablanca*, the movie that transformed Bogart into a Hollywood icon. By the time Raft left London, his acting career was pretty much over but not his lifelong association with gangsters. He was seventy-nine when he died of emphysema in Los Angeles in 1980.

Mr. Gordon Scott's real name was Gordon Merrill Werschkul. As he told Miss Tempest, he was working as a lifeguard at the Sahara Hotel in Las Vegas when, despite his complete lack of acting experience, he was picked from two hundred others to become the eleventh Tarzan. The producer, Sol Lesser, didn't like the twenty-six-year-old's last name and changed it to Scott. After six Tarzan pictures, Mr. Scott tired of the role and moved to Italy. There, in an age before comic book superheroes, he

played everyone from Samson and Goliath to Zorro, Julius
Caesar and Buffalo Bill. Perhaps most notably, his impressive
physique made him the perfect Hercules in *The Beast of Babylon
Against the Son of Hercules* and *Hercules Against Moloch*. Toward the
end of his life, Mr. Scott made a living signing autographs at film
conventions. He came to visit Mr. Roger Thomas and his wife,
Mrs. Betty Thomas, in Baltimore, and ended up living with
them in their row house until he died at the age of eighty.

The Walsinghams spirited Edward and Wallis, the Duke and
Duchess of Windsor, back to Paris without incident. Restless
and seemingly bored members of international café society, Bertie and Wallis spent the rest of their lives moving between their
fourteen-room Paris mansion at the edge of the Bois de Bou-
logne (where they were sustained by a staff of thirty-two) and
the Waldorf Astoria Hotel in New York. So far as is known, the
duke never again visited England. Whatever their far-right sym-
pathies, and despite the constant reminders of their scandalous
pre-war support of the Nazis and Hitler, they kept their views
to themselves. In ill health for years, the duke finally succumbed
to throat cancer in May 1972 at the age of seventy-seven. Wallis
attended her husband's funeral in the chapel at the Royal Bur-
ial Ground in Windsor and then promptly flew back to France,
where she died in 1986 at the age of eighty-nine. She was buried
beside her husband.

FROM THE SAVOY NEWS DESK

The Savoy is sad to report that two of its most esteemed guests, Prince Teodoro, the Duke of Vento, and his cousin, Prince Constantino, Prince of Parma, have both died in London. The Savoy sends its heartfelt condolences to the families of both the princes. No further information about their deaths is available.

General Manager Clive Banville announces that Major Jack O'Hara (Ret.), after a brief stint in the press office, has been returned to his former job as the Savoy's head of security. Major O'Hara brings years of experience as a valued hotel employee to his position. Miss Priscilla Tempest will continue to head the press office.

The photography exhibit by the noted photographer Antony Armstrong-Jones, 1st Earl of Snowdon, titled *A Day in the Life of a Great Hotel*, has been cancelled due to scheduling difficulties. No other details are available.

ACKNOWLEDGEMENTS

Among the many delights writing the Priscilla Tempest adventures is the way in which we are able to make use of real-life celebrities as characters who inhabit the Savoy Hotel of the late 1960s. How could we ignore the rich, royal and famous who have passed through the hotel's Front Hall and occupied its exclusive river suites?

It helps that during the years she worked in the press office at the Savoy, Prudence hobnobbed with just about everyone who was anyone, including Noël Coward, Britain's most famous playwright, a reoccurring character in our novels. Prudence helped to organize his seventieth birthday party.

She arranged the tickets for Prime Minister Pierre Trudeau so he could attend the party where he met Barbra Streisand whom he famously dated for a time, enjoyed nightcaps with the American actress and comedienne Elaine Stritch, befriended Louis Armstrong and hosted the notorious press conference at which Liza Minnelli announced that she was marrying Peter Sellers—before announcing less than a month later that she wasn't marrying Sellers.

Prudence never met the American actor George Raft while he was in London. More's the pity. Raft was one of Hollywood's most curious and intriguing characters. Ron's fascination with him dates back to *Magic Man*, one of his earlier novels, in which a young Raft appears in 1928 Hollywood.

Years ago, Ron spent some time with Lewis Yablonsky, Raft's biographer. Like Ron, Yablonsky was interested in the fact that Humphrey Bogart and James Cagney were actors who played gangsters, whereas Raft was a real-life gangster who became an actor.

For Yablonsky, Raft was the enigma he could never quite crack. One of the last times Yablonsky visited him in Los Angeles, they lunched together at the Beverly Wilshire Hotel. Yablonsky confronted Raft about walking away from the roles that made Bogart a star. Raft would have none of it. He had no regrets. "He didn't dwell on the past or the errors that he made," remembered Yablonsky.

After lunch, as they were about to cross the street, Raft heard someone behind him mutter, "Hey, George Raft. Hey, he had his day." Raft gave no sign he had heard the comment, Yablonsky recalled. He started across the street and never looked back.

Our mutual experiences with the famous have certainly been helpful when it comes to bringing them to fictional life. But our efforts alone would never get these books into print. A team of talented editors is required. First reader Kathy Lenhoff, a.k.a. Ron's wife, identified early problems. James Bryan Simpson, as he always does, contributed a sharp pencil and a forensic eye for inconsistencies.

Editor Pam Robertson has worked with us on all three novels. Always encouraging, she nonetheless identified plot holes that needed filling and characters who benefited from fleshing out. Line editor Caroline Skelton, back for a second time, did a quick, masterful job tweaking the small things that, taken together, made the book a much better read.

Many thanks to everyone at D&M for sticking with us through a third novel.

Prudence reserves a special place in her heart for Carl Young-bloed, Kate Wood and Amber Liberatore, a trio of friends who have been there for her during some recent tough times.

Finally, one more big thanks to agent Bill Hanna who got us into all this and to whom we are forever grateful for his unstoppable energy and unfailing enthusiasm.